# FEAR NO EVIL

## THE DIARY OF JULIE HAMMOND

NAOMI W. STAN

Fear No Evil

The Diary of Julie Hammond

Naomi W. Stan

The Lazy Lizzy Press

ISBN (Print Edition): 978-1-09831-379-1

ISBN (eBook Edition): 978-1-09831-380-7

# PROLOGUE

My father was a tall, handsome man who possessed the terrible gift of second sight. I say terrible because his predictions weren't the happy sort that most sought, but those that foretold of misfortune, tragedy, and death. On my eighth birthday, and a week before he committed suicide, he told me my future. *"Be wary daughter and don't be deceived. You were born under a dark cloud and I see loss and sadness in your future. Choose your friends carefully for evil wears many faces and finds pleasure in deceiving. It pains me that one day you'll be forced to forfeit your life in order to save it."*

Frightened by what I heard, I hid his words away in the dark recesses of my mind and there they remained till the Air Force transferred my husband Mark, our adopted son Andrew, and myself to a base in England. We rented a house called Thornwood, and it was there my father's prophecies became my reality. Twenty-five years have passed since then but never once have I felt free of its disquieting implications.

It all began anew a year after our son's death and six months before Mark's long-awaited retirement. An unexpected job offer arrived from a company on the outskirts of London that Mark said was too good to turn down. He assured me it was just what we needed, but I had a hard time agreeing, but as usual his enthusiasm won me over. Besides, maybe this was for the best, I had lived with the past for far too long. Now one way or the other I'd be in a position to end it.

We located a house in the picturesque village of Wicklesbee and settled down. In mid-October Mark went off to Inverness on business. There was danger in Inverness, but I dared not say for fear the old arguments would begin again.

Normally Mark would call upon his arrival, and talk about the trip, the condition of his room and what he had to eat, but this time was different. This time Mark and the storm of the century had arrived at the same time and made communicating with the outside world impossible. According to the BBC, roads were flooded, rivers were overflowing their banks and the police warned people to stay in their homes and not venture out. Three days passed without word, and then on day four I received a call from Lieutenant Donaldson of the Inverness Constabulary.

According to the Lieutenant Mark had apparently swerved to miss a downed tree, skidded on the wet pavement, and after jumping the guard rail, wound up in the loch. If an approaching motorist hadn't seen his headlights disappear, they might not have found him. Trying to be kind he said a female liaison officer would meet me and help get me settled in. I thanked him and went to pack.

Arriving at the hospital, I went directly to the ICU ward. The nurse said Mark was in room seven, but it took seeing his wedding ring to convinced me. Battered and broken, his chances of recovery were slim. I stayed for a time then returned to the hotel, contacted his family then called Connie Johnson. I met Connie when Mark asked her husband Charlie who served with him in Vietnam to be his best man. Over the years we became close friends and now were more like sisters.

"Slow down and stop crying. I can't understand when you're blubbering," Connie said.

"It's Mark—"

"What about him? What's going on?"

"There was an accident; he's in a coma. They don't think he'll live."

She was silent for a moment then responded. "We talked about what might happen before you left, but you assured me you had a plan." I didn't answer. "Julie, you have a plan, don't you?"

"Sort of," I managed. "I just never thought—"

"Oh, for God's sake Julie—tell me you weren't naïve enough to assume she'd give you time to plan."

"Of course, I didn't," I interrupted. "I'm dumb not stupid."

"So where do we go from here?"

"I don't know. I need time to think."

"Well, while you're thinking I want you to write down everything that happened at Thornwood. Everything—leave nothing out. At least that way when everything goes pear- shaped, and it will, they'll be a record."

I tried to say no, but Connie could be dogged when she wanted to be, so I agreed. I bought some paper and several pens and set to work. At the top of page one I wrote, *"Fear No Evil—The Diary of Julie Hammond,"* and below that; *This is a complete and accurate account of all that took place before, during and after my time at Thornwood. Make of it what you will.*

# CHAPTER ONE

By the time I was nine both my parents were dead, and I was living with my Aunt Bertha; my only living relative. Aunt Bertha didn't like children, me in particular, and daily found reasons to blame me for what she called 'my parent's untimely passing.' When I turned seventeen, having fulfilled her obligations, she married me off to John Dickson. Fifteen years my senior his only aim in life was to have a son. I was seven months pregnant when a speeding car crossed the center line and hit mine head on. In the hospital for several months, I lost the baby and any possibility of having another. Undeterred, John found a woman willing to do for a price what I couldn't. Andrew, wrapped in a shabby blue blanket, came into my life eleven months later.

But as usual there was a problem. While out drinking with friends, John discovered Andrew wasn't his. When threatened by John's left fist, the surrogate admitted she had no idea who the real father was. Made to look a fool, John arrived home in a drunken rage and threw us into the street. Not knowing what else to do I asked my aunt to take us in. Instead she handed me what she said was a small inheritance left me by my father. It wasn't much, but it kept us going till I could find work and a place to live. Six months later I filed for divorce and sole custody of Andrew.

Having no life outside work, I took a chance and attended a dance at a nearby Air Force Base held for men returning from Vietnam. Never having attended a dance I was nervous but determined. The party was already in full swing when I arrived, so I found a place to sit and waited for someone to ask me to dance. When they didn't, I collected my damaged pride and headed for the door where a young Captain blocked my way.

He apologized for being late and suggested we find a table. He said his name was Mark Hammond and had just arrived stateside from Vietnam. His next assignment he hoped would be England. He talked about his job, that his folks lived on the East coast, and then self-consciously laughed and asked about me? I explained that I had a four-year-old son named Andrew, and that I worked as a bookkeeper for a local construction company. Nothing about our conversation was earth shattering, or even out of the ordinary, but by the end of the evening I was in love with this man.

It wasn't because of his hazel eyes, or contagious laughter. Nor was it his blondish brown hair or his slightly cockeyed smile. All that was wonderful, but what I fell in love with was what I sensed was underneath it all. I didn't believe in love at first sight; I didn't believe in love at all, but something about this man made me want to put my arms around him and never let him go. After John it was an insane idea, but that's how it was. The wonder of it was Mark felt the same, and four weeks later we married, and were looking forward to England. My life had become a dream.

We assumed we'd go together, but housing being in short supply Mark would have to find a place before we'd be allowed to join him. He was about to give up the search when a man stopped to help him change a tire. He didn't give his name, but when asked, said he knew of a place just a few miles further on that might be available. "There's a sign on the gate," he said, then drove off. Mark followed his directions and there it was. 'House for Rent or Lease. Inquire within.' Mark could hardly contain himself. On the other hand, he'd driven along this stretch of road at least six time and never once noticed what was in fact impossible to miss.

A Mr. Devlin Black answered the door. Having recently sold his business, he and his wife Edna intended to do some extended traveling. Afraid to leave the house empty they decided to lease it out till they returned.

That night Mark called with the news. "It's large, twenty-two rooms, but most of it's been renovated, and what hasn't we can close off. They call the place Thornwood. We'll have to sign a two-year lease and promise to find another tenant if we move but the way things are at the moment moving would be out of the question. If there was enough time I'd send pictures, but Devlin says someone else is also interested. So, what do you think? If we wait it could be months maybe even longer before something else becomes available." Said like that it was an easy decision.

* * *

Our plane was late due to a weather hold, and by the time we located Mark, got a bite to eat and started for home I was close to exhaustion. We were driving through Bury St. Edmund's when Mark mentioned the fire. Nothing serious, a little ozone and burnt wallpaper, but enough to make the Black's feel the place needed rewiring. Why it wasn't done during the remodeling was a mystery. Tom Bates a local electrician would do the work.

"How long will it take?"

"He figures about two months." Mark said, keeping his eyes glued to the road.

"Two months! What's he going to do, tear it down and rebuild?"

"Very funny. He's only going to tear down the part we live in."

My first view of Thornwood was a depressing one, and for a moment thought Mark had turned into the wrong driveway. Except for its size nothing was as Mark described, and I couldn't help but wonder if he leased the place in a moment of sheer madness. Why else would he even consider moving us into this brooding old ramshackle mausoleum?

I left Mark to unload the luggage while I wandered back down the drive for a second look. A young woman, first a shadow, then a figure, stood looking out the bedroom window. At first I thought her a figment of my trip weary imagination, but imagination gave way to reality when looking down at me my heart grew cold. The whole thing only lasted a moment, but she was there, I knew it. Unnerved, I hurried back to where Mark waited for me on the porch.

Once inside I had to admit to being pleasantly surprised. Yes, it was large and at the moment rather cold, but it has possibilities. Yes, I thought, this will do just fine. Our own furniture and a few pictures on the wall would make the world of difference.

Mark, seeing my state of exhaustion, took charge of Andrew while I dug through my luggage looking for my flannel pajamas. The expensive see-through nightgown I bought to wear on our first night would remain tucked away.

"What are you doing?" Mark asked from the doorway.

"Looking for something warm to put on."

"You won't find me in there," he said with a wink and a smile. "It's the boiler. It won't stay lit. I've been meaning to ask Tom, but I keep forgetting." Mark went to lock up then crawled in beside me. "Geez, I thought you'd have the bed all warmed up by now."

"Will Andrew be warm enough?" I asked as he settled in beside me."

"I put a heater in his room, so he'll be fine."

"Tell me about the landlords. What are they like?"

"Devlin's all right, a little creepy, but not bad. I haven't met his wife." Mark kissed me on the forehead as I snuggled closer. "One thing was odd though—he insisted the house had been on the market for almost a year."

"What's odd about that?" I asked getting up to put on another sweater.

"He lied. I talked to every estate agent in the area at least three times. Even said I'd consider anything that's livable, but no one mentioned Thornwood—no one. In fact, I drove past here several times and never saw the sign. Here's something else that's crazy, he wouldn't shake my hand. Not sure why, but he wouldn't."

"Then I guess we should be thankful for the helpful stranger."

Reaching over Mark took me in his arms and though we tried to find each other through the layers of clothes we had on finally gave it up as a lost cause. "Oh well, something to look forward to tomorrow night," Mark joked as he rolled over on his back and tucked his arm under his head. For the next twenty-minutes he explained in detail what our life for the foreseeable future would be.

"Navigators are in short supply so we're doing double duty till we get more people. I'll be sitting alert four days out of every week. When I'm on, I can't come home at night. You can come to the club for supper or a movie but come nine o'clock home you go. Then we have month long deployments to Spain and Italy. After that we have surprise exercises, and some that aren't surprises. When that's all over, our time is our own."

I sighed, half asleep. "That's nice." I didn't mention the woman.

# CHAPTER TWO

Mark had already left for work when I woke next morning, and if it hadn't been for the sound of someone using an electric drill I would've gone back to sleep. I tried to ignore it, but in the end realized that if they didn't stop they'd wake Andrew and I'd have a grumpy child for the rest of the day. Fighting my way out from under the knot of sweaters and coats we'd piled on during the night I raced down the stairs. A white-haired old gentleman met me at the bottom.

"I'm Tom Bates, and you must be the Captain's wife?" He said, extending his hand. "Didn't mean to wake you but I'm a little hard of hearing so can't always tell how noisy I'm being."

"Mark tells me you're doing all the work yourself."

"That's right, but I'll get it done and done proper." With nothing to add, I went to the kitchen for a needed cup of coffee. "Did I hear the kettle going on?" Tom asked coming in from the hall. I overlooked his selective hearing and invited him to join me. I explained about Andrew and Tom said for the child's sake he'd start at eight instead of six.

"Was that dad hammering?" Andrew asked, climbing up on my lap.

"That was me I'm afraid, and who might you be?"

"I'm Andrew Hammond, and my dad flies a plane."

"Well, I'm glad to meet you Mr. Hammond, and since I'll be working here for a while, you can call me Mr. Tom." He was about to return to work when I mentioned the heater.

"Mark can't figure out how it works."

Tom roared with laughter. "Why didn't the Captain say—the place has been colder than a wife's greeting when your late home for dinner. I'll check it first thing."

Breakfast over, Andrew insisted we go out and explore. He raced off toward the grove of trees on the far side of the house while I walked back down the drive. I prayed that the house would be different; more welcoming, less gloomy, but in the dim light of a cloudy winter's day the house looked even more depressing. Sadness oozed from every joining of Thornwood's ivy-covered bricks, and I could almost picture tears slipping out from under the sill and trickling down its facade.

The woman was back. More gossamer than flesh, she stood staring off into the distance as if expecting someone's return. I doubt she saw me for her gaze never wavered, yet I knew instinctively she'd be disappointed. Depressed by the idea I found my son and returned to the house.

"These old houses—a whole week's work wasted." Tom threw down the coil of wire in disgust.

"What's the problem?"

"Upstairs. The room at the back."

"You mean the nursery?"

"Yes," he said with a surprised expression. "I'll have to get more wire." I wanted to ask about the woman, but Tom was already out the door and Andrew suffering from jet lag needed a nap. Once he was settled I made a cup of coffee and took a seat on the bottom step of the front stairs. "This house," I said looking around. "What surprises do you hold."

Built in 1865, it boasted fifteen-foot ceilings, elaborately carved cornices, and marble fireplaces in every room. The staircase on which I sat encircled the main entrance hall and was divided by a landing. Above the landing the entire wall was stained glass, while below French doors opened onto what had been a glass enclosed conservatory.

Too many rooms, too many dark corners. And then there was the atrocious wallpaper; white lilies on a grey background. Rather morbid I decided for when the sun hit the paper just right the flowers appeared to droop and die. The other feature that made me shiver was the large chandelier hook sticking out from the ceiling just above my head. I couldn't help but think it looked more like a beckoning finger than anything else. The sound of tires skidding on loose gravel signaled Tom's return. Maybe having Tom around wouldn't be so bad.

\* \* \*

I admit Thornwood was a challenge, and even though our household goods hadn't arrived, I did my best to make it feel like home. I thought I was succeeding until things began to go wrong. Random items would disappear only to reappear days later in places they didn't belong. Furniture was moved or overturned, doors left shut were open, curtains left open were closed. All of it maddening, but with Mark so busy at work I knew I'd have to deal with it myself. That changed on the first of March.

Andrew and I had gone out to enjoy a day without rain. He ran off to play soccer, while I sat reading on the front porch. I closed my eyes for a moment against the sting of the wind, but when I reopened them the warmth of summer had replaced the chill of late winter. The roses in the once dormant flower garden where now in full bloom and in amongst them strolled a young man and woman deep in conversation and wearing clothes that dated back to the Victorian era. Over by the conservatory a young girl was sitting with a boy who looked to be about eight. The woman in the garden laughed, the scene disappeared, and winter returned.

Concerned for Andrew's safety I ran to find him, but he wasn't where I expected. Instead he was standing beside an old tree swing which I was certain hadn't been there when we came out. After testing to make sure it was safe I lifted him unto the seat and gave it a gentle push. At the same time I heard a child crying. Turning toward the sound I was surprised to find both the woman and the child sitting together on an ornate garden bench less than five yards away. Like the swing, it hadn't been there earlier. The child kept pulling on the woman's sleeve in an attempt to get her attention, but she ignored his cries and focused her hate-filled gaze on me. Only after the child began struggling to breath did she stand and reaching for his hand disappear.

Terrified, I carried Andrew back into the house, and locked the door behind me. "Is Nathan okay," Andrew asked, taking off his coat. "He can't breathe sometimes."

"What did you say?"

"He told me he's going to die because he can't breathe."

I stared at my son as if a stranger. "You know those people?"

"Yeah, they live here. He's real nice. He gave me this." Digging down into his pocket he pulled out a toy soldier.

Later when Mark and I were alone I explained what happened. He laughed in response. "You want to move because Andrew has a make-believe friend?"

"How can they be make-believe if I saw them—they're real, and I won't live in a house with people who appear and disappear at will. We could be in danger."

Mark smiled. "I'm not in danger, I'm never here."

"Don't you care about our safety?"

"I care," he said, putting his toothbrush away, "but you're talking about an imaginary friend and a few tricks of the light. Andrew has a vivid imagination. It's nothing more than that." I tried again during breakfast but got nowhere. "Julie—please. I know you don't like the house, but you need to learn to cope. Andrew has no one to play with so he makes them up. It's not that unusual."

"I'm not unhappy with the house. I like the house . . . or did."

"Even if we wanted to, the housing office wouldn't allow it. Too many people are still waiting for a place."

"Fine. But when you come home and find us dead in our beds, you'll be sorry. And when you are, I hope I'm here to see it." Mark made as if to comment, then stopped himself and smiling picked up his keys and left for work. He'd be sitting alert for the next four days.

Tom arrived shortly after Mark left and Andrew anxious to show off his new airplane ran upstairs to get it. "She's a beauty, and that's for sure," Tom said when Andrew returned.

"I gave my old one to Nathan." Tom took a seat and reached for a scone and some jelly.

"So, you've made a friend then?"

"His mom took him away a long time ago, but then she brought him back."

Tom's expression went from curious to concerned. "What's Nathan's last name?"

"Stanley, I think." Tom's rosy complexion turned pale, and he returned to work without touching his food.

# CHAPTER THREE

It was pouring rain the day our things arrived, and eager to get everything in, I didn't see the little white-haired gnome in the huge yellow rain hat standing off to the side.

"I'm Tom's wife Maggie," she said as I hurried toward her. "Have I come at a bad time?"

"No, not at all. Please, come in out of the rain."

"He never said I was coming, did he? Tom, I mean."

"Sorry, no. Come back to the kitchen and I'll make tea."

"I've often wondered what this place was like inside." Then beginning to laugh, "Must be hard to keep warm."

"What are you doing here woman?" Tom asked, coming in from the pantry.

"I'm here to tell Julie we aren't going into town, but since no one told her we were and left no number for me to call, I had no choice but to come in person." Tom looking sheepish made a hasty retreat.

"Is he in trouble?" I asked pouring her a second cup.

"Heavens no, but it doesn't hurt for him to think so." Maggie glanced at her watch. "I didn't realize—I need to be going or I'll miss my bus. I told my sister I'd stop in. She suffers from arthritis and in this weather—" Refusing to let her walk I drove her to the bus stop. "Tom says you're having problems with the house?"

"Mark said I'm being silly," I said, slightly embarrassed.

"Well, if needs be, you and the little one and come stay with us. We've plenty of room." She hurried for the bus and I thought no more about it.

By mid-afternoon everything was off the truck and accounted for. At four, with the weather worsening Tom left to pick up Maggie, and shortly afterward I called Mark to cancel our dinner plans. By nine-thirty Andrew and I headed up to bed. An hour later lightening knocked out the power and Andrew began screaming that he was scared.

"Can I sleep with you mom? Please? I don't want to sleep here. I think someone's in my room."

I aimed the flashlight into all the corners and under the bed but found nothing. Still, figuring it wouldn't hurt, I picked him up and started back across the hall. Halfway there I noticed a light shining out from under the nursery room door. Since that was impossible I'd have to go check it out. I got Andrew settled than started down the hall. Flashes of lightening accompanied by window rattling booms of thunder did little for my already frayed nerves, but I continued on. Reaching the door, I stopped to listen. Someone was moving about inside the room. Then the tapping began. Slow at first, *tap-tap—tap-tap—tap-tap.* Then louder and more frenzied.

Bravery gave way to panic. The door was in front of me, my hand was on the knob, and then the flashlight died. Having come this far I wasn't about to turn back, so taking a deep breath I pushed the door open and went in. The light was gone, and the tapping had stopped, but someone was here. I could hear them breathing.

The high-pitched howling of the wind as it seeped through the cracks and down the chimney brought memories of my aunt. "*Those are the* whistlers," she told me. "*They search out bad little children to carry them away in the dead of night.*"

The words had barely crossed my lips when a shadow moved past me and out into the hall. As I hurried back down the hall the nursery door closed, and the light returned. Climbing into bed, I pulled Andrew into my arms and swore that whenever Mark was away Andrew would sleep with me.

* * *

The following day was a struggle. On edge, I jumped at the slightest sound. By bedtime my nerves were stretched to the limit, and when I found the dining room door, a door normally kept closed standing open, I considered taking Maggie up on her offer. Insisting I was braver than that, I hid in the recessed area behind the door and tried to peek through the crack to what was happening.

This wasn't the moldy, mildewed room Mark spoke about, this one overflowed with the extravagances of the rich and just outside my line of vision, two people were having a violent argument. So intent was I on finding out who they were I almost cried out when one of them rushed past me and out the front door leaving only the slight scent of lavender behind. It was a scent that since childhood had held an odd fascination for me. Now it was here in the hall wrapping itself around me like a warm blanket on a cold night.

Next morning I sent Andrew out to play and hurried back to the dining room. I admit I was disappointed. Where yesterday everything was clean and bright, now huge cobwebs hung like Spanish Moss and dust nearly an inch thick blanketed everything in sight. On the floor Persian rugs, rolled and tightly bound lay scattered about like so many downed trees in a forest. But it was what I saw peeking out from behind a molding Chinese silk screen that held my interest.

"My bureau—" I said hurrying toward it. Pushing the screen aside I pulled out one drawer after another. "It's not here. Why isn't it here? It had to be, it just had to be." I began to panic. My heart racing I reached inside and ran my hands over the runners. I was out of control and it took a splinter sliding under my nail to bring me to my senses. What was I doing? That wasn't my bureau—how could it be? Backing away I tripped over the carpets and hoping not to fall reached out my hand to brace myself against the wall.

My balance restored I intended to leave the room as I found it, but the wall would not release my hand. It was being held by some force within the wall itself, and like before I saw what took place here.

Someone devoid of those tender feelings necessary for love, deliberately shattered the heart of another. Whoever the perpetrator, they viewed love not as an emotion to cherish, but as a weapon to destroy. My hand wasn't pressed against a wall it was covering a broken heart, and once I understood, my hand was freed, and I ran from the room.

* * *

Driving out to meet Mark that evening for dinner I was torn as to what to do. If I told him would he laugh like before and say it was my imagination? Or, if I said nothing and something happened, would he blame me for not saying? Unable to decide Andrew made the decision for me.

"So, what's the matter?" Mark asked. "You've hardly said two words all evening?"

"There was someone in my room," Andrew blurted out.

"We're not moving Julie, and I don't appreciate your using our son against me," Mark said as we were getting ready to leave.

"I'm not using him, and I resent your—"

"But you wanted to," he interrupted.

I left without saying goodbye and arrived home to find the nursery room light shining down onto the lawn. Like my father would say, *"you can't run away from a problem. You've got to face it straight on,"* and this was definitely a problem. But what if I did leave? It would mean never knowing what was hidden in the bureau, or why lavender affected me so, and then there was Andrew's poor little friend. All these things needed answers and I needed to find them. No, I would stay until I discovered the why behind all those things. With my decision made I carried my sleeping son into the house where a man stood waiting.

"Miss Julie." He gave a slight bow as we entered. "I'm so glad you're back."

With my decision made, I still wanted proof that the light was real. I called Tom to come and regretted it at once. Like Mark he'd probably laugh and say it was my imagination, but it was too late to change my mind. The hour late, he arrived in his pajamas and robe. I explained as best I could about the light, and Tom though hesitant, went to check.

"I'm not lying Tom; the light was there last night and again tonight. It was shining down into the yard." Through one cup of tea and half of another he seemed hell bent to convince me I was mistaken, but when an impasse was reached I sent him home.

"What did Tom say?" Andrew asked as I kissed him goodnight.

"About the same as Dad. Who was the man in the hall?"

"That was Silas the butler. Nathan said he takes care of things."

* * *

Next morning Maggie, red faced and out of breath arrived at my door. "What happened last night?" She placed her coat over the back of the chair and took a seat. "I've never seen Tom so upset. He didn't sleep a wink."

With no reason not to I explained I did. By the time I finished the color had drained from her face and her eyes darted about as if expecting a ghost to appear any moment.

"See how you are?" Tom said coming in. "White as a sheet. That's why I didn't say." Tom sat down beside her and helped himself to a biscuit.

"So, what will you do?" Maggie asked.

"I was thinking of writing them a letter. Something about leaving them alone if they'd do the same. I'll give it to Andrew who will give it to Nathan." Maggie wondered if perhaps it would be better to find another place, but since that was impossible and Mark would never agree, the letter would have to do.

"Then you believe me?"

"Of course we do—don't we Tom?" she said giving him a nudge.

The whole situation was absurd. I was writing to a dead person and worse, expecting an answer. I penned what I thought a reasonable compromise then sent it on its way. Now there was nothing for it but to wait for a reply. I returned to my unpacking while Andrew went to start on his room. Moments later he came running in with a small box in his hand.

"Look what I found," he said trying to catch his breath. "I couldn't close the drawer, so I pulled it out and there it was."

My box. The black lacquered box I had hidden behind the drawer of my bureau. But how was that possible? And how did I know its contents?

"Is it magic?" Andrew held it up to the light and gave it a gentle shake.

"No, not magic, but special. Inside is a pearl brooch, and a hand-written poem."

"Open it so we can see." Andrew could hardly contain himself. I undid the latch then carefully removed the contents. My suspicions were correct. Inside was a simple poem written by a love-sick young man to the girl he hoped to win. Andrew insisted I read it aloud.

*"For J, My Heart's Desire."*
*I want so much to tell you of the love within my heart,*
*To let you know the longing grows each moment we're apart.*

*I have no right to beg your love, or even dare to dream*
*That you will see and pity me and end my agony.*
*I do so deeply worship you, I'd die a thousand tortured deaths*
*If only I for one sweet hour, could hold you to my breast.*
*My heart I freely give, my love, I entrust it to your care,*
*Hoping that you'll see the true devotion hidden there.*
*Much Love, Edmund. (summer-1868)*

*It was the summer of 1868. Giddy with excitement I ran to meet Edmund in the garden. "This is for you," he said, "for your birthday." He held out a small black lacquered box. "There's something for you inside. Don't open it now, wait till you're alone." He took my face in his hands and kissed me. The first real kiss of my life. As I started back toward the house a phone rang in the distance.*

\* \* \*

"Mom," Andrew said tugging my arm, "It's Mrs. Bates. She needs to talk to you."

Tom, having suffered a mild heart attack was now in the hospital. I asked if I could do anything, but she said no, her sister was with her. She thought it best to call so I wouldn't worry when he didn't arrive. I told her to let me know if she needed anything than rang off.

It had been a long trying day, so Andrew and I headed up to bed. Going over to close the curtains I stopped for a moment to study my reflection in the darkened glass. At first I was looking at myself, but then my reflection changed, and I was staring into the face of the girl in my vision. Raising her hand, she pressed it to the glass and waited for me to do likewise. At once the glass between our hands turned warm. She smiled and was gone.

Why was I being made privy to these things, and how could I know what was in a box I'd never seen before? At first it all seemed like random events, but now appeared to be so much more. Were they using these small enticements to draw me into the past? Did the idea excite me, in a way yes, but it was also frightening.

I found the answer to my note lying on my pillow. Below my signature she wrote, "Why should I bend to your wishes? This is my house!" Endora.

# CHAPTER FOUR

Because we lived some distance from the base making new friends was difficult, so when Connie wrote saying they were being transferred to our sister base a mere ten miles away, I was overjoyed. Even better she was pregnant with their first child.

For several months I'd been trying to convince Mark that with Andrew about to start preschool now would be the perfect time to bring another baby into the family, but Mark's continued ambivalent was beginning to cause problems between us.

Over lunch Connie got straight to the point. "Confront Mark and demand an answer. It's not fair for him to keep you dangling this way. Maybe he just needs a gentle push, and if that doesn't work try a kick in the pants," she added laughing.

* * *

Two weeks later Tom returned looking pale and tired. I argued the job could wait, but he insisted on finishing. "If I stay home Maggie will fuss and I'll get no peace. Better to keep busy till they find me a bed." Later he asked about the note. Had I heard anything? I took out the letter and gave it to him. "What am I supposed to be seeing?" Tom turned the letter this way and that but saw nothing.

"It's right there under my signature. See I said pointing. And there's her name."

"Well, if you say so, but all I see is what you wrote."

There was no sense arguing, if he didn't see it, then he didn't, but things changed after that. He became distant, less talkative and more furtive.

Two weeks later a bed became available, and I'm ashamed to say I was glad. Still, we were friends so when Maggie called saying Tom was home I went round. Looking frail Tom let Maggie do most of the talking and when it was time to leave she invited me back, but some time would pass before I saw them again.

* * *

After a long dismal winter, spring arrived. The sun rode higher in the sky and the days lengthened and grew warm. Windows opened, lawn chairs reappeared, and people were out and about. At the end of May Connie delivered a healthy baby girl named Samantha, while any hopes I had of another child ended with a spilt glass of milk.

"What in the hell's going on?" Mark, home early stood in the doorway hands on hips surveying the mess. "I could hear you yelling clear down the drive."

"Ask Andrew. I told him to wait, but no, he had to do it himself and now he's made mess."

"For Pete's sake, it's just a little milk. It can be cleaned up."

"But I just did the floors."

And you wonder why I don't want more kids." For an instant my heart stopped. Had I misunderstood? I thought he said he didn't want any more kids. I confronted him once we were alone.

"I just think Andrew's enough."

"And you waited till now to tell me?"

"It never occurred to me you'd want more." Mark tested the water and climbed into the tub. "Now please, let me take my bath in peace. I've had a long day."

"And I haven't? Andrew's growing—"

"Up, yes, I know."

"I don't want him growing up as an only child like we did."

"That's all well and good, but if you can't cope with one how will you cope with two?"

"Since you're never home how would you know how I'm coping?"

Mark dried himself off and headed for the bedroom. "So why now? You're not jealous of Connie, are you? I mean her having a new baby?"

"Of course I'm not jealous." Mark studied me for a moment, and I tried not to cry.

"Julie, come here." Reaching out Mark pulled me down beside him. "You're right, Andrews growing up, but having another baby won't keep him a child or make you miss him less. For now, one is enough. Once we're home, if you still want to adopt, we'll look into it further."

"I don't want to keep him a child. I want another child for him to grow up with. Now you tell me I have to wait four years—Andrew will be almost a teenager by then." I was too angry to continue so went to bed. Did I sleep, not much. In time I gave up the fight. Not because I agreed with Mark but because things at Thornwood had taken a turn for the worse and having a new baby would only make things more difficult. It required a lot of tears to get there, but eventually I came to terms with it.

Though unseen, Endora was making life a misery. Closets were ransacked, sheets were shredded, items were broken and anything containing liquid was spilled out onto the floor. It came to a head when she destroyed my new dishes. I was on my knees picking up the pieces when Mark and Andrew arrived.

"What happened?" Mark asked as he began to sweep up the mess.

"Ask Endora, she did it." I expected him to ask who Endora was, but he said nothing until we went to bed.

"So, who the hell's Endora?"

"I've only told you a thousand times. She's the woman that lives here. The one I saw in the garden. Nathan's mother."

He was quiet for a moment then rising up on one elbow looked over at me and said, "I think before dragging Andrew into your illusions you should talk to Dr. Connelly—"

"You want me to talk to a psychiatrist? And say what? That you're never here, that you don't want more children, that you never listen to what I'm saying, or take my fears seriously?"

"Julie, come on. That's not fair. I'm not—" But I had stopped listening. Tomorrow he'd be flying a plane back to the states then joining the squadron in Spain. He'd be gone for a month. How, I wondered lying there in the dark, could he say something like than then fall blissfully asleep? I didn't have an answer, but my father did.

*"You were born under a dark cloud Julie."*

# CHAPTER FIVE

Mark was gone when I woke next morning, and it hurt to realize he didn't wake me to say goodbye. I told myself it was just as well, but I wish he had. Since there was no way to change it, I got up to start the day and that's when I saw her—hanging from a rope tied round both wrists, thrown over the chandelier hook and fastened to the newel post. Her clothes shredded and bloodied barely covered her and when she tried to breathe, it came in quick desperate little gasps. A slight breeze, as though someone suddenly opened a door turned her so I could see her face and was horrified to find I was staring at myself.

This had to be some insane nightmare. I needed to wake up. But I was awake . . . dreadfully awake . . . so awake I could feel the coldness of impending death radiating off her skin.

There was nothing to do, she was far beyond human help, yet somehow she managed to open her eyes and look into mine. I expected to see pain, despair, maybe a cry for help, but instead saw victory and perfect peace. Frozen in place I watched as her lips curled into a soft triumphant smile and with her last breath whispered, "My life for theirs," and nothing more. Exhaling she died.

Holding tight to the banister I made my way down the stairs. Reaching the bottom my legs gave way and collapsed beneath me. A trail of blood snaked across the Spanish tile floor and reaching down I ran my hand through it and found it warm. For the first time since my arrival, I experienced absolute terror.

I don't remember getting Andrew out of bed, or driving to Maggie's, I only remember begging them to open the door. "Mark says I'm crazy, I don't know—maybe—I don't know."

"For heaven's sake Julie, come in." Maggie directed me down the hall and into the sitting room. "Go sit with Tom while I get Andrew settled." When she returned, she poured a glass of brandy and insisted I drink it. "Now tell us what happened."

Over the next hour I explained all that took place. I told them what Mark thought I should do, and about the girl hanging in the stairwell. It was Tom who spoke first.

"The guilt is ours I'm afraid," Tom said without being asked.

"Not that he meant to hurt you by not saying, but he figured when things got too bad Mark would come to his senses and do something."

"I don't understand," I said, looking from one to the other.

"I'm not quite sure where to start."

"At the beginning," Maggie said annoyed.

"What you need to know is that Thornwood has been sitting empty for the best part of fifty years. Back in the forties they fixed it up and made it livable, but no one would live there. Said the place was haunted. Eventually it was boarded up and left to rot. Sad because it had been a beautiful home."

"But what about the Blacks, Devlin and Edna? They showed Mark around. Showed him the repairs they made; said they'd lived there for over thirty years."

"If that's true," Maggie said, "why did no one ever see them? Never see a car in the drive, a light on at night—or anything. One minute it was about to fall apart, and a week later it looked as it does now. No one could figure it out. Why do you think no one came to welcome you. They were afraid of the house. Couldn't figure out how you could manage to live there. Especially you being alone a lot."

"My great-grandfather, Silas Bates was butler to the Stanley's. Came down from Scotland when Edmund Stanley built the house. He was a wealthy man, was Edmund Stanley. Had a head for inventing things. Farm machinery mostly. Had a factory on the outskirts of town. A big place but gone now. He built Thornwood as a gift for his wife."

"Never could figure out why he married her. Beauty she had in spades, but not much else. The only lady-like thing about her was her title," Maggie added. "A real troublemaker my grandmother said. Thought the world of herself she did. If the house is haunted, she's the cause."

"At least that's what granddad said," Tom added. "And he would know."

As I prepared to return home Maggie argued that I should stay with them till Mark returned, but Tom said it wasn't their place to say. "Mark wouldn't be happy if he thought we tried to interfere. Not that we aren't on your side Julie, we are. Our door will always be open to you, but it's not our place."

"If he refuses, go on your own to prove you mean it," Maggie added, as she walked me out to the car, "Regardless, be careful how you go Julie—just be careful."

Once home I told Andrew to stay in the car till I came for him. He wasn't to follow me. Parents aren't supposed to be afraid, and I was, but I didn't want Andrey to know. The man was there again waiting. He nodded at my entrance then left. Standing by the stairs a rhyme my father loved came to mind.

> *As I was going up the stairs*
> *I met a woman who wasn't there*
> *She wasn't there again today*
> *I wish, I wish, she'd go away.*

"Please Father," I said moving up the steps "please don't let your predictions come true. Not this time."

That evening Mark called. He'd arrived without incident and was spending a few days with his parents before continuing on to Spain. He asked if Andrew had everything he needed for school and would I please take lots of pictures. He didn't mention our last conversation and neither did I.

Andrew started school the following Monday. I knew he needed to spend time with real children, but it hurt to realize he was growing up and in time wouldn't need me anymore. It wasn't until he ran up the steps and disappeared into the building without look back that the tears came.

* * *

Back at Thornwood I found I was at sixes and sevens. I'd never been completely alone in the house and found it rather disconcerting. What was I to do with myself? I hadn't been back to Nathan's room since the night of the storm so decided it was time to face my fears. After all, Andrew went there all the time and was quite happy to do so. If he could, so could I.

It was nothing like what I expected. No wonder Andrew loved coming here. This was the sort of room any child would love. Brightly color wallpaper, toys of all descriptions, and children's books galore. Even better in the corner near the window was a magnificent dapple-gray rocking horse waiting to gallop out across the fields. Unable to resist I gave him a gentle push to get him started. *Tap tap—Tap tap*, nothing to fear, nothing at all.

Street noise drew me to the window, and I stood amazed by what I was seeing. Horse-drawn carriages, carts of all sizes and descriptions, and standing over by the lamp post, a hurdy-gurdy man played for the amusement of the passer-byes while his monkey collected coins in his hat. Fascinated by the sight, I failed to notice the room growing dark or the walls beginning to run with damp. It was the furious rocking of the hobby horse that drew my attention back inside and caused me to run for the door before it closed against me.

Back in the hall I thought myself safe, but the darkness followed me down the stairs to where I discovered the house like the nursery had gone back in time. A newspaper lying on the hallway table said it was June 10,1868. Somehow in a matter of moments I had traveled back over a hundred years. Was this what Andrew experienced when going to see Nathan? A mere moment and you were there?

My reflection in the hallway mirror showed that I had changed as well. I had been wearing jeans and a sweatshirt, now I was dressed in a neat, long sleeved blouse with pin-tucking across the front, a sensible floor-length skirt and high button shoes. My hair had been pulled up into a rather neat little bun and was held in place by two tortoiseshell combs.

You'd think traveling back in time would be frightening, perhaps even terrifying yet the only thing I found upsetting was not knowing how to get back. I was trying to figure it out when I was called into the dining room.

"So, there you are," Endora said, sitting at the far end of the table. Radiant in a dress of pure white lawn she had around her neck five strains of waist length pearls, and in her auburn hair, two diamond studded mother-of-pearl combs that sparkled in the candlelight. Her beauty was unmistakable, but the coldness in her emerald green eyes exposed her inner self.

Having acknowledged my presence, she turned her gaze toward the fireplace where a tall, well-dressed man stood watching the flames. At first, I thought it was Mark, but Endora reading my thoughts corrected me.

"No, not Mark, Edmund. Strange how two men born a century apart could share such a strong likeness."

Things became even more surreal when Nathan arrived with his nursemaid to say goodnight. If not for the difference in age, Nathan was two years older than Andrew, and the boy's frail appearance, they could pass for twins.

"Odd then that you and I should have nothing at all in common?" Said in a manor intended to demean it carried me back to my aunt's house and the daily ritual of leaving for school.

*She stood just inside the front door waiting to give me my final inspection. My hair was cut short in no particular style, my dress was a nondescript green, and my black Mary Jane's were scuffed from use. My eyes as always were glued to a spot in the carpet just beyond the toes of her shoes. Like a bird of prey ready to pounce my aunt would make her pronouncement. "How could two such handsome people produce such a plain, unattractive, stupid child? Oh well, go on. You're as good as you'll get, I'm afraid."*

"I came to say goodnight Mother," Nathan said, bringing me back to the present. Offering the boy only a meager smile she sent him to his father who laughing, picked him up and hugged him. "Sally tells me you're making good progress with your studies."

"Yes, Father I am."

"Then as a reward what say we visit Grandpapa at Haddonfield." Nathan, his expression brightening shock his head vigorously, but Endora interrupted and ordered his nursemaid to return him to his room. "Your mother's right, it's time you were away to your bed," Edmund said. "Especially if you want to see me off in the morning." Reluctantly he passed the boy off to his nursemaid who carried him back upstairs to his bed.

"What good are studies when he'll be dead before he understands them? A waste of time and effort if you asked me. As for Haddonfield he won't be going."

"Come on Endora, stop being childish."

"If I'm not welcome, neither is my son."

"That's our son, if you don't mind," Edmund corrected.

"My God Edmund—when are you going to stop pandering to your parents? It's so demeaning."

"I'm not pandering to anyone, I'm respecting their wishes, nothing more. As for demeaning myself, since I know how much you enjoy it, I would never deny you the pleasure." Edmund poured himself a whiskey and tipped it in her direction.

"A real man wouldn't allow his parents to bully his wife."

"Ah—back to that are we? Be a man and confront my father or a disfigured cripple and crawl away into the darkness? It's a conundrum for sure, but until I can work it out, I'll not deprive Nathan of their company. You know my family is close to the Queen and more so now she's in mourning, yet you made deliberate remarks intended to wound her. Apologize and they'll welcome you back."

Going over to the bell pull Endora gave it a fearsome tug and at once a girl no older than seventeen appeared to clear away the dishes. I smiled. Edmund had struck the first blow and Endora was using this slight interruption to regroup. The girl had barely left the room when the onslaught continued.

"Considering your father's past indiscretions, he should be the last to lecture others on proper decorum. As for Nathan, if you weren't so tight fisted, we could take the boy to a warmer climate where he wouldn't have to fight for every breath."

Edmund's features hardened as his hands tightened their grip on the chair back. "Do you think me so hard, so calloused, that I'd allow Nathan to suffer rather than spend a few pounds?"

"Yes, I do."

"So where would you have us go?" Edmund asked.

"Anywhere away from this dismal, tiresome place and that ridiculous business of yours."

"That ridiculous business pays for all this."

Like a petulant child Endora threw herself down onto the divan, and though she didn't kick her feet or pound the sofa arm, she appeared ready to do so. "If Nathan dies, it will be your fault for keeping us here."

"I keep us here because you've spent the money needed to move us elsewhere."

Endora sprang to her feet and marched about the room with hands on hips. "What are you trying to say?"

"If the Americans don't buy my harvester, you won't need to worry about living here because we'll have to sell the place to survive." Again, Edmund landed a blow, and I applauded his efforts.

"But what about the money your father gave you? The money you had in your own right?"

"Look around you," Edmund said spreading his arms, "the chandeliers, the carpets, the furniture. Go open your wardrobe. Touch the jewels around your neck. Any money we had, you've long since spent."

Endora's expression changed from shock to loathing. "Damn you Edmund. Damn you to hell! You're speaking to the eldest daughter of a Duke. Not some common whore that takes in washing to survive."

"I'm afraid you're more familiar with hell than I am. The only reason we're here now is because of what you did."

"Yes, blame me."

"Who else should I blame? If you hadn't taken advantage and wormed your way into my bed—"

"How dare you—"

"How dare I?" Edmund said turning on her. "I'll tell you how I dare. Your father might be a Duke, but he's a tightfisted one for all his pomp and bluster. Everything you have is because of me, not him. And why, because he refused you your dowry rather than allow me to have it. I've given you everything to the point there's nothing left and still you want more."

"You poor pathetic fool what you gave me was a man so overwhelmed with self-pity that he'd rather drink himself under the table every night than face his responsibilities. Why you didn't die on the battlefield instead of crawling home to become an embarrassment is beyond me."

Endora had struck the decisive blow and Edmund's demeanor showed it. His shoulders drooped, his voice softened, and his eyes turned dark and empty. It was clear he was tired of her taunts and tired of her.

"From the moment I learned you were with child I attempted to do what was right. I confessed to your family the child was mine, then built Thornwood so you'd have a home worthy of you. I bought you diamonds, and trips abroad—yet for all that you make it clear in every way possible you despise and loathe me. If it hadn't been for Nathan I would've died out there and been done with it, but the thought of him being left in your care kept me fighting to live."

Limping slightly Edmund turned, left the room, and in the absolute silence of the moment left the house. At once I was standing in the alcove behind the dining room door, as the scent of lavender faded down the hall.

* * *

What before I had only imagined, I now admitted was true. I had become a part of Thornwood's past, a past I found hard to share even with Tom and Maggie, and when they questioned me, I'd say as little as possible. Noting the change Maggie argued that I should leave Thornwood before it was too late, but I laughed at her concerns. Still, they were my friends, and I found peace and comfort when with them.

After a month's absence, Mark returned and took a few days leave. Andrew couldn't be happier, but I found his presence unsettling. "I went over to Tom and Maggie's while you were gone." Mark looked up from his newspaper. "They talked about Thornwood and how we were the first people to live here in over fifty years."

"So where is this going?" Mark asked, laying the paper aside.

"I thought you'd want to know that's all. I mean if the Black's had lived here like they said, someone would have seen them. Seen their car in the driveway, or people making repairs, or something."

"To hear you, our finding this place was some sort of witchcraft or something. It's utter nonsense and I'm going to bed."

"You have to admit it's strange," I called after him.

# CHAPTER SIX

I found it while rearranging the attic to make more room. An old steamer trunk tucked away in a corner and covered by a centuries-worth of dust. As usual my curiosity went into overdrive and I had to open it. Inside there were several magazines dating back to the 1860's, two old photo albums filled with faded photographs and a package wrapped in paper and tied with black ribbon. Fearful of damaging the contents I cleared a space and laid it down with care on the lid.

Inside was the most beautiful gown I'd ever seen. Made of powdered blue silk, this was no ordinary gown and though the ages were taking their toll and the dress was beginning to fray, it was still possible to see that this dress was made for a special occasion.

Holding it up to the light I was stunned to find that the back was stained with blood. Why would someone keep something so damaged? Then just as it was with the poem I was there watching what took place.

*I was standing in the upstairs hallway looking down on a crowd of people very finely dressed. Off to my right, a door opened and a young girl of about seventeen appeared wearing the blue dress. Appearing happy but nervous, she waited for the orchestra to begin then made her way towards the stairs. Endora appearing out of nowhere shoved the girl back against the wall, and though I couldn't hear their conversation, I could see she was furious about what was taking place. After a brief struggle, the girl freed herself and hurried toward the steps where Endora caught her and giving her a slight push caused her to stumble and fall to her death. Thinking no one saw her Endora allowed herself a quick satisfied smile.*

Sickened by the spectacle I placed the dress back in the trunk, gathered the items I wanted to take down with me and left the attic with more questions than answers. Why would she do such a terrible thing? I needed to find out but how when the Stanley's had been absent for almost a month? Tom and Maggie naturally were relieved by their absence and suggested things might now return to normal. Even my father—*"If the devil walks out the door, don't call him back."* Then I had a thought. If I were alone like before maybe they'd appear. I went to see Connie. She owed me a favor.

"What did you say?" Connie asked rummaging through her diaper bag.

"Will you keep Andrew for a few days?"

"What's going on?"

"Nothing, I just need a little time to myself."

"Are you and Mark having problems? He sounded stressed out on the phone last week."

"I'll drop him off Friday after school and pick him up on Sunday."

"At least give me a hint?" Connie said.

"Fine, pretend I never asked."

"Don't be like that," Connie said wiping carrots off Samantha's cheek. "Go do what you want, I'll watch him. I'll be in town on Friday anyway, so I'll pick him up."

I waited all day and into the evening for them to appear but when they didn't I closed up the house and headed up to bed. Endora was waiting on the landing.

"You wanted me, so here I am."

"I want to know about the girl in the blue dress."

"That's none of your concern—but I did try to warn her. She was such a stubborn little thing. When she refused to listen well . . . It's a lesson you should take to heart."

"Are you threatening me?"

"Stupid girl. Why would I threaten you?"

"For the same reason you like to make my life a misery."

"Perhaps it's time you understand who you're dealing with."

With a wave of her hand the house began to shake and for a moment seemed about to come apart. Raising her arms toward the heavens she rose slowly off the floor and floated above me. "The power is all mine Julie."

Seeing someone floating in the air is rather disconcerting, but how was I to respond? If I did nothing she'd think I was weak and afraid. This will sound mad but looking around to find some way to defend myself I noticed a piece of that vile wallpaper had come away from the wall. Immediately I heard someone whisper "tear it from the wall." It was a ridiculous idea that I disregarded immediately. What good would tearing off a piece of wallpaper do when she could hover in the air? Again, the voice, this time more demanding, said tear the paper from the wall. With nothing to lose I did as I was instructed with amazing results. Endora began to scream as if I were tearing the flesh from her bones. Finding another piece, I did the same and this time I noticed spots of blood appearing on her clothes.

"You're not the only one with power," I shouted up at her. "Like my father I can see into the future, and if you don't stop, I'll tear down Thornwood brick by brick and crush it beneath my feet."

It was all a bluff, I could no more destroy Thornwood than fly Mark's plane, but for a moment her expression was one of terror.

"You'll be gone long before you have the chance," she said then disappeared.

\* \* \*

You don't sleep well after an incident like that so next morning I staggered down to the kitchen for a cup of strong coffee with lots of sugar. "Hello there," a man called out as I passed the living room door. I had been wanting to meet him ever since I saw him in the dining room and now there he was, and I was asking if he'd like to join me in a cup of coffee.

I found his answer almost Mark-esque. He joked and said he doubted we'd both fit. When I returned, he smiled, apologized for the joke, then pulled out a chair and suggested I join him. "I'm Edmund, Edmund Stanley, but I guess you knew that. Where did you find these?" He nodded toward the photo albums spread out in front of him.

"In a trunk in the attic. I hope you don't mind?"

"Heavens no. To be honest, I thought them lost. Would you like me to tell you who they are?" Nodding, he began. He was showing me a picture of his mother when I saw her on the opposite page. The girl. The one in the blue dress. The one with the poem.

"Edmund, who is that." I asked my excitement growing.

"That's Jennifer Glenn with William her father." He didn't elaborate.

"I know that girl. I've seen her—she has a blue dress. Tell me."

Again, he hesitated. "Jennifer was my stepmother's maid."

"And" I encouraged. "I've seen her, and I need to understand." Edmund's tone changed, his eyes narrowed, and he implied without saying that nothing more would be forthcoming.

"This is one of my favorites," he began. "That's Matilda Brown our maid-of-all-work. Over by the carriage is Sally Shaw, Nathan's nursemaid—nanny, really. He's too old for a nursemaid. That's Clara Jordan the cook. Oh, and that's our butler, Silas Bates. Clara and Silas have been with me since childhood." Edmund stopped and looked toward the doorway. "I'm sorry, I'm needed upstairs." He replaced his chair and hurried toward the stairs leaving the faint scent of lavender behind.

I achieved little that day for my mind was on the girl and Edmund's response. Why was he so unwilling to talk about her? Did he still love her? And what about the wallpaper. What was that all about? Clearly Endora had some connection to it but what? Even stranger who told me to do it, because someone did, of that I was certain.

Andrew went to bed early that night with a slight temperature, so having nothing to do I pulled out the magazines I'd taken from the attic. I was reading an article on lace making when I heard shouting out in the hall. Edmund was leaning over the banister calling down to Clara who had hurried in from the kitchen. "Get Silas to fetch the doctor. Hurry." Clara curtsied and disappeared down the hall.

"Can I help?" I asked running up the stairs.

"Yes, please. Nathan's in trouble, and I could use your help."

The scene was chaotic. Nathan was barely able to breath. In my world they called the condition Cystic Fibrosis, but this was the 1800's and little was known about the condition at that time. Remembering a program I'd seen on TV some years earlier I decided to do what they showed on the screen. Methods had advanced since then, but it was all I could think to do. Cupping my hand, I laid him on his stomach and began pounding on his back in an attempt to break up the congestion. Sally horrified that I should treat the Master's son in such a manner tried to stop me, but I refused to stop. By the time the doctor arrived the seriousness of the situation had eased, and Nathen was breathing more comfortably.

The doctor, impeccably dressed, with a well-trimmed lampshade mustache stood surveying the room. Small in stature he nevertheless had an air of authority difficult to ignore.

"You said the boy couldn't breathe?" he said opening his bag. "Well, no sense wasting a visit." He gave Nathan a cursory examine then turned his attention toward me. "I don't believe we've met." He extended his hand which I shook. "Dr. Albert Wood. And you are?"

"Julie's a distant cousin visiting from America," Edmund said hurrying forward.

"Well, she seems competent enough. Yes, she seems competent."

The crisis over, Edmund saw the doctor out while I stayed behind to help Sally get Nathan settled. Afterward I went to find Edmund. "I don't mean to intrude," I said from the doorway of his study, "but I'm not sure how I got here or how I get home?"

Edmund looked embarrassed. "How foolish of me. Picture where you want to be, and you'll be there. It works both ways. Oh, and before you ask, no, I'm not a ghost I'm flesh and blood like you. Here see for yourself." He placed my hand in his. "See, flesh and blood."

# CHAPTER SEVEN

Just after ten next morning Connie called to ask if she could keep Andrew an extra day. They were having a children's matinee at the theater and she wanted to take the kids. With an extra day to myself I decided to pack a picnic lunch and head down to Shingle Street, my favorite place to sketch.

I was all packed and ready to go when the house returned to the past and Endora came in with a man on her arm that wasn't her husband. Wanting to avoid a confrontation I hid behind the Aspidistra plant by the French windows.

To be fair, women's taste in men differ. But that woman, with that man? Graying around the temples I guessed him to be in his mid-forties. His clothes were expensive, but much too flamboyant for my taste, and his overall air of superiority was off-putting. His most prominent features were his mouth, wide with full fleshy lips, and his eyes, set deep and a cold steel gray, that looked through rather than at you. He reminded me of John. Pleasant enough on the outside, but underneath dangerous and cruel.

"Touring the continent with Mother wasn't my idea of fun but running into the Mortimer's made things a bit jollier." He dropped his walking stick into the umbrella stand and threw his coat on the chair. "As usual, the crossing was dreadful."

"There's someone I think you'll want to meet." Walking over to where I was hiding, she dragged me out from behind the plant. "This is Julie Hammond. Julie, meet Charles Ambrose Lester, the Baron of Kilgore."

"Enchanted," he said reaching for a hand I didn't offer. Then running his tongue over his lips, he pressed them into my palm. "Please, call me Bunny. My friends do." I didn't care what his friends called him, I wanted my hand back, and pulling it away cut myself on the sharp edge of his ring. "Oh, I am sorry." Taking a hanky from his pocket he wiped the blood away. "There, all better. He held the soiled hanky to his nose as if smelling a rose then returned it to his pocket. "Delicious, absolutely delicious. I'll keep it as a memento." Hearing Endora call he followed her upstairs.

I intended to continue on to Shingle Street, but as usual curiosity got the best of me and sent me sneaking up the steps behind them. The bedroom door, open just enough to allow the bed to be reflected in the hallway mirror made me wonder if that wasn't done on purpose.

"Come to bed Endora. I didn't come to look; I came to partake." Endora, naked, climbed in beside him. Without waiting, Bunny, grunting like an old bore rolled on top and with growing intensity, slammed his body into hers with the force of a pile driver. Wet with sweat, he came with a long, guttural moan then relaxed back onto the bed and reached for his cigar case. "You said by my return everything would be settled." Endora resting on her elbow played with the thick mat of dark curly hair on Bunny's chest.

"You of all people should understand these things take time."

"Time yes. Eternity no."

"Since the Councils gotten involved, we have to be more cautious."

"She's rather an innocent, isn't she?" Bunny took a long drag on his cigar and blew smoke rings toward the ceiling.

"Just remember who she's here for."

"I understand Edmund's still dragging Nathan up and down Harley Street looking for a cure."

"What else does he have when I've convinced everyone he's nothing more than an abusive drunk?"

Intent on their conversation, I didn't notice Sally with an armload of clean linens, coming down the hall. If she put the sheets in the airing cupboard, then returned to the kitchen, everything would be fine, but Endora chose that moment to knock her wine glass onto the floor. Assuming she was alone Sally hearing the noise hurried to investigate but stopped short when she looked into the mirror. Her checks turned red, her eyes widened, and with a gasp of surprise dropped the linen on the floor.

"Now look what you've done you stupid girl," Endora screamed as she rushed out into the hall barely covered by her flaming red kimono. My first thought was that it was all too convenient. Did she really hear Sally gasp, or did she expect her to be there? And why, if Sally saw me last night did she not see me now when I tried to wave her away? It was all too convenient for my liking.

"I don't like people who spy. Especially those that think it's a ticket into the Master's bedchamber. I've seen you making eyes at him," she said circling the girl. "Laughing at everything he says. Making everyone believe you're all innocence and light. Will, I've seen through your little ploy and as of today you're done. I want you out of this house by sundown. Is that understood?"

"But Madam—"

"Don't Madam me you little slut. And don't expect a reference because you'll get none." Lowering her voice, she moved closer. "And if you tell one person, one person mind you about what you saw here today you'll have to prostitute yourself to survive. Do you understand?"

Too frightened to speak Sally barely nodded her head. Satisfied, Endora returned to her room where gales of laughter filtered out from under the door. Sally, in a near state of collapse collected the soiled linens, ran down to the kitchen and throwing herself into the nearest chair, buried her head in her hands and began to sob. Clara, back from the greengrocers, took charge.

"Now what's all this?" Clara asked. "Calm yourself and tell me what's happened."

"It's Madam—her and that Bunny Lester. She says I've been sleeping with the Master, but I never did—never."

"Of course, you didn't. Why Master Edmund would never do a thing like that."

"I've got to leave today without a character." Clara appeared ready to explode.

"Look here my girl, you're going nowhere. That woman's done more hurting than one woman should be allowed. I'll take it to the Master. Till then you're to stay put, understand?"

"But Madam said—"

"Never you mind what Madam said."

"But—"

"Go have a lie down. I'll see to things till you're more settled."

\* \* \*

The crisis over, I continued on to Shingle Street a desolate strip of land at the mouth of Orford Ness. It could, depending on the weather be dark and foreboding, or eerily beautiful. When the tides were at their lowest, you could walk out onto the exposed sandbars, but care was needed for if you missed the tides turning you could be cut off and washed away.

The sun warm, I spread my blanket, ate my sandwich, and spent the next several hours absorbed in my work. Off to the west a storm was gathering. I hoped to finish before it arrived, but miscalculating the distance lost all my work to the sudden downpour. Soaked to the bone I headed home, dropped my equipment by the door, and hurried upstairs for a quick shower. Hearing the water running I assumed Endora was up to her usual tricks.

"What do you think you're—" Mark with a startled expression looked up from his bath. "Sorry, I thought you were someone else," I said without thinking. "You didn't say you'd be home early."

"I wanted it to be a surprise. I see you've already showered," he said laughing. "Where's Andrew? I brought him something."

"He's over at Connie's. I wanted to go into London, so she said she'd watch him. I thought he'd be home today, but she asked for him to stay another night."

"Who did you think I was?" Mark grabbed a towel and climbed out of the tub.

"The neighbor's cat."

"You've met the neighbors?"

"Their cat went missing—"

Mark interrupted. "So, did they find it?"

"Yes," I said, trying to make a lie sound truthful, "she was all curled up in one of our empty bedrooms. I took her home, but she keeps coming back. I've tried to find where she gets in but haven't yet." Dropping my wet clothes on the floor, I took a quick shower, then joined Mark in the bedroom.

"You don't seem very happy to see me."

"I am," I said, "want to see how much?" I threw my towel aside and pushed him down onto the bed. At that moment I didn't care if he said I was crazy, or we hadn't been getting along—Mark was home and wanted me as much as I wanted him. It was only afterward when he lay exhausted by my side that the darkness of the past few months came stealing back. We vowed never to lie to each other, but since arriving at Thornfield lying had become a way of life. At least for me.

# CHAPTER EIGHT

Thursday night a pea soup fog rolled in off the channel, but Mark's five a.m. briefing had not been canceled.

"It's all right for the guys on base, they don't have to drive, but for the rest of us it's suicidal. You can't see a hand in front of your face out there." Mark finished his breakfast and headed for the door. "If you don't hear from me send out a search party."

"But you're the best navigator in the squadron."

"Yeah. when I can see."

\* \* \*

On top the wardrobe was a large box filled with toys Andrew no longer wanted. Deciding Nathan could have them he climbed up on a chair, the chair slipped, and the wardrobe fell on top of him. Trapped underneath I tried to lift it and pull him free, but it was too heavy. I sent Nathan to fetch his father while I did what I could for Andrew.

A few moments later Edmund arrived and lifted the wardrobe while I pulled Andrew out from underneath. A bone was sticking out of his right arm. Regardless the weather I had to get him out to the clinic. Edmund held him while I called Mark in hopes he could join me, but Mark had managed to get away and would be spending the night in Belgium.

"I know this isn't the best time," Edmund said as he carried Andrew out to the car, "but I need to ask a favor. Once Andrew is well again, would you consider looking after Nathan? There's no one else I can ask at the moment, and he likes you. Would you think it imposing?" My emotions on overload I agreed believing someday I might need his help. "I know you will," he said as I drove away.

By the time I reached the clinic Andrew was showing signs of shock. They did what they could then sent us by ambulance to the main hospital at Dunmore. Dr. Phillips, expecting us, rushed Andrew into surgery while I paced the floor and worried. Afterward, the doctor explained what they did, and that Andrew would remain hospitalized for at least a week. "It a severe break but hopefully we've got it stabilized. The next few days will tell, and of course there's always a chance of infection with this sort of injury."

Mark arrived late that night looking tired and worried. I explained how it happened, and what the doctor's said, then suggested he get a room at the BOQ. I'd remain with Andrew till he returned. Over the next few days Andrew's condition appeared to improve, but on day five he became delirious, his fever skyrocketed, and his arm showed definite signs of infection. Mark stayed with Andrew while I called his parents and Connie. When I returned Mark was a changed man.

"What's wrong with you?"

"You said you loved me—but now—I'm not sure what to believe," Mark said.

"What are you talking about?"

"How long did you think you could keep it a secret?" Mark asked. "Because it's not a secret anymore."

"What's a secret?"

"Don't play innocent with me Julie. I can't do this, not now, I can't." Mark grabbed his jacket and headed out the door.

"Where are you going?"

"Home."

"You can't go home. You're needed here. What will I tell Andrew? How can you do this? Tell me what's wrong," I said running after him.

"I love Andrew, I do, but I can't stay. Not now. I'll call to see how he is, but . . ."

It was touch and go for several days but slowly Andrew seemed to improve. Two weeks later they sent him home. I called to tell Mark the good news, but Edmund answered. His crisp manner said something was wrong.

"I don't mean to burden you further, but after Mark came home, he rummaged through your things. The wardrobe, the bureau, everything. Even looked under the bed. I tried to discover why, but he was so angry I couldn't get through."

Stung by this unexpected news, I felt ill. The brooch and poem—I hid them in my bureau intending to give them back. Now Mark had them . . .

The next day we headed for home with a strict warning from Dr. Lambert to call the clinic at the first sign of trouble as Andrew had several weeks of healing ahead of him. Nathan was waiting at the door as we pulled in the drive. When he saw the cast on Andrew's arm he began to cry. Patting him on the shoulder Andrew assured him he'd be fine, and not to worry. As I made their lunch Andrew told his friend in gruesome detail the indignities he had to suffer and how everyone told him he was very brave. Afterward I tucked them in for an afternoon nap.

"Any noise, which includes giggling, "and I'll put Nathan back in his own I room." I gave them both a kiss, then joined Edmund sitting on the top step of the stairs.

"Everything all settled then?" he asked, as I sat down beside him.

"Nothing will ever be settled again."

Edmund looked at me quizzically. "Explain."

"The box you gave Jennifer. I found it and intended to give it back and should have but couldn't. Now Mark has it and thinks I'm cheating on him."

It was clear Edmund had something he wanted to tell me, but each time he started I interrupted. Perhaps because I was afraid of what he'd say, I don't know. Moments later I made everything worse by blurting out that if he ever needed anyone I'd be there for him. Being married, it was a ridiculous thing to say, yet I didn't take it back. And again, like with the wallpaper, I felt as if someone was talking through me.

* * *

Mark and I shared a home, but a coldness had crept into our relationship. I tried explaining about the brooch and poem—tried to make it better but Mark having felt betrayed refused to listen. When I asked if he was still leaving for Spain in the morning, he said, "We're on weather hold till Saturday, but I can go tonight if you prefer. You probably had plans." He then implied that I'd be glad if he were killed in a plane crash.

Angered by his insinuations I shot back. "That's a sick thing to say—I love you and if you can't see that it's your problem not mine."

"I just figured that if I were dead you wouldn't have to sneak behind my back with the guy Andrew kept talking about. The one that gave you the stuff in your bureau."

"Oh, for God's sake Mark. Is that what this is all about. A little boy says something while delirious with fever and you take it as gospel? He didn't know what he was saying."

"But he knew about the box. He knew about that, didn't he?"

# CHAPTER NINE

Over the following months travel between the past and present became second nature and with Edmund's help the servants accepted me as a member of the family. As for Endora, her cruel nature was on full display when Matilda, the parlor maid came to fetch me.

"Please Miss Julie, please you have to come. I can't make Madame stop—please, hurry."

I found Nathan huddled in the corner with his arms wrapped around his head to shield himself from the blows his mother was raining down upon him. Grabbing her arm, I tore the belt from her hand and spun her around to face me. Surprised that I would interfere, her expression changed from anger to indifference, and with a shrug she returned to her room.

"Get away from me—leave me alone." Nathan, his arms covered with large red welts huddled deeper into the corner.

"It's Julie honey, not your mom. I'm here now and no one's going to hurt you." In a burst of tears Nathan threw himself into my arms.

"She hates me because I'm sick."

I carried him over to the rocker and began rocking him gently back and forth while Matilda called for Clara to bring warm water and towels. Afterward I asked Matilda what happened.

"Nathan needed his medicine, but the bottle was empty. I went to get more, but I swear I was only gone a minute, honest. When I got back Madam was here, and I couldn't make her stop. She just kept hitting him and screaming that she was sick of his constant coughing and wheezing. Said it was driving her mad."

"She's always hitting him," Andrew said joining us. "I told Uncle Edmund, but she still does it."

Furious that Edmund would allow such cruelty, I took matters into my own hands. "If you're going up to Madam, Lester's with her," Clara said. "Been there since tea-time."

There was no way Bunny Lester would stop me from telling Endora what I thought of her, but Edmund having returned unexpectedly from America dragged me into his office to hear the news.

"Do you remember me saying that if the Americans didn't buy my harvester I'd be ruined?" I nodded. "Well that wasn't quite true."

"You knew I was there?"

"Yes, but even better the Americans loved my invention and offered a deal beyond anything I thought possible." Humming a dance tune, he waltzed me around the room then stopped in mid-step. "I must tell Nathan." Before I could stop him he was halfway up the stairs.

"Father, your home." Nathan reached out for Edmund's hand.

"Did she do that," he asked when he saw the bruised on his son's face and arms. It didn't require an answer. "The Council promised this wouldn't happen. Does their word mean nothing?"

The house fell silent as Edmund made his way down the hall to her room. As he passed, I touched his arm. "She's not alone Edmund, Bunny's with her." He nodded and continued on. I figured he'd fling open the door and confront her. Instead, he stood silent as their conversation seeped through the door.

"You're playing with fire Endora. When Edmund sees what you've done—"

"Don't be ridiculous. He'll do what he always does—drink himself senseless then stagger home."

"How much longer must this charade continue? I'm getting bored with the entire situation."

"Patience, we're almost there."

"How you can stand living with a whore's bastard . . ."

A short burst of laughter was followed by the rhythmic squeaking of bedsprings and Endora's deep guttural moans of pleasure. Not till she reached the frenzied pitch of impending climax, did Edmund burst into the room and with one powerful shove unseat her from atop Bunny's throbbing member. Having robbed Endora of her pleasure he took hold of the bedsheet and giving it a tug, rolled Bunny onto the floor. Attempting to retaliate Bunny sprang to his feet and charged headlong into Edmund's clinched fist.

"That's for the comment about my mother. Now for God's sake cover yourself, no one wants to see that." Realizing his state of undress Bunny grabbed Endora's kimono and wrapped it around himself like a toga.

"If I've learned anything," Edmund said, concentrating on Endora, "it's you'd fornicate with the devil to hurt me, and since I wrote that I'd be home today, I assume that's what this was all about."

Surprise spread across Bunny's face as he stared up at Endora sitting half naked on the edge of the bed. "But you said—" he sputtered.

"Shut up Bunny," she ordered, keeping her eyes fixed on Edmund.

"Sadly, it now appears I'm faced with a dilemma. Until today your little dalliance didn't interest me. But now—well—now you've placed me in the untenable position of having to do something about it."

"You have no right--"

Edmund gave Bunny a look that would melt steel. "I have every right. This is my home and that—though I regret to say it, is my wife."

Wrapping his fingers through Endora's hair he forced her head back so she couldn't turn away. "From now on, if you so much as look sideways at Nathan I'll take a horse whip to that white skin of yours, and my scars will be nothing to those you'll carry. As you say, I might be a bastard, but Father isn't and if not for me then for him, they'll drive you from England." Edmund stormed out of the room and reaching for his coat left the house.

* * *

Later that evening Nathan's condition required a call to Dr. Wood. "So, where's Edmund," he asked taking off his coat. "No, don't tell me, out drinking. I'm afraid he'll do what he wants regardless what I say. Now take me to the boy." Tensions increased when he saw the damage his mother had done. "She won't be happy till they're both dead."

He did what he could for Nathan, then ushered me into Edmund's study and closed the door behind us. "I've known Edmund since childhood, and never once did he mention a cousin in America. So, who are you?"

Being honest at this point was impossible, so I said we met onboard ship. Edmund was returning from a business trip and I was running away from an abusive husband. I had no place to go, so he offered to let me stay at Thornwood. In exchange, I'd care for Nathan. He thought saying we were cousins would shield me from any embarrassment."

"I don't believe you," he said pouring himself a whiskey, "but others might. Yes, others might." He returned to his seat and asked, "Do you intend to stay—here I mean, at Thornwood?" I shrugged my response. "Perhaps if I told you a little about the family—"

"Shouldn't Edmund be the one to do that?" I asked.

"Edmund's not here so it's up to me. If you didn't know, Edmund is the illegitimate son of Sir John Owen Stanley the Marquis of Swansgate. His grandfather is John Horatio Stanley the Duke of Cambrea. His mother, Sarah Budge was lady's maid to the Duchess. Or was, till she became pregnant with Owen's baby. Owen loved the girl and wanted to marry her, but that didn't sit well with his father. The Duke ranted and raved and sent Owen off to the Continent and Sarah onto the street.

"Owen was kept away for three years, then without permission returned to search for Sarah. He found her dying of consumption and too weak to explain where their son was."

"How old was Edmund when his father found him?" I asked.

"About seven if memory serves, or maybe eight, but no more. You'll laugh, but Owen offered a reward for the boy. People even brought their own children, hoping for the money."

"The Duke must have been livid?"

"He was, but Lady Flora reminded him that if he disinherited his son, the estate would go to a nephew he disliked even more. A fine woman was Lady Flora. Told Owen the child was his, and he owed the boy a decent life."

"Did Owen ever marry?"

"Yes, the Lady Beatrice. The youngest daughter of the Duke of Cumberland. A nice woman, but shy. Edmund could be a handful, but she did her best by him. Well," the doctor said glancing over at the mantel clock, "it's time I go home to my bed. When Edmund comes in it won't be pretty but do what you can."

I checked on the boys then carried my now dry sketches into the living room to see what could be done with them. I was just sorting things out when Endora strolled in.

"Put that stuff away, I'm lonely and want to talk. What did the quack have to say?" She poured herself a glass of wine and took a seat on the sofa.

"Nothing you'd want to hear."

She smiled, "Worried about Edmund I suppose?"

"Someone has to be."

"Oh, come now. Don't be such a prude. He'll come home when he runs out of money."

"Then you know where he is?" I asked.

"Where he always is, the Stags Head." I rang for Silas and sent him to fetch Edmund home. "Why are you so concerned about Edmund when you have Mark?"

"Why do you sleep with Lester when you have Edmund?"

"Touché. My relationship with Bunny is of a peculiar nature and nothing you need concern yourself about. So, answer my question. Why chase Edmund when you have Mark?"

"I'm not chasing anyone."

"Then why do you talk about him in your sleep? Not quite the thing to do with Mark lying next to you."

"I don't talk in my sleep and I don't cheat on my husband. I would never do that."

"You should never say *never*," Endora said pulling back the curtain to look out at the sudden rain shower. "It means under no circumstances. When you say never, you're setting yourself up for a fall. Oh well, at least you've got two fine specimens in Mark and Andrew. All I've got is a sickly child, and a drunken—"

I interrupted. "You can't blame Edmund for being wounded any more than you can blame him for his son being born with a life-threatening illness. Things happen."

"Oh, here they are now." Endora let the curtain fall back, then turning to face me said, "I don't remember saying Nathan was Edmund's child."

# CHAPTER TEN

Both men were soaked through by the sudden downpour, but only Edmund smelled of whiskey and needed support.

"Julie," Endora called from the middle landing, "do try to control him. He gets rather rowdy when in his cups."

"Don't worry my pet, I'll be as quiet as the grave," Edmund called up to her.

"Come now Sir. No more of that." Silas removed his wet coat and edged him toward the stairs. "It's time we got you into bed."

Getting Edmund anywhere proved difficult as he insisted on flinging his arms about in dramatic fashion while reciting poetry. "To die in the arms of the one I adore, what bliss would such death afford, if in the spring, when the Robin's sing, we'd lay side by side once more."

"The only place we'll be lying is on the floor if you don't stop," I said struggling to hang on.

"Oh, fair maid thy angry words hath brought me to despair. For I with fondness do recall the tender ones we shared." This time his theatrics almost sent us over the railing. By the time we recovered Edmund had broken away and was pounding on Endora's door promising to be quiet. Afraid he'd wake the children, we manhandled him into his room and dumped him on his bed.

"The Master would prefer I do that," Silas said, as I began to remove Edmund's wet clothes.

"The Master's in no fit state to prefer anything. Now go change before you catch pneumonia."

"What are you doing?" Edmund demanded.

"I'm getting you undressed because you don't seem able."

"I'm able—I'm just a little tipsy. See," he said pulling himself into an upright if shaky position. "Someone's sewed the buttons closed."

"No, they haven't. Keep trying."

"My fingers won't work. Help me." Attempting to do so Edmund flopped back onto the bed. "Endora hates me. She calls me a freak, a deformed monster. I don't know why. I never meant to be." As the alcohol drove him deeper into despair Edmund quoted from another of his poems. "From the heart love doth come, and all the emotions passion evokes. Yet is not the heart the first to suffer when all love's promises turn to dust?" Turning away Edmund wept. "Jenny—Jenny—you promised you'd come back. Why didn't you come?"

At the mention of her name a sudden madness overtook me, and once again I felt as if someone was speaking through me.

"Tell him—tell Edmund all will be well. Tell him—"

*I was sitting in the park with Father eating an ice cream cone. He seemed burdened by something and when I asked he said, "Sometimes when people die unexpectedly they leave unfinished business behind. Something they wanted to say to a loved one, or something they hid away that needed to be found. At other times it's to say they're all right and not to worry and that they'll wait for the one left behind. When the time is right, they speak through me and I forward their message. I know people think me strange, even fearsome, and perhaps I am, but I never asked for this terrible gift, it was passed on to me."*

I was too young to fully understand, but now I had to believe that in his own way he was telling me what my future would be. He knew that someday someone would use me in that manner. A girl that died before she could tell Edmund not to worry that she'd be alright, and that she'd come back in time.

I managed his shirt, but the trousers proved difficult and in the struggle I accidently hit his wound with my hand. He moaned and I moved away fearful of hurting him again. It was a terrible wound running from his hip to just below the knee. In several places little pockets of inflamed flesh poked out from where the stitches had come loose. An ugly scar, yes, but to degrade and humiliate him for it?

"Sergeant Jeffery's, get the men back behind cover," Edmund shouted. "No! Follow orders. Now! Where are they? I've lost them in the smoke." Silas, returning, rushed over to help. "Don't let them see you, their up on the ridge. Stay down, stay down!" Edmund cried out as he struggled to get to his feet.

I slapped him hard across the face. "Major, get hold of yourself. The battles over—we must see to your wounds. Lie still so we can care for you."

"So much blood—"

His nightmare over we finished what we were doing and turning down the light left him.

Silas stopped me as we made our way downstairs. "Thank you for what you did. When I tell him—"

"No, say nothing. We'll keep this between ourselves."

I was late going back next day as Andrew's follow-up appointment at the clinic took longer than expected. Unable to find Edmund, I asked Silas. Once again Edmund had gone to Lathan at his father's request. Renovations were being made and Sir Owen wanted Edmund's input.

"He'll be gone a week, maybe longer," Clara said, clearing away the supper dishes. "It's a fine big place just outside Inverness in Scotland, but why they think it needs enlarging is beyond me."

* * *

Three weeks later Edmund returned and did his best to avoid me. Endora hinted it had something to do with a passage in my diary. When I said I didn't keep a diary, she shrugged and walked away.

As planned I dropped Andrew off at Connie's for a children's party she was giving. She invited me to stay but being preoccupied I said I'd come another time. "You've been saying that for weeks. What's wrong? You've lost weight and you look unwell. When I bring Andrew back, I'll expect answers."

Maybe she was right, I was a little run down and true, I'd lost weight, but for now my relationship with Edmund was more important. I found him hidden away in his study and it took several minutes for him to notice me.

"You've been avoiding me, and I want to know why." He looked up briefly then continued his work. "I need an answer Edmund."

"You already know the answer."

"If I knew I wouldn't ask."

"Liar." Reaching for a bottle of Scotch, he poured a small amount then downed it all at once.

"If this is about the diary, I'll tell you right now I don't keep one. Never have. My life isn't that exciting."

He managed only a cursory glance in my direction. "What do you take me for? Your name was inside. It was your handwriting."

"Like I said. I don't keep a diary. But even if I did, what right have you to read it?"

"Then why leave it lying about."

"So what am I supposed to have written that's got you so upset?"

"Maybe the part where you call me a pathetic drunk with a grotesque leg. Or perhaps your description of me as a poor excuse for a man and not worth caring about."

I almost laughed out loud. "Does any of that sound like me? There's nothing grotesque about your leg. It was just—"

"Then why pull your hand away?" he interrupted.

"Because you cried out when I touched it."

"I've got work to do. Now please, just leave."

"What do you want from me Edmund? I'm a married woman, yet I told you to come to me, that I'd be there for you. Why would I say that if I didn't care?"

"Because you needed a shoulder to cry on and mine was available. Foolish me for believing you meant it. Poor Edmund, too stupid to understand he's being played for a fool."

"Yet is not the heart the first to suffer. That's what you said, and you were right. I would rather die than see you hurt?"

"Then you'd best go see to it, because you already have."

Crushed by his words, I ran from the house and drove to Shingle Street. Why did his words upset me so? Mark was the man I loved, the man I married. Edmund was in the past, pulled up from the dust, yet I told him I'd rather die. Those are the words you say to your husband not a friend. "Oh God," I whispered falling to my knees, I can't do this. I can't . . ."

A man was walking out onto the sandbar. The tide was turning yet he paid no attention and walked out as far as possible. Watching, I cried out for him to come back, but the wind caught my words and carried them away. Perhaps it was the way he stood, head down and arms hanging limp at his side. Whatever, it touched me, as if he were saying, "watch, witness my end. Don't let my death go unnoticed." And then he disappeared, carried off by the tide.

From out of the mist a boat appeared, and the oarsman rowed toward the scene. Coming alongside, and with some difficulty he pulled the body on-board and headed for the shore. Anchoring the boat above the waterline the boatman laid the man on the ground, looked over at me, climbed back into the boat and disappeared back into the mist.

Running toward the abandoned body I was horrified to discover the man lying dead on the stones was not some stranger, but my father. Once again, I was a child watching from the doorway as the blood-tinged water splashed onto the bathroom floor as they lifted Father out of the tub. I tried to go to him, to say don't leave me, but a woman took my arm and said, "Come away, there's nothing for you here."

# CHAPTER ELEVEN

I was in a room no more than ten by ten. There was no light, or door that I could find, and if I wanted to stay warm had to keep moving. Water was dripping somewhere I could hear it *Drip, drip, drip stop, drip, drip, drip, stop.* Never two drips or four, always three, and the more I tried to ignore it the more difficult it became. I was afraid of water.

My aunt said being afraid was for weaklings, then she'd drag me out and throw me in the pond yelling that if I didn't want to drown I should swim. It always ended the same, she'd come in and pull me out. Now I was in this room with the dripping water and was beginning to panic when Endora arrived. At first I thought she was there to rescue me, but I soon learned that she was the reason for my imprisonment.

"These aren't the best accommodations, but they'll do for the time being. You're probably wondering why you're here, but all I'm willing to say is that we needed to move things along."

"What things," I managed.

"Convincing Mark you ran off with Edmund your secret lover. I thought a few whispers in his ear, and a couple nights talking about Edmund in your sleep would move Mark to believe the lie. It didn't, and so—the need for more drastic actions."

"I told you before I would never cheat on Mark and he knows it."

"There's that word *never* again. You must stop using that. As of now you've been gone just short of a week and Mark has no choice but to conclude you've gone off with your lover."

I interrupted. "I've been away for a week?"

"More or less."

"But Mark knows I'd never go off and leave Andrew on his own."

"He's not on his own. He's staying at Connie's house—remember."

A narrow light behind her made me believe that it was coming from a crack in the door. Taking advantage of her inattention I made a run for it. I didn't see Bunny and ran straight into his arms.

"Someone will come looking for me," I said struggling to free myself. "You wait and see. You can't keep me here forever, you can't."

"Oh, I don't intend to keep you here forever. This is just the first step in a series of steps. You'll be going home fairly soon now."

They left without a word, but I didn't keep walking. I found a corner and sliding down to the floor wrapped my arms around my knees. I was beginning to lose control when someone came into the room.

"Get up," Bunny demanded. When I didn't, he slapped me and taking hold of my arm yanked me upright. "When I say get up I intend for you to obey." Taking my face in his hands he forced his tongue down my throat. "Most men when presented with such an opportunity would take advantage at once. But I'm not most men. Take a woman physically it's just another encounter but take her mentally and she's yours for life. Shoving his hand inside my blouse he caressed my breast. "You're shivering. How delightful. You like it don't you? I can tell."

Using his thumbnail, he cut a long gash across the base of my neck and pulling me to him licked the blood from the wound. "It's an acquired taste, but soon you'll crave it as much as I do. Running his finger through the blood he smeared in on my lips and tried to make me taste it. When I refused, he struck me with his fist and tore my blouse away.

"What in the name of hell? No one gave you permission to do that," Endora screamed, pushing Bunny aside.

"She refused to obey."

"Then she's smarter than I thought. This isn't about you it's about me, and if you ruin my chances—"

"It'll teach that bastard husband of yours a lesson. He'll think twice before striking me again."

"Fool. He'll think nothing of the kind," Endora countered.

"You knew what I was when you asked for my help, so why the surprise when I take advantage."

"Get out of my sight before I do something I'll regret." Endora shoved him out the door and slammed it behind him. "The fool," she said. "Get dressed, we're taking you home."

A few minutes later Bunny returned, covered my eyes with a blindfold, then led me down a series of corridors that eventually led us to a waiting carriage. I was barely seated when Endora forced a vile tasting liquid down my throat. "What was that?"

"Just a little something to help complicate the situation. Your pain level will increase, and now you'll remember nothing at all about what took place. Oh, here we are. Home at least."

Lifting me from the carriage Bunny carried me to the foot of the stairs then removing the blindfold left me. A woman was looking down at me from the mirror and when she saw me began screaming. I told her to stop but she refused and continued on. I thought perhaps if she couldn't see me she'd stop, so I crawl up to the second floor, but she was there before me.

"You can't get away," she said. "I'm you and you are me." Was I mad, loony—perhaps like Alice off my rocker?

The woman turned and looked out the window, so I did as well. Out under the oak trees Nathan, his head resting on a satin pillow, appeared to be sleeping on the garden bench. A man dressed in black appeared, folded Nathan's arms across his chest, then tipping his hat in my direction walked away. "Soon that will be Andrew," the woman said, her voice full of conviction, "and Endora will go free."

Going over to the bannister I leaned out over the railing. It was a long way down. If I jumped would I die? Would they lay my head on a satin pillow and cross my arms? Deciding to find out I climbed over the banister, but before I could jump someone took hold of me and pulled me back. His strength was far greater than mine, but when I continued to struggle, he picked me up and carried me to the graveyard.

"Please, don't bury me alive," I pleaded. "Don't bury me alive."

* * *

Andrew sat beside me stroking my face. "Wake up Mom," he whispered. "Please wake up. I don't want you to be dead. Daddy said you were saying crazy things about a screaming woman, so he gave you a pill. Is she here?" he asked moving closer, "the screaming woman."

"No, she's gone."

"Clara said Daddy hurt you and that Uncle Edmund should send him packing. Daddy wouldn't hurt you, would he Mom?"

"No, Daddy wouldn't hurt me."

"But Daddy's really mad because he pounded on the table and said a lot of bad words."

Mark called for Andrew to come, so after a hurried kiss he ran to join his father. Later they brought me supper on a tray. Andrew stayed to keep me company. Mark didn't return till almost eleven. "Do you want anything?" he asked.

"I'd like to get washed." Mark helped me into the bathroom and as I stood waiting for the water to warm noticed several bruises on my arms and face and a large gash at the base of my neck. "Mark, why do I look like this? Was I in some sort of accident or something?"

"Get done, I want to go to bed."

"Mark, please, I need to know what happened."

"So, do I . . ."

# CHAPTER TWELVE

The clock was striking twelve when Nathan began coughing, but when no one came I struggled to my feet and went to him. By the time he was settled I was in too much pain to return to my bed so climbed in beside him.

"Julie," Clara said from the doorway, "what on earth? Well never mind, since you're already here I'll sit with you for a spell." She pulled up a chair and sat down. "I guess you know Madam's gone off with Lester again. We figured since the Master was in one of his black moods there'd be hell to pay, but he didn't seem to care a wit."

"Black moods?"

"Had them since childhood. Gets frightful angry then shuts himself away. Silas said it had to do with your husband taking you off against your will. Then Madam, egging him on says he should be more careful about telling people what to do. They might think he means it. So off he goes to the mill and Madame calls after him, 'You'd best go see to it then, because you already have.' Right away he comes roaring back and all hell breaks loose."

"They're both shouting and going on, I tell you, I never saw the like. He's asking what she did, and she's yelling he needs to stop sticking his nose into her business. He says something about Lester, and she picks up a vase and throws it at him."

"'You hideous deformed bastard. You'll be sorry for that,' she screams at him."

"So he says, 'End it Endora, or I'll expose you for the fraud you are.'"

"Edmund's always a gentleman, but there was nothing gentle about him that day, and that's for sure."

Clara patted my shoulder, replaced the chair and returned to her bed. I remained with Nathan and thought over what she said. If I left the house was that when the accident happened? So, where did I go and how did I get back?

"Julie, why aren't you in bed?" Edmund said, standing over me.

"He needed help."

"Listen Julie," Edmund said, carrying me back to my room. "What can you remember? Anything at all will do. What the place looked like. Sounds, voices, anything that might help."

"Why would Mark take me away?"

"He didn't. It was just easier that way."

"But now everyone hates him, and he can't defend himself."

"No one will ever see him, so it doesn't matter."

Next morning Mark helped me down to breakfast. A sad affair, and when the squadron called saying they needed him to fill in, his relief was obvious. When he returned, he'd expect an explanation, and when I didn't have one . . .

He brought home fish and chips and afterward played soccer with Andrew on the front lawn. The game over, they sat on the porch talking over the finer points of the game. Andrew slipped his arm threw his fathers and Mark reached over and kissed him on the top of his head.

Shortly after eight he put Andrew to bed and joined me in the living room.

"Tell me where you were, and who you were with, and don't lie." He sat down across from me and waited.

"I can't tell you what I don't know."

"Will I do. I know exactly. You were with Edmund, and when it didn't work out, you thought you'd come home, tell some crazy story about an accident and all would be forgiven."

"Then how did I get all these bruises?" I asked holding out my arms.

"You don't have any bruises. So where were you last night because you weren't in bed?"

"Nathan needed help."

"You tell me you're in pain. That you can hardly get around, and then you want me to believe you got up, walked all the way down the hall and back in order to help someone that doesn't exist? Do you think I'm that stupid?"

"No."

"At night you talk about him in your sleep. How you love him and want him with you. Can you imagine what that does to me?" I love you and all you can do is talk about someone else." Getting to his feet he raged about the room.

"Admit you were with him and get it over with? All this I'm hurt only makes it worse."

"I need to understand how it happened—what's so wrong about that?" I asked.

"Because nothing happened. If you'd think about me for a change instead of yourself, maybe we could work this out, but no, you won't stop. If it's not me you're upset with it's the house. I don't know what to do anymore. You know we're short-handed at work, that I'm doing the job of three men, but then when I come home all I get from you is nothing. I think I deserve better than that."

# CHAPTER THIRTEEN

Mark left a note on the kitchen table reminding me to pick Andrew after school. At the bottom he wrote, "You seem to have trouble remembering things."

Meanwhile, Connie was still banging on the front door. She'd been doing so for some time, but I wasn't in the mood for a lecture. I figured eventually she'd get tired and go away, but I forgot how persistent she could be.

"Well, it's about time." She pushed past me and headed for the kitchen. "Is that coffee I smell?"

"It's on the stove."

"Holy Toledo, you call that coffee? Sit down and I'll make a fresh pot. What's going on between you and Mark?"

"Nothing?"

"Oh, please—you drop Andrew off for the party, don't stay for dinner, disappear for a week, and nothing's wrong?" Connie poured each of us a cup then leaned against the counter waiting for an answer.

"I'm supposed to be having an affair."

"Well if you are, and the guy's name is Edmund his life's in danger—because Mark's ready to kill him."

"You can't kill someone who's already dead." Realizing that was way too broad a concept for her to follow, I asked why the visit?

"After everything that's happen you need to ask. I'm trying to stop you from destroying your marriage. Two days ago, Mark sat in my kitchen choking back tears."

*"Julie's having an affair with a guy name's Edmund."*

*"Don't be ridiculous. Your everything to her."*

*"She talks about him in her sleep, and hid the gifts he gave her? The other night I went to check on her and she was gone. I searched everywhere, even the basement, and then there she was back in bed asleep. So next day I asked her point blank where she was, and you know what she said? She looked me straight in the eye and said she had to check on Nathan. Nathan, a kid that doesn't exist."*

*"But maybe to her, he does. She was heartbroken when you said no to having more children. This could be her way of coping."*

*"I didn't say no, I just said we have to wait."*

*"Yeah for four years. Would you wait that long for something you badly wanted?"*

*"I don't know. But does that justify her cheating on me? Or her constant lying? I told her to talk to Dr. Connelly, but she hasn't, and I doubt she will."*

*"You told her to talk to a psychiatrist?"*

*"She's sick and needs help. This whole thing is killing me."*

"This is serious Julie, and you need to make it stop."

"And that's your advice—make it stop?"

"Yeah, I guess it is."

"Nothing's been right since the day we moved in. Stuff would disappear then reappear days later, furniture was moved, doors would open on their own. Then Andrew started talking about his new friend Nathan. Mark said there was nothing wrong with a kid having an imaginary friend. But it wasn't imaginary, because I saw him. I saw them all. One day as I came down the stairs the whole place changed. Suddenly it was June,1868. Now I can go back and forth in time whenever I want. I've become more comfortable in their world than mine own. It's hard to believe, but it's the truth."

"Julie slow down. You're not making any sense. All this stuff of about traveling back in time—"

"Just come out and say it. You don't believe me."

"I don't know if I believe you or not. It's not like you're telling me it's going to rain. I need time to digest it all . . . In fact, I need more coffee."

I followed her out to the kitchen. "So, tell me what I'm supposed to do?"

"Leave."

"Everyone says that, but where do I go? Back to my aunts? She'd laugh in my face. Besides, I love Mark." I took out one of the photo albums and handed her a picture of Edmund. "Tell me who that is. She gave it a brief once over and handed it back.

"Don't be silly, it's Mark."

"No, it's Edmund."

Grabbing the picture from my hand she took a closer look. "My God, they could be twins. Are there more in there? I mean of these people you see?" She took the album, returned to the living room and took a seat on the sofa. She opened the album slowly as if expecting it to disintegrate in her hands. Slowly turning the pages she would stop every once in a while to ask who someone was. "If that little boy didn't appear so sickly I'd say it was Andrew."

"That's Nathan."

"Has Mark seen these? At least he could see they were real people."

"Real people that died over a hundred years ago."

"Do you love this man?" she asked going back to Edmund's photo.

"It's not that easy. If it was only about how they looked I'd say no, but it more. It's the way they talk and move. The things they say and how they say it. Even their sense of humor. If it wasn't for how they dress I'm not sure I could tell them apart."

Without commenting Connie leafed through the pages but stopped when she saw the picture of Jennifer. "That girl—the one in the apron. I'd swear that's you. And look on the back. He wrote, 'my heart's desire,' and then the letter J."

The hall clock struck twelve. "Oh, God. I forgot about Andrew." Without thinking I ran for the door.

"Wait," Connie said grabbing my arm. "I'll go." She came back twenty minutes later empty handed. Mark had already been there.

"What in the hell is he playing at?" I said pacing back and forth. "He never picks Andrew up. Never. Why is he even in Ipswich at this time a day. He's supposed to be flying." He did this to get even. He wants to show everybody I'm a bad mother."

"You're being ridiculous. Mark isn't the sort of guy that do something like this deliberately. He just isn't," she said defending him. "You're letting you imagination get the better of you."

"How do you know what sort of guy he is? And why is he confiding in you? You're not married to him. I want you to leave." Better to be alone than with a friend who betrays you.

# CHAPTER FOURTEEN

It wasn't fair for her to take Mark's side. She was supposed to be my friend, not his. I wasn't sure which hurt more. This was a side of Mark I'd never seen before. Was I so desperate for love that I deliberately overlooked his faults? How could I have been so wrong about him?

"Miss Julie," Silas said, as I sat on the settee crying, "what's wrong? You seem very low today. Come and let Clara fix you something to eat. You'll feel better with a little food inside you." Before I could respond Clara had a plate containing a rasher of bacon, eggs, toast and marmalade sitting in front of me.

"Now get that lot down you," she said, "and you'll be right as rain."

Four steaming pies sat cooling on the table. "Is someone coming for dinner?"

"Businesspeople mainly. Americans. Want to look over the mill." Clara wiped her hands on her apron and poured me a cup of tea. "Imagine questioning the Master's finances."

"That's what people do when investing in a business."

"Well, it don't seem right somehow."

"Is Endora back?" I asked pushing aside my empty plate.

"Thank heavens no." Clara refilled the creamer then handed it to me. "Can you imagine what she might do with all those Americans coming? Ruin things for sure."

"Well I'm not going to curtsy to that fancy man of hers—I'll tell you that right now."

"Matilda—" Silas warned.

"And I'll tell you something else, my girl." Clara added. "If you don't want to end up like Sally, you'll keep your opinions to yourself."

Removing his sleeve protectors Silas sat down next to me. "I think everyone agrees that things around here aren't what they should be and haven't been for some time. Even the Master. The way he's been acting lately, I just can't figure it. I went to him and told him straight out what he was doing was wrong."

"Mr. Bates—" Clara said placing her hand over her heart as if about to faint.

"So, what did he say," Matilda leaning forward asked.

"He looks up from his work and says in that gentle voice he has when he doesn't want to hurt you but has to tell you anyway, that it was none of my concern. He'd do what he thought best. So, I said the way he was behaving wasn't the best for anyone." Clara gazed at Silas in awe as I reached over and squeezed his arm.

"Tell me about Edmund's leg. How did it happen?"

Silas started, but Clara cut in. "He was wounded in the siege of Magdala. They were set up on a ridge, but a bomb went off tore open his leg and sent him falling some thirty feet into a ravine. Even though he was badly wounded he managed to save several other men who were trapped. It was a terrible time for him, and as you can imagine, she didn't make it any easier.

Anyway," Silas interrupted, when he got home she made a fuss about him being unable to walk—well you've heard how she carries on. I think if it wasn't for having Nathan to see to he'd never have made it through. The boy kept him going."

* * *

Noting the time, I excused myself and returned to the future. Mark came in just after mid-night with Andrew asleep in his arms.

"So where were you?" Mark ignored me and carried Andrew up to bed.

When he came down he answered. "Tell me where you were, and I'll tell you where I was."

"Did you plan this before or after last night's conversation?"

"What conversation? You lied and I didn't believe you—but conversation, I don't think so." Mark started up the stairs then stopped and looked down at me. "And don't blame Connie she had nothing to do with it."

The mention of her name confirmed my worst fears. "Funny, I don't remember saying anything about her."

"I saw her at the BX. She said she'd been out to see you."

How convenient. Had they worked it out together? Did she know Mark would be there waiting? The thought made me ill and I needed to go to bed, but as I tried to pass him on the stairs he stopped me and pushed me back against the wall.

"Please Julie, for the sake of our marriage, stop seeing him before it's too late."

"You're hurting me."

"If I'm not enough then tell me? Don't go behind my back." He tried to kiss me, but I broke free. "I bet you don't push him away."

"What do you want me to say?"

"That you'll give him up."

My heart was pounding, and the warmth of his breath on my face made it hard to breathe. What I wanted was to reach out, take him in my arms, and demand that he take me to bed and love me till there was nothing left of me, but I didn't because my best friends name was still pounding in my ears.

\* \* \*

I had grown close to the Bates' and spent many happy hours in their company, but now Tom's heart was weakening, and they thought it best to move to Brighton so they could be near their daughter. Saying goodbye was heart wrenching and by the time their car disappeared down the road, I was in tears. I'd write as they insisted, but it wouldn't be the same.

Endora, with a long list of complaints was waiting at the door when I returned.

"Aren't you afraid to be out during the day?" I asked pushing past her.

"Hilarious. Now tell Silas to move Nathan downstairs. All that going back and forth to his room is bad for my nerves."

"Since I won't be doing that I guess you'll have to learn to put up with it."

"Or he could die and get it over with," she called after me.

I didn't respond.

\* \* \*

It was late when Bunny brought Endora home and it was clear both were drunk. Standing in the shadows I watched while they said goodnight. Edmund watched as well and once Bunny left, he made his presence known.

"What do you see in him?" Edmund asked, causing Endora and I to jump at the sound of his voice.

"More than I see in you."

I waited till they went into the study then crept down the stairs to stand just outside the door. Endora, her face flushed from her night out, shrugged off her cape, then relaxed into the chair opposite Edmund's and sighed.

"Better now, are we?" Edmund asked, refilling his glass.

Endora unlaced her shoes and kicked them across the room.

"Much. Pour me one of those."

"So, where did you go?"

"We agreed not to interfere in each other's business, remember?"

"I'm curious that's all. The man nearly ruins everything, and you go out dancing with him."

"He can be reckless at times, but he's a good dancer. A very good dancer."

"You're not doing your reputation much good by being seen out with him so often."

"I might say the same about being seen with you."

"True, but we're not talking about me, we're talking about you, and regardless what you might think, I'm still your husband and it's my place to remind you of yours." Edmund leaned back, propped his feet up on the desk and continued. "Lady Lester isn't pleased. She's got a lot invested in Bunny marrying the lovely Rolanda Nethercutt, the Earl of Sunderland's daughter."

"You're talking nonsense." Endora swirled her drink with her finger then licked it off.

Edmund was studying Endora intently when suddenly he slammed his hand down on the desktop. "You didn't know. I can see it in your expression. This is all news to you," he said as he burst out laughing. "Well, well, well."

"Laugh all you like, because soon Bunny won't need Rolinda's money."

"That would be news to Lester," Edmund said wiping his eyes. "He needs all the money he can get at the moment. In fact, Lady Lester made it clear that if the marriage doesn't take place Hillborn and the money, goes to Lester's cousin, John Lucas. If the choice comes down to Hillborn or you—I'd say you'd be the loser. On the other hand, he's taken quite a fancy to our Julie."

"Bunny's only interested because I am. He knows what's at stake."

"For a woman who considers herself to be infallible, you can be incredibly stupid. You're the one with everything to lose, not Bunny, and believe me, Bunny would willingly risk everything if he wanted something bad enough, and from what I've seen, he wants Julie."

"You're insane."

"In this grand scheme of yours, have you considered what you'll do if she says no? It is her choice remember, or have you forgotten? She has to come to it on her own."

"And she will. Once Nathan's dead and buried Julie will do whatever is needed, and all will be right with the world. At least mine." Angered by her comment, Edmund pulled her from her chair and throwing her onto the sofa tore away her clothes.

"Tell me Endora, tell me you want me like you did before."

"Fool," Endora said, struggling to free herself. "I never wanted you. It was James Harcourt, the Marquis of Westerbrook. Nathan's father, that I wanted."

For a moment it seemed the earth stopped rotating. Edmund got to his feet, backed away and then in a voice barely audible asked, "Are you saying James is Nathan's father?"

"I thought I made that perfectly clear." Endora sat up, wrapped herself in what was left of her dress and turned the knife. "We were in a fix and needed someone to blame, so we decided it would be fun to blame you. I mean with your background who would question the truth of it? Everyone would assume you were following in your mother's footsteps. If you doubt me check with Johnathan Browbecker, James' solicitor. If Nathan survives to eighteen, he'll inherit fifty-thousand pounds from Westerbrook's estate. If not, the money's all mine and Rolanda will no longer be a problem."

With smug satisfaction Endora walked past him and out into the hall. She wasn't surprised to see me and in passing asked if I'd like to know what really happened while I was away. When I said yes, she smiled, snapped her fingers and continued up to bed.

# CHAPTER FIFTEEN

In an instant I saw it all and realized everything I thought true was a lie. There hadn't been an accident, or fall down the stairs, there was only Endora and her desire to drive a wedge between Mark and me.

On the other side of the door Edmund had fallen to his knees, his world crumbling around him. It was a pain I understood yet I found it hard to sympathize. Nathan wasn't lost to him, unless he wanted him to be. The voice in my head said to go to him, but it was a decision I'd already made.

"Come to laugh at my humiliation?" Never had a man looked so defeated or cast down.

"I came because I thought you needed someone." I reached out my hand, but he brushed it away.

"All I ever wanted was to belong. To have something to hold on to. Something of my own. I slept under newspapers, ate from rubbish bins. When Father found me, I was told things would be better, but instead no one could see past the blood that ran through my veins.

"I was a bastard child with a washerwoman for a mother. I was bullied and called names. When I fought back I was punished. I wanted to show them, to prove I was as good as they were, and I did. My inventions have given a living to over two-hundred men, and for what? A wife that despises me, and a son that isn't mine. We were friends. James stood with me at my wedding and all the while . . . How do you do something like that?"

"It's easy if you have no soul. So, what are you going to do, deny that Nathan's yours? Tell the world your son is a bastard? Disown him and break his heart?"

"I don't know—I don't know!" I helped him to his feet and led him over to the sofa.

"If you let this destroy the relationship you have with him then you don't deserve him. Nathan worships the ground you walk on. You're his number one topic of conversation. Father this and Father that. Are you going to let him go to his grave believing you don't love him anymore? What you decide will either destroy you both or bring you closer together, the choice is yours."

"You don't understand. You have Andrew—" Edmund interrupted.

"Yes, I have Andrew, but when I was eight months pregnant a speeding car hit mine head on. The baby I was carrying was killed, and my injuries left me infertile. Andrew is my adopted son." For the first time since entering the room Edmund looked directly at me.

"What are you saying?"

"My husband paid someone else to carry his child. When he was born John brought him home for me to raise. So Nathan is just as much yours as Andrew is mine. You would be lost without that little boy just as I would be lost without Andrew. They might not have our blood, but they have our hearts and nothing else matters."

Edmund sat for a moment studying his hands, then without responding walked over to his desk, slumped down into his chair and turned it to face the wall.

\* \* \*

"The first rays of sun were peeking out over the horizon when I stepped into the tub and eased myself down into the water. Exhausted by events I allowed the warmth of the water to soothe me.

"Julie," Mark said, coming into the bathroom.

"I'll be done in a minute."

"Since when do you take a bath at five in the morning?" I shrugged in response.

Needing to be near him I dried off and as I had done a thousand times before came up behind him, wrapped my arms around his waist and laid my head against the cool flesh of his back. Always before he would turn and take me in his arms. This time I felt his body stiffen. "I'm not Edmund."

No, he wasn't, and trying to make things better, if possible, would take a great deal of work. But if I couldn't fix things with Mark perhaps I could make my peace with Edmund. The key was the diary. Until I could locate that and prove it was all a lie any effort to make things better would be for nothing. Returning to my room I threw myself onto the bed and tried to figure out where Edmund might hide the blasted thing.

His bedroom seemed the most likely place, but a thorough search found nothing, and I was forced to move on to his study. I checked everywhere and over-looked nothing. Even searched for hidden compartments in his desk or a wall safe hidden behind the pictures.

On the bookshelf behind his easy chair I noticed a book was out of place. Edmund, neat to the point of obsession would never allow such a thing, and I was right. Taking the book from the shelf I found that it had been hollowed out and now contained my diary.

So, now I had it and knew what it said. To think that anyone could think me capable of such perversion was humiliating. The question then became what to do about it? My first thought was to somehow make Endora confess her part in this, but how? It would require a great deal of thought. I didn't want her twisting my words so I practiced what I would say and how to say it daily till I had it down pat. I even practiced entering her room. With everything at the ready, I made my move.

I didn't knock as I normally would, instead I pushed open the door and went in. Waving the diary in her face I told her straight out that she had better look like telling Edmund the truth or else I would—

"Or else you will what?" she interrupted. "It was a question I expected her to ask, but not so soon. Consequently it threw all my practiced lines out the window leaving me with no response. "If you don't have an '*or else what*' in your pocket it's just an empty threat. Now go away, you're making a fool of yourself."

"Endora's right, Julie." Bunny folded the newspaper and laid it aside. "You needed a clear cut *or else what* to bolster your threat. Besides, you have no power over us."

"But I do have power don't I Endora? Tell him about the wallpaper. Go on—tell him."

"What is she talking about?" Bunny gave Endora a quizzical look.

"Parlor tricks, that's all. Parlor tricks."

"Then why did you scream out in pain? And don't deny it, you did."

"You're being ridiculous."

I decided to change tactics. "You say I'm here because you need me to do something, right? Something you can't do yourself."

"That's right."

"Tell Edmund the truth and I'll do it. No questions asked." Uproarious laughter followed.

My brilliant plan had fallen apart. What made me think they'd go against their own self-interest? The only thing to do was to make a tactical retreat, which Bunny blocked.

"Someday," Bunny said, his voice low so Endora wouldn't overhear, "we'll finish what we started earlier." Smiling Bunny made a sweeping bow in Endora's direction then hurried down the stairs. Infuriated by his actions she demanded I leave as well.

"You missed a golden opportunity tonight," I said from the doorway. "I would've done whatever you wanted but now—"

She interrupted. "Easy to say when you don't know what that something is."

"Whatever it is, the decision is mine to make. If I say no, it's over. You could have avoided that possibility if you had agreed to tell the truth, but you choose not to. How sad."

I was already halfway down the hall when she started screaming. "Come back here, Come back here this instant."

When I ignored her command she came after me and attempted to push me over the railing. Shoving her back against the wall she stumbled and falling, hitting her face on the banister. Blood gushed from her nose and down the front of her dress. "You bitch. You stupid little bitch. I'll see you pay for this."

"It's just blood Endora, lick it off. It's an acquired taste." Reaching out her hand she shouted 'come' and at once the diary flew from my hand to hers. Blowing on the cover it turned to dust.

"Parlor games," she said, "nothing but parlor games."

* * *

With the destruction of the diary any chance of reconciling with Edmund vanished. I was depressed and disheartened. I thought I could make her confess, but all I did was to make a bad situation worse.

Over the next few days I could think of nothing but how badly my plan had failed. Tormented by my failure I went out onto the porch hoping to find peace in the early morning air. Instead I found Endora pacing back and forth down by the oak tree. What was she doing? She never left her room before twelve, but there she stood with what looked like a rather large book in her hand.

Finding a place to watch unseen I waited. For a moment she hesitated then thumbing through the pages stopped and reread what was written several times. Satisfied she threw the book aside raised her arms toward the sky and began speaking in an unknown tongue. When finished she bent forward and cupping her hands pretended to throw water in her face. Straightening, she was no longer Endora but Matilda.

Each time she performed the ritual she became someone else. Satisfied, she retrieved the book and laughing, returned to her room.

\* \* \*

In June, the squadron would be deploying to Spain for a month, so Mark decided to take Andrew to the beach for the weekend. When I ask why I wasn't invited he said that he did ask, several times, but I refused.

"Why would I turn down a trip to the beach? I love going there."

"Look, I asked—you said no. I won't ask again."

"Come on Mark. I'd be happy—"

"Maybe you would but I wouldn't," he interrupted. "I stopped being happy months ago, and if you don't soon get help our marriage will be over."

"I don't need help. I need a husband willing to believe me." Next morning, they left for the beach without so much as a goodbye.

"Not much of a fond farewell." Endora said buttering the toast Andrew left behind.

"It was you he asked wasn't it? You changed yourself to look like me."

"I haven't the foggiest idea what you're talking about."

"I saw you down in the garden—"

"Am I interrupting something?" Edmund asked from the doorway.

"Julie's just trying to start a fight." Picking up the last slice of toast, she left.

"Is that true?"

"What do you want Edmund?"

"Sorry, just wondering why you didn't go?" He poured a cup of coffee and took a seat.

"Maybe because your bitch of a wife told him I didn't want to go."

"You mean Endora?"

"Yes, I mean Endora. How many other wives have you got?"

"Just her I'm afraid. Julie—I was wondering if you'd be willing to have dinner with me tonight?"

"Why? Have I done something else wrong?"

"Of course not, I just thought maybe we could work things out, that's all. Say around eight?"

"All right, yes, eight would be fine." Appearing relieved, he left for the mill.

* * *

Connie showed up around eleven and insisted we go out for lunch. I didn't want to go, at least not with her, but I went anyway. We ate at one of the newer places down by the river. Connie did most of the talking and made it all the way to dessert before asking about Edmund. When I refused to be drawn in, she changed the subject, and started gushing about a new dress shop she'd discovered.

"You've never seen anything like it," she said urging me along. "It's just the type of place you'd love. See, didn't I tell you?" she said pushing me through the door.

"Yes, you told me." What sort of shop was this? No one wore clothes like this anymore. Nothing in this entire dress shop was newer than 1920. And most much older. "For Pete sake Connie, no one wears this stuff anymore. It's years out of date."

"Not at Thornwood. Come look at this, the blue matches your eyes."

"My eyes are brown." Though it had a remarkable resemblance to the blue dress in the attic I knew for a fact that my blue dress was tucked safely away in the trunk in the attic.

"Go try it on," she insisted. "Let's see how it fits. It's made for you", she said as I stepped out of the dressing room. "Perfect."

By the time I joined her at the checkout counter the dress was bought and paid for. "A gift," Connie said, but it didn't feel like a gift. It felt like a mistake. "Now you'll have something to wear to dinner."

It was getting late, so I made my way upstairs to change, but the blue dress preyed on my mind. How odd that two dresses could look so alike, though I did think this one was a darker blue. And the embroidery was definitely not as fine.

Noting the time I removed the dress from the box and slipped it over my head. At once my legs grow weak, my head pounded, and I had the odd sensation of having died and come back to life. With no time to think, I shook off my misgivings and headed down for dinner.

# CHAPTER SIXTEEN

Edmund stood at the foot of the stairs with an orchard in his hand. Hearing me on the steps he turned to watch me descend, but by the time I reached the bottom his smile had turned to a scowl.

"What in the hell are you playing at? I thought we could work it out, that we could start over, and then you do this?"

"Do what?" But instead of answering he stormed off to his office slamming the door behind him.

Feeling suddenly ill, I raced up to the attic, opened the trunk, and found it empty. The dress was gone. I never went to lunch with Connie, and we didn't visit an amazing dress shop. The dress I was wearing was Jennifer's dress. I could almost hear Endora whisper "*parlor games, nothing but parlor games.*" "Damn you Endora, may you rot in hell." But what was it about this particular dress? I needed to talk to Silas.

"He's taking the Master a fresh decanter of whiskey," Clara said as she came in from the pantry. Perhaps I can help."

Unable to breathe I pulled out a chair and sat down. "It's this dress. I need to understand why it's so important."

"Then I'll tell you," Clara said sitting down next to me. "When Edmund was young," seventeen if I remember, he fell in love with a girl called Jenny whose father worked on the Stanley estate up in Scotland. She was a lovely thing, full of life, and pretty. Edmund wanted desperately to marry her, but his grandfather refused permission. Determined to make his own way Edmund took any job he could find from working in the fields to driving horses. Didn't matter. Three years it took him and by then he'd come of age and there was nothing they could do to stop him. Since he couldn't inherit there was little they could do. It was a beautiful dress as you can see, and she looked absolutely stunning in it, but then on the day they were to announce their engagement—" Her voice trailed off and I was there.

*I was waiting for Edmund to come and escort me down the stairs to where he intended to announce our engagement. I couldn't take it in. And the dress—I had never had such a dress—or been so happy.*

*For weeks Endora had demanded that I give him up, but I refused to be cowed by her threats. Appearing out of the shadows she pulled me back into my room and again promised to destroy me.*

*"Edmund is mine and nothing you do here today will make any difference. I have plans for Edmund that don't include you?"*

*"Then they'll come to nothing." Breaking free I ran toward the stairs, but Endora followed and took hold of my sleeve. As I fought to free myself. Endora gave me a slight push and I tumbled backward down the stairs to my death.*

"Julie, Julie," Clara's voice, tense and worried, broke through the fog of my vision. "Are you all right, love? You passed clean away."

"I need to talk to Edmund—"

"The Master's gone out and didn't say when he'd be back."

"But I need—"

Clara sat down on the edge of the bed. "Look, you rest and when he comes in I'll wake you."

*I lay at the foot of the stairs, blood flowing from the wound on the back of my head.*

*Edmund, sobbing, knelt beside me pleading for me to stay, but the Council was calling, and I had to obey. Endora looked down from the landing and smiled. Edmund would be hers now, and there was nothing I could do.*

"Julie, love, he's back. He's in his study." Making my way down the hall I felt Endora's presence close by.

"I know you're here Endora, show yourself."

"I can't, I'm a part of you now. Together we're going to show the Council just what Edmund's capable of. I tried to tell them, but they wouldn't listen. So I'll show them, and then they'll be forced to do something about it."

"What does any of this have to do with me? I don't even know what the Council is."

She laughed. "Ah, but they know you, and you have everything to do with it. You're just too stupid to realize. Edmund will see you but will hear me. And don't think you can fight me because you can't. Now let's go in."

The only light came from a small lamp on Edmund's desk, and if not for the squeak of his chair we would never have known he was there. I turned on the light and stared down at him. "Drinking already? Well, no surprise there. You do a lot of that don't you?"

"Get out!"

"Halfway into a drunken stupor and all because of a rather ugly dress. But then I guess for someone of her class . . ."

"Yes, someone of her class. Just like me. Low born, low class."

"I found where you hid the diary."

"You don't keep one remember?"

"You didn't expect me to admit it? So, tell me, would you let Bunny treat Jennifer the way he treated me?"

"Are you saying I let it happen?"

"Yes, I think I am."

"Well, just so you'll know, I didn't. I pleaded with the Council—tried to persuade them to stop, but they rebuked me. Said I was meddling in things that didn't concern me. Don't they realize everything about this sadistic melodrama concerns me? Endora is trying to save herself by destroying us and I'm the one that's meddling!"

Endora was nervous. This wasn't going as she planned. Edmund was being too honest. What Endora wanted was for Edmund to condemn himself with his own words. Intent on making it happen she started for the door pretending to leave.

"No, please don't go. We can fix this," Edmund said rushing over to block my way. "You must know how much I care? That I've tried to protect you."

Endora burst out laughing in her high-pitched cackle. "I told the Council you were interfering, but they needed proof and now they've got it. You've condemned yourself with your own words."

I saw it in his eyes, a sudden awakening. "You stupid, selfish, cow. It was you all along, wasn't it?" The diary, the dress—all of it?"

"Every bit." Driven by rage Edmund charged toward her but grabbing his walking stick Endora smashed it across his injured leg. With a scream he collapsed onto the floor. That's when something remarkable happened. Throwing down the cane Endora helped him into his chair. It was the first and only act of kindness I ever saw her grant him.

"You left me no choice."

"So where is she?" Edmund asked his face grimaced with pain.

"With me of course. She even promised to do whatever I wanted with one stipulation."

"What was that?" Edmund said holding his leg.

"She wanted me to admit I wrote the diary and to promise I'd leave you and Mark alone. What made me laugh was her thinking I'd actually keep a promise."

"Why would she do something like that? I could see for Mark, but me—I doubt it."

"If you want her back, you're going to have to agree to my terms."

With that a battle of wills took place. Both spoke in a language devoid of human understanding and both were out of control. If emotions were an indicator, both would willingly have killed the other. Back and forth, each jostling for position, but it was Endora's ruthless nature that won the battle. Whatever concessions Edmund was forced to make it was clear by his expression that he wasn't happy.

# CHAPTER SEVENTEEN

At first I thought it a dream, Edmund and Endora having a violent argument about something I couldn't understand, but then I realized what I saw was real. Edmund sat at his desk his head in his hands.

"Edmund, what's wrong? What's happened?"

"I . . . I need to talk to you, but I'm having trouble finding the right words. If I were writing a poem, the words would flow without pause from hand to paper. But it's not a poem and I struggle to say what needs saying. When I think of what you did, the things you said, it fills me with loathing. I can't even look at you without feeling ashamed. I tell myself it will pass, but instead it grows stronger with each passing minute. I thought about saying nothing, but that would be cowardly, and regardless what Endora thinks, I'm no coward." How do you respond to something like that? Unable to bear the pain I returned to the future.

Over by the window Aunt Bertha stood watching. *"There's a darkness hanging over you Julie. It's been there since the day of your birth, and though I hate to say it, there's not a thing about you that's worth loving. Someone might take you on, but I doubt it will last."*

Edmund arrived, but the ghost of the past lingered. "Go away Edmund, I have company enough already."

He looked surprised. "I'm not going till you let me finish."

"Please, Edmund, go away and leave me alone. I've heard it all before."

Edmund seemed perplexed, then laughing, pulled me into his arms. "You silly, silly, little goose. When Endora said how you tried to protect me, it broke my heart and made me realize how unworthy I was. To hear you defended me . . ." He took my face in his hands and kissed me with increasing passion. "You are my one true love, and I want you with all my heart."

What I was doing was wrong in so many ways, yet I continued on and wallowed in the luxury of his touch. In all of time before or after, there were only the two of us. Only our lips, our flesh, our whispered words of love. Passion? What was that to what we were feeling?

I answered his touch with a sigh as his fingers like feathers blown on the breeze, glided over me, touching, exciting, going away, then coming again to carry me higher. Hypnotized by the sound of his voice Edmund lifted me toward the heavens, then stopping just below the stars brought me back to start again. His lips warm and moist against my flesh only caused my need to grow. Lost in exquisite blackness, his nearness inflamed my desires and when he whispered, "now my love," my body arched toward his in anticipation.

And so, we came together, floating up beyond the heavens to lie content in each other's arms in that dark, silent void. In time we returned to earth, but now, with our passion spent, Mark's shadow cast a pall over my heart. Edmund tried to reassure me, but the guilt remained.

To say I regretted what happened would be a lie, but with passions spent and my emotions settled, my heart screamed that I'd made a monumental mistake. I loved Mark, but never again could I argue that I had been faithful.

* * *

Mark and Andrew returned later that afternoon. Rain had come to the seashore and there was nothing for it but to return home. As I unpacked Andrew's suitcase Mark noticed the blue dress hanging on the wardrobe door. "A new dress? Rather old-fashioned don't you think—but I guess being old, he likes that type of thing."

"He's not old, he's your age."

"How nice. Did you sleep with him?"

"Mark please, not in front of Andrew."

"But you said Andrew knows all about the guy?"

"I do," Andrew said. "Edmund's my friend."

"Andrew take you suitcase and put it away." I waited till he was gone to continue the conversation. "I don't appreciate you talking like that in front of Andrew."

"Why? Afraid he'll find out what his *friend* has been up to with his mother?"

Later, Mark went upstairs to take a nap, so Andrew and I got out his coloring book and crayons. "I missed you, Mom," he said, looking for green.

"Then we missed each other. Did you have a good time?"

"Yeah. They had pony rides and everything, but Daddy cried during the night. It made me sad, so I hugged him."

Supper was a disaster with conversation limited to what dishes needed passing. Mark asked for the potatoes twice. To be honest, I was surprised he was still here, but then it wasn't about me, it was about Andrew.

"So, how much did it cost—the dress I mean? I know how much the affair's costing us," Mark said as I came into the kitchen later that evening.

"I don't know."

"A gift, how nice."

"Did you have fun at the beach?"

"Yeah, before the rain came," Mark said, looking up from his check-book. "Was it good?"

"Was what good?"

"The sex."

Ignoring his question, I asked if he couldn't be a little more civil. He shrugged the answer and continued balancing his checkbook. "Mark, I asked a question."

"I'm being as civil as I can be."

After pouring myself a glass of wine I went out on the porch hoping to clear my head. Why in God's name did Andrew say Mark cried? A few minutes later Mark joined me, and sitting only inches away, I found his nearness comforting. Reaching for my hand he managed a quick smile. "I don't know. What I said in there . . . what I said before I left, I can't figure it out. I promised never to let anyone hurt you again, and now I'm the one . . ."

"Mark you don't—"

"That's not who I am but hurting each other is all we seem to do anymore." Mark picked up a stone and threw it out into the yard. "It's hard for me, putting things into words. I'm not a word person like you are. You need words. You need to hear me say what I feel for you. I want to, I have them—those feelings, but I can't get them out."

"I know."

Mark's fingers tightened around mine. "Why can't we be like before?"

"It's this house. We need to find another place. As long as we stay here things won't change. We need to get as far away from Thornwood as possible."

"What is wrong with you?" Mark said getting up. "I'm trying to explain my feelings and all you want is to talk about the house. It isn't the house it's your damn fantasies."

"Mark thinks your looney, round the bend," Endora volunteered from behind me.

"I shouldn't have bothered," Mark continued. "Why I thought you'd be rational is beyond me. I'm going to bed."

Taking Mark's place Endora said, "I've never been called a ridiculous fantasy before. Perhaps getting the two of you together wasn't such a great idea."

"Oh, please. We were fine till you showed up."

"You've got that wrong. I didn't show up, I arranged everything. Your divorce, your meeting Mark, everything. And remember, Mark did say he was sorry for being late. Years ago, my governess, Miss Prime and Proper, taught being good was its own reward. But Mother showed being self-centered if done right far outweighed the rewards virtue afforded. Using Mother as an example, I turned self-indulgence into an art form. What I didn't realize was that minor mistakes often blossom into major problems. Hiding you away in America made things more difficult, but then I found Mark and things moved in my direction."

"Why would anyone hide me away?"

"Now, now, you can't expect me to give away all my secrets, but your father knew and tried to warn you."

"You're talking rubbish. I'm going in."

"Oh, come on, there's nothing for you in there. Stay and keep me company."

"Why?"

"Because I'm the only friend you've got." She had a point. Well, Connie, but even that was iffy. The night turning cool, Endora pulled her wrap tighter about her shoulders, and studied the heavens. "People assume everything up there is all goodness and light, but they're wrong. The battle between good and evil never stops."

"So what side were you on?"

"As usual the wrong side. It was actually Mother's fault. If she hadn't fobbed James off on my cold, pale sister Victoria, none of this would have been necessary."

"How could you love James, but hate his child?" I asked, following Endora out into the yard.

"Illness frightens me. The ugliness of it." Arching her back, she stretched out her arms and twirling round called for me to come push her on the swing. Once she got started, she leaned back and kicked off her shoes.

"I'm going in, Endora. It's getting cold." Endora agreed, but insisted I stay and help her find her shoes.

"At least now Mark can go to bed."

"What do you mean?"

"Didn't you know? He's been watching from the bedroom window. Imagine watching your wife push an empty swing and hunt threw the bushes when it's nearly midnight. Only a mad woman would do that." She laughed and ran off ahead of me.

# CHAPTER EIGHTEEN

Over the ensuing weeks Mark began questioning everything I said or did, and if Andrew was involved, it became an inquisition. Then in mid-October friends invited us to a housewarming party. Most of the squadron attended and as the evening wore down our host mentioned finding a dead body tied to a chair and bricked up behind a false wall in their basement. Contacting a local historian, they discovered that their house had been a place to hid contraband coming in from France in the late seventeen hundred's. The dead man was probably a customs officer caught spying on the smugglers or perhaps a smuggler that stepped out of line.

Others had similar stories, so I decided to share mine. Now perhaps having too much to drink I said more than I should. How does one judge, but at some point Mark, losing his temper declared enough was enough and practically dragged me out to the car.

"Why, must you always make a fool of yourself whenever we go out? You saw how they were looking at you."

"You didn't say that to Larry or Joan, or any of the others. What did I say that was different from them?"

"They never said they talked to ghost or traveled through time. God, they must think you're mad."

"Then they agree with you I guess." He said nothing more and left for Italy the following day.

* * *

Normally when returning from a trip Edmund would seek me out to hear how Nathan was doing. This time however he went straight to his study and remained there till bedtime. My emotions were mixed. My heart wanted to see him, to be with him, but my head said no, pretend that night never happened. I was reading in my room when Edmund pounded on the door.

"We need to talk about the other night." Pushing past me he went and stood by the fireplace. "What I should've done was to remain in the past. To let that be an end to it. Instead, fearing I'd left you with the wrong impression I followed you back. If you hadn't looked so lost and hurt . . . I knew I wasn't strong enough to resist but hoped you'd be strong for the both of us. That you'd say no, but you didn't."

My response to this betrayal was instant. "That's a lie. I told you to leave, several times in fact, but you said I was your one true love, that you wanted to make love to me. And now you tell me—"

"All right," Edmund interrupted. "Yes, that's what I said, but only because you intoxicated my mind. I got carried away by emotions I couldn't control."

"And that's my fault?"

"No, that's not—"

"Well, that's how it sounds."

"It's not just about us. We have to think about the others and what our relationship would do to them."

"Our relationship? We had a one-night stand, thanks to you. Not a relationship."

"But there's Endora and the others to be concerned about."

"You already said that. Why Endora deserves your concern is a mystery. She'd like nothing better than to see you dead."

"I'm an honorable man, and honorable men protect their homes and families. My loyalty must be to Endora and Nathan. It's not my fault you hate her. You even called her a bitch."

"Yes, because I was angry, not for any other reason. Or am I the only one not allowed to get angry."

"Come on Julie, let's not play word games. You hate Endora because she's everything you aren't."

"Get out! Get out of my room. Now—before I do something else I'll regret."

"Julie, please. You're only making this harder. Hate me if you must but it's over. We can be friends and nothing more."

"I don't want to be your friend. Now leave."

On his way out he started to say something, but I was way past listening. Instead I shoved him out the door and locked it behind him. Again my aunt chimed in.

*"Why are you surprised? You know it's your fault? It's always your fault. That's how you are."*

Yes, that's how I am. Crazy, like Mark said. Maybe Edmund does love Endora, and maybe this is all just a horrible nightmare and I need to wake up.

\* \* \*

Nathan was failing, so Edmund began working from home. Everyone knew the boy could go at any moment so when a telegram arrived from Haddonfield, asking Edmund to come at once it came as a surprise. Believing his father wouldn't call on him if it wasn't absolutely necessary he felt obligated to go. He was barely out the gate when Endora began making demands. Exhausted from lack of sleep and worry, I angrily suggested that perhaps it would be best to just smother the child and have done with it.

Shortly after eight that evening Nathan began to fade, and Dr. Wood was summoned. Not wanting Andrew to witness his friend's death I asked Connie to take him for a few days. She agreed but said it would be the last time she'd cover for me. If I wanted to cheat on Mark, I should do it without involving her.

"Where's Edmund?" Dr. Wood asked, throwing off his coat as he hurried upstairs.

"Haddonfield." I called up to him. "He thought he'd be back by eleven."

"He'll never make it. They're doing repairs on the line and everything's running way behind schedule. He'll be lucky to be back by morning, and that I'm afraid will be too late." He checked on Nathan then racing back down said he was needed elsewhere but would be back momentarily."

The doctor saw himself out while Silas went to send a telegram. I returned to Nathan's room and found Endora standing over him with a pillow in her hand.

"Endora! In God's name! What have you done?"

"You told me to smother him, so I did." Said without emotion, she threw the pillow onto a nearby chair and started back to her room. "Perhaps now I can get a decent night's rest," she called over her shoulder.

Checking for a pulse and unable to find one I carried him over to the rocking chair and as I had done a hundred times before, began rocking him. Nathan loved to be rocked. Back and forth, back and forth, humming his favorite tunes. He wasn't really dead, just pretending. Nathan loved to pretend. Back and forth, back and forth.

"Julie!" Clara hurried to my side and asked what I was doing, but I was too busy to answer. "Julie I asked what you're doing?"

"I'm rocking Nathan. He's pretending he's dead, but I know he's just playing."

"Oh, dear God," Clara hurried to the head of the stairs and called for Silas to come at once. "The boys gone but Julie won't give him up."

"Come now Julie," Silas said kneeling beside me. "Nathan needs to be in bed. Here, let me help you."

"No! I said holding him closer. "I promised Edmund I'd see to him and if I don't he'll get someone else. Nathan will be fine in a minute and then I'll put him to bed."

"Julie, listen." Silas said, his voice growing sterner. "If the Master comes home and finds Nathan out of bed he'll be upset. Remember the little rhyme you made up for him? In bed by seven you'll go to heaven. In bed by eight they'll lock the gate. Now we wouldn't want Nathan locked out of heaven would we?"

"No, I wouldn't want that. I placed him back in his bed, laid his favorite toy next him, then noticing he was cold, wrapped his covers around his chin and turned down the lamp.

"That's better," Silas said. "Now let's get Clara to make a pot of tea." Guiding me out of the room we continued down to the kitchen.

"I can't be gone long. Nathan worries when I'm gone."

"A nice cup of tea will do us all good and once you're done, you can go back." While Clara poured the tea, Silas slipped out and went for the doctor who came at once. Later I escorted him into Edmund's study while Clara, with grief-stricken Matilda, saw to the body.

"It's all my fault," I said beginning to cry. "I told her what to do." Dr. Wood put down his pen and studied me. "Explain."

"As God is my witness, I never—but Endora kept demanding I do something. So, I said fine, let's just suffocate him with a pillow and get it over with. I didn't mean it I was just tired."

"Come now Julie." Dr. Wood came and sat beside me. "You weren't to know."

"But I did. She wants a divorce and believes with Nathan gone Edmund will grant it."

"Endora doesn't want a divorce."

"Oh yes she does. She wants to go off with Bunny Lester, her lover."

"Bunny Lester! Why in heaven's name . . . Look, would you feel better if I told him?"

"No, it's my fault so I should be the one—"

"Don't be so hard on yourself," the doctor interrupted. "Nathan out lived his lifespan by several years. I'll put respiratory failure as cause of death. Edmund will have to decide the rest."

Silas saw the doctor out, and I rejoined Clara and Matilda. I laid out the suit Edmund wanted Nathan to wear, then went down to the living room to await his return. The silence was maddening and several times I thought I heard Nathan calling. Auntie Julie, Auntie . . . Once I even started up the stairs, then stopped and whispered,

*"When I was going up the stairs*
*I met a woman that wasn't there*
*She wasn't there again today*
*I wish, I wish she'd go . . ."*
*When I came home last night at three*
*The woman was waiting there for me*
*But when I looked around the hall*
*I couldn't see her there at all!*

# CHAPTER NINETEEN

Edmund arrived home just as the dawn was breaking with his coat slung over his shoulder and a worn expression on his face. Assuming I'd been up all night he told me to go get some rest he'd check on Nathan before he did the same.

"Edmund, wait—" I called out as he made his way up the stairs. He stopped and stood unmoving. "Nathan's gone." Now he turned to face me and almost in a whisper asked when. I explained then told my part in it and why, and when I finished he rubbed his face as if wiping away a bad dream.

"And you gave Endora the idea?"

"She kept insisting I do something. I hadn't been to bed for several days—"

"Are you saying lack of sleep was sufficient reason to suggest killing him?"

"No, that's not what I—" But he turned away and continued on to Nathan's room where Clara was sitting the first night's vigil. As Edmund entered Clara curtsied and left the room. Passing me in the hall, she gave my arm a gentle squeeze.

"My darling boy, my precious child, Edmund said kneeling by his side. "I should never have left you on your own."

For a time, the house stood silent, waiting. Then a tiny shaking, like a brief earthquake shook the foundation, and I knew something bad was coming. Edmund stood, removed his suit jacket, regained his composure, and more to himself than to me said, "Now it begins."

There was no pounding on her door pleading for help; he didn't spout poetry or beg to go in, he made no sound at all until in deadly earnest said, "I'll give you three minutes to come out. If you don't, I'll burn the house down around you."

"You wouldn't dare," Endora called through the door.

"I don't make idle threats Endora. I'll burn Thornwood to the ground and laugh while doing it."

The slow and determined way he spoke left no doubt he meant to carry through on his threat. Endora's situation desperate, her only choice was to comply. The moment the latch clicked Edmund burst in, picked her up and carried her back to Nathan's room.

"I want you to see what you've done," Edmund said, forcing Endora to look at her son. "Was he such a nuisance you couldn't wait another six hours for his passing?"

"No—you're lying. No one knew how long."

"We all knew. You would have as well if you hadn't been out whoring every night with that pig." Breaking away Endora made for the door but Edmund caught her and carried her back.

"Please, Edmund, let me go back to my room. Death frightens me."

"Not enough." The corners of his mouth rose in a momentary smile than vanished. "Poor Endora, you committed murder to get the divorce I was more than willing to grant once Nathan was gone."

Endora's demeanor brightened. "But you said—so now I can—"

"No, you can't. For now, I shall hang myself around your neck like a millstone."

"You have no power to keep me here."

"Maybe not, but I do have the power to remain your husband."

"Damn you! Nathan wasn't your son."

"You vile little bitch," Edmund said slapping her across the face. "I should've thrown you into the street the moment I caught you in bed with that swine."

Insane with rage Endora tried to strike back, but Edmund grabbed her arm and tearing her sleeve uncovered the tiny scratches made by Nathan's fingernails as he fought to live. Horrified, Edmund moved away as if she were poison.

"Blame Julie not me. She told me to do it," Endora screamed, pointing a shaking finger in my direction. "Ask her. Ask Julie if she didn't tell me."

I thought Edmund would kill her. Going to the head of the servant's stairs I screamed for Silas. Taking charge Silas pulled Edmund away, and I took the rather disheveled and hysterical Endora back to her room. Calm restored, Edmund remained with his son while Silas and I returned to the kitchen.

For the next several hours the servants discussed what needed doing; which rooms to prepare, what amount of food needed ordering and preparing—the mundane things that are necessary when someone dies. But nothing would happen without Edmund's approval, so they sent me to remind him of his duty. I found him in the attic, surrounded by childhood memories.

"Am I intruding?" Edmund looked over and smiled.

"Father never sent for me," Edmund said pulling up a box for me to sit on, "It was a fool's errand to get me away. She had planned to do this all along." He held up a tiny handmade lace gown. I wore this for my christening, and Nathan for his. Mother took on extra work to buy the lace. I have so few memories of her. Grandfather told everyone Mother seduced my father hoping for money, so naturally no one would have her. For a time she wandered from place to place, then when I came she used what little she managed to put aside to get us a place on the outskirts of Sudbury. It was only a room, but it kept us out of the weather. Mother took in laundry to support us."

"It must've been horrible for her."

"Yes, it was," Edmund said, slipping back into the language of his youth, "but Mother always said once Father returned we'd be right as rain. I was too young to help much but when I turned five Mother showed me how to use the mangle and such. It was hard cause I had to stand on a stool, but I did it. Sometimes when things got really tough, I'd sneak out and go sweep the streets. The wealthy ladies, they'd give me sixpence to sweep a path so they could cross. Then one morning this real posh gent shows up wanting me mum to do his ironing and maybe a bit of cleaning. Seems his wife had passed, and he needed the help."

"So, things go on, and one day Mother finds three guineas tucked down in one of his pockets. Three whole guineas. It was like finding a gold mine, but she gets her shawl, puts on her bonnet, and says, 'Edmund, we're taking this money back to the gentleman,' and off we go to his place. Murray was his name, Mr. J. Constant Murray. Turns out, he put the money there on purpose. Mr. J. Constant Murray was testing her like, to see if she was an honest sort of woman. It turned out Mr. Murray had a place at the back of his house, and he moved us there.

"It had three rooms, not including the loft. How I loved being up above everything. And warm, like duck eggs just laid. We lived there about two years when she took sick and sent me to live with Great Auntie Budge up in Manchester."

"Going must have been hard."

"I hated leaving, and I guess she did too. I figured it was because I was one more mouth to feed. Not that she ever said. But kids, they get queer ideas. Talk about homesick—the whole world turned black that day. When I found out she'd passed, I thought I'd drown from the guilt welling up inside me. If I hadn't been born . . . she was everything you see—everything. I should've stayed, but I guess Mother didn't want me to see her when she was ill. Then just like that, Auntie Budge falls off a ladder and kills herself."

"What did you do?"

"Lived rough till they caught me and put me in the Orphans' Home. A hateful place. I ran off so many times they stopped looking for me. Winters were the worst. I thought a couple times I might die from it, but then Father found me." He paused for a moment and looked away. "I loved that little boy, Julie. How shall I get on without him?" Tears welled up in his eyes, and though I could've reached out to comfort him, I didn't.

By evening Thornwood was in a subdued state of turmoil. Edmund handled the sadder aspects while Endora kept herself locked away. Two things worried me. First, over the last few weeks with the added stress of having to help tend Nathan, Edmund's leg had grown weaker so that at times he would stumble and nearly fall.

Second, I had no idea what a Victorian funeral entailed so worried that the servants would notice my ignorance of something that should be common knowledge. Not wanting to be asked about it I did what I could then found a place at the head of the stairs where I could watch unobserved.

Edmund's parents, The Earl and Countess of Swansgate arrived just after six next evening and went directly in to view their grandson. Tomorrow at four Nathan would go to St. Paul's Church for the service, then on to Inverness for interment.

I waited till the house was settled for the night, then went in to say my goodbye's. As I sat by his small white casket, I came to a decision. Once the funeral was over, I would slip away and return to the future to try and rebuild my marriage. I would not return to the past again.

I placed the picture Andrew had drawn of them playing together along with Nathan's favorite toy soldier in the pocket of his jacket, then straightened his hair gave him one last kiss, and returned to my room. Nathan had found his peace and now I must find mine. The past would be a memory and nothing more.

# CHAPTER TWENTY

I did what I could to help with breakfast, then returned to my vantage point on the landing. My time with Nathan weighed heavy on my mind and tears soon followed.

*"Look, Auntie Julie, a rainbow." Nathan called out from his day bed on the porch.*

*"They say there's a pot of gold where its end," I said.*

*"Father said the stairway to heaven starts there, and when someone undeserving tries to climb it, it disappears."*

*"Well, your father's a very smart man."*

*"If I grow up, I want to be like him."*

*"You already are, my love, you already are."*

"Don't mean to interrupt, but do you mind if I joined you?"

"Your Lordship—I'm sorry, yes, please—" I said brushing away my tears.

"It's a sad affair for everyone I'm afraid. Nathan was a wonderful child for all he suffered."

"At least he's at peace."

"If only Edmund were. He tries, but under the circumstances . . . That's why Lady Beatrice and I are so glad you're here."

"Only till after the funeral, then I'm returning home."

"But—you'll stay till everything gets sorted?"

"With Nathan gone, I see no reason to stay."

"My dear girl, are you mad with grief? Edmund will be devastated."

"I rather think he'll find my absence a blessed relief." Unwilling to discuss it further I excused myself and returned to the future. Edmund was waiting when I arrived.

"Is what Father said true? You're leaving?" He didn't wait for an answer. "How can you do that?" The sorrow in his voice cut deep into my soul. "All right, maybe things aren't what they should be between us, but to leave now. Now when I've just lost my son? Please stay, if only for a while."

I was determined to leave, yet here I was telling him I'd stay. Not for long just until things got settled, and once again I was speaking words that weren't my own. Unaware of my inner turmoil, Edmund, relieved, said he'd lay out a dress for me. And would I give Clara a hand in the kitchen? She was growing desperate."

"All right," I called out as he faded back to the past, "but only for a few days and no more. Do you hear me? I won't let you involve me further. I'm done."

I put on the dress he left for me then went to help Clara in the kitchen. Afterward I intended to return to my alcove, but Edmund escorted me into the living room to be introduced. Lady Beatrice sitting alone by the window waved for me to join her. A small, soft spoken woman, with a rosy complexion and bright blue eyes, she appeared much younger than her sixty-five years.

"Please, come and sit with me. I feel rather out of place on my own." She patted the seat next to hers and waited. "Nathan was such a darling child and so mature for his age. Very much like his father."

"How old was he when he came to you?"

"He was eight going on nine, and I must admit his independent nature seemed rather frightening."

"Little boys can be difficult."

"I should've tried harder to win him over, to reassure him I wasn't trying to steal his affections away from his mother. I'm sure at times he thought so. Mistakes are easy to make but difficult to repair." She sat reflecting for a moment then nodded toward the gaggle of relatives over by the doorway. "They're here for Endora," she said with a hint of bitterness. "It's always been about her."

"On that Lady Beatrice, I agree."

"His Lordship and I felt blessed knowing Nathan was in your care. And darling Andrew. Nathan could talk of nothing else. Perhaps I'm being impertinent, but please reconsider and stay. Edmund would be lost without you." She reached over and took my hand. "Even if he doesn't always show it, he needs you now more than ever."

Our conversation ended when a whirlwind of a woman came bursting into the room carrying all before her. She nodded here, gestured there, then disappeared up the stairs. Once gone, Lady Beatrice exhaled. "That was Endora's mother, the Duchess of Overland. I shouldn't say, but I can't abide her."

Unlike her daughter, the Duchess was a woman short in stature and wide in girth. She had a moon shaped face and flushed complexion. Her hair, pulled back into an unbecoming bun, caused her expression to be one of constant amazement. As for Endora's father, there was little about him to like. Tall, conceited, and loud, Lord Spencer the Duke of Overland appeared the perfect picture of spoiled nobility. If Nathan's death meant anything to him, he kept it well hidden.

Later Endora's brother Richard Spencer, Viscount Grandville, his wife Lady Barbara, and their two sons arrived. Stewart, the eldest, having spilt funeral punch down his shirt argued it was his brother Arthur's fault. Taking them in hand I marched them upstairs in search of a clean shirt and a game or toy that would keep them out of harm's way.

"He won't take it off, Miss Julie. He gets embarrassed when anyone sees his mark."

"No, I don't," Stewart shot back. "I'm just too old to get undressed in front of girls."

"Boys, please. Have a little respect for the dead."

The embarrassing mark was nothing more than a large birthmark which I explained was there because an angel had kissed him. Arthur, unhappy with the idea insisted an angel would have to be crazy to kiss Stewart for any reason.

With the boys finely settled, I stood off to the side and studied their father. Not as tall as Edmund, Richard dressed more to his position. Handsome, with brown eyes and thick, wavy dark brown hair, he had a way of smiling that hinted at mischief. Silas mentioned the two men had been close, but now avoided each other. He didn't share why but I couldn't help thinking Endora was involved somehow.

At three o'clock the undertaker arrived and placed the tiny casket inside the hearse. As it moved down the drive and out into the street a procession of carriages each adorned with black plumage followed. At the church a large contingent of mill workers stood waiting to offer their condolences. Each man doffed his cap while the ladies nudged their children forward with small bouquets secured with black ribbons. A small thing, but Edmund received each with humility and thanks. Endora, surrounded by family, looked neither left nor right and gave no hint she knew they were there.

At the head of the center aisle and left of the altar, sat Nathan's little casket. Called forward to say their final goodbyes, Edmund led the way followed by the Earl and Lady Beatrice. Endora followed, but once out in the aisle she refused to go further.

"You can't make me look at him. You can't. Tell them Edmund. Tell them I didn't know he only had a few hours. It wasn't my fault. I didn't mean—"

Before she could finish Edmund swooped her up and carried her out of the church and into a waiting carriage with instructions to take her home. Only after the carriage pulled away did I notice Edmund holding his leg and stumbling toward his father who kept him from falling.

The service in disarray, the pastor brought the proceedings to a close, escorted the coffin back out to the hearse and watched as it disappeared from view on its way to the Utica train station. From there it would proceed to Edinburgh then on to Inverness. Edmunds father wanted Nathan buried at Haddonfield, but Edmund refused saying at Latham, "*There was a peace there that passes all understanding.*"

Back at Thornwood, Endora's behavior was the main topic of conversation among those returning from the church, and though food was laid out, few remained long enough to eat. Most were eager to get away and agreed that a breakdown was imminent. Surely they whispered she didn't mean what she implied?"

The guest having left, Matilda went to clear away the bedrooms. I went to the kitchen and found Clara in tears. "Two day's work in a hot kitchen and no one ate a thing. What am I to do with all this?" On the brink of collapse, I insisted she go lie down and try to rest. I'd sort out the kitchen.

Now the question was how to tell Andrew? I placed the dishes on the rack and started on the pans. He knew Nathan was dying, but did he understand the finality of it? With everything put away I took off my apron and was about to leave the kitchen when a hand went over my mouth and I was forced down into the basement.

"Hello pet," Bunny said, as I heard the latch on the door click shut. "I thought it was time you and I had a little chat."

"If you don't let me go, I'll scream."

"Go ahead, no one will come."

"Edmund will."

"Wrong again I'm afraid."

"He won't let you hurt me."

"Of course he will. Do you think I could be in his house without his knowledge? He knows I'm down here and he knows you're with me."

"Liar." My response got me a slap across the face.

"Watch what you say Julie, saying the wrong thing could get you into trouble."

Footstep's overhead meant someone was in the kitchen and fearing I'd scream Bunny quickly covered my mouth. "Be still and you won't get hurt. Did you see Rolinda?" he asked when the footsteps faded away. "A pathetic creature I admit, but rich. Very rich. It's you that fascinates me. I can't get you out of my mind." Biting my shoulder, he sucked the blood from the wound. You are the blank canvas on which I'll paint my masterpiece."

"And what makes you think you'll ever get the chance?"

"I know I will. You've intoxicated my mind and I'll have no peace till I own you completely." Again he licked the blood that trickled from the wound. "Now however I must leave you." With that he was gone, and I was alone. I made my way back to the kitchen but overwhelmed by events couldn't remember how to get home.

"I thought I saw Bunny?" Edmund said hurrying in from the yard. "What did he want?"

"I need to go home but can't remember how."

"I'll take you, but then you must tell me what happened."

"Please, just leave me in peace."

"Do you think I'm blind, that I can't see your torn dress or the blood on your neck. I want to know what happened."

"It's none of your concern, now go bury your son." Frustrated by my refusal he joined his father and drove off to the train station. I took a long hot shower and went to bed.

# CHAPTER TWENTY-ONE

Depressed, worn out and alone, my intention was to forget the past and try to rebuild my marriage, but every effort failed. Harmless questions became arguments and lack of a response an incitement. Regardless, I was determined to stay in the future and fight for my marriage, but with each passing day it seemed more hopeless.

In July, two letters arrived. One from Maggie, saying Tom had passed away in his sleep. At the bottom she wrote, "My door is always open to you. Come if you need a place to run to."

The second letter was from the Blacks. It was addressed to Mark but fearing what might be in it I took the liberty to open it. I had to laugh out loud. Supposedly I had written begging them to break the lease. I found the whole thing utterly absurd. Mark would never contemplate moving regardless the reason.

"I don't know what you intended by this Endora, but whatever it was, it won't work." I tore it up and threw it in the trash, but a week later during a heated argument, the letter mysteriously resurfaced.

"So now you're rummaging through my trash?"

"It wasn't in the trash; it was on the table with the other mail. Isn't it enough that the whole squadron thinks you're insane without sharing that fact with our landlords?" Tossing it aside he continued out the door.

Damn! Why hadn't I seen that coming?

* * *

With my marriage disintegrating, returning to the past seemed more enticing by the day. At least there I told myself I could find peace and friendship in Clara's welcoming kitchen. What I found however, was anything but. Open rebellion had broken out. "Talk to the Master," Silas pleaded. "Tell him we can't keep on this way."

"If the servants aren't happy, let them go elsewhere," Edmund said as he hurried down the hall. "I've other things to concern me."

Surprised by his answer and knowing how it would be received I decided it was best to say he'd see to it the moment he returned. It was only natural they'd be unhappy as Edmund would be gone for a number of weeks in which the situation would only grow more contentious. Meanwhile the friction that had grown up between Clara and Silas continued leaving poor Matilda caught in the middle. Everything about Thornwood was out of kilter and made me wonder if the last bits of goodness had been torn from the house and buried with the child.

* * *

If the past was in turmoil, the present had become a mystery. Mark, seldom home, was now constantly under foot. Even more curious having been assigned two weeks duty with the RAF in Skegness, a seaside resort on the North Sea, he was anxious for Andrew and me to join him.

Everything seemed perfect. Mark was in good humor, Andrew loved the rides and games, and I the solitude that came from long walks along the shore. Having just finished a wonderful meal at a local restaurant we decided since the night was warm to take a stroll along the promenade. Ahead of us a young woman lost her hat to a sudden gust of wind. Handing it back I discovered the woman wasn't a stranger. Endora thanked me then melted into the crowd.

"Julie, where are you going?" Mark called out as I ran to catch up with her.

"It's her. She shouldn't be here."

"Who?" Mark asked catching up.

"Endora—the woman with the hat." I asked several people walking by, but no one saw her.

"Julie, stop! Everyone's watching. If that was her why didn't she introduce herself." Edmund said.

"Go on, make fun. You're good at that, but I know what I saw, and I saw her."

A crowd having gathered, a passing policeman came and ask if he could help. "It's my wife," Mark told him. "She's been ill and sometimes thinks she see's people who aren't there. If you could help me get her back to our hotel I'd appreciate it."

Andrew, afraid his father was having me arrested pleaded with the officer who assured him he was only helping me back to the hotel. When the officer left Mark tried to explain, but Andrew would have none of it.

"You think you know, but you don't. Just because you can't see Endora doesn't mean she's not there. She is. Ask Uncle Edmund. He'll tell you." Furious, Mark walked out. Next morning there was a note on the nightstand. I was to take the car and go home. He'd come back by train.

On the evening of Marks return I went to bed early hoping to avoid a scene, but Mark appeared hell-bent on having one. Bursting into my room, he demanded that I talk to Dr. Connelly or else.

"Or else what?" I said remembering what Endora said about needing one.

Only he had an *or else what*, all ready and waiting. "I know about the photo albums. How you spend hours looking at the pictures and pretending the people are real. Only they're not real Julie. They're dead and buried and you can't bring them back. Call them Edmund or Endora or the man in the moon, but it doesn't change the fact it's all in your head."

"I don't have to look at the albums, they're living with us."

Now the anger came. "Listen to me Julie, because I'll only tell you this one time. If this doesn't stop and I mean soon, I'll have to decide whether Andrew should remain here with you. He's only six and you've got him so confused he can't tell what's real from what's not. Last week I found him crying in his bedroom because his friend had died. Now that's sick Julie and it has to stop—now!"

"What's sick about it? He really did die. It's only natural he'd cry about losing a friend."

If Mark was a shouting man he would have shouted, instead he stood over me and told me that he'd reached the breaking point and if it didn't stop he'd be gone and Andrew with him.

He didn't wait for an answer which was for the best as I didn't have one, but there was no doubt in my mind that it was Connie who told him about the albums.

I was angry with the world when I went back next morning, and it didn't help that Endora was in the middle of one of her rages. Nathan's room was in shambles and she was now intent on destroying Edmund's study.

"So, what's got you all bent out of shape?" I asked from the doorway.

"I'm sick of this house and everything in it. I'm being kept a prisoner in my own home."

"How can you be a prisoner if you can go to the beach whenever you like. If you're unhappy, leave. Walk out. I'll help you pack."

"I could tell you the same thing," she said tossing a book at me.

"If you hadn't killed his son, you wouldn't be having this problem."

"It wasn't his son," she corrected.

"How much longer will Edmund put up with all this before he has you committed?"

Endora paused for a moment. "Probably as long as it takes Mark. I understand Connie told him about the albums. Not something a friend would do, is it? Pretty painful finding out your best friend can't keep her mouth shut. Oh well, they've always been close."

She said no more till the room was a complete disaster. Content, she pushed passed me and returned to her room. I called Matilda to help repair the damage. She took the study while I started on Nathan's room.

Home on school holiday Andrew came to help. He was picking up Nathan's nine pins game when he vanished under the bed, and reemerged with Nathan's miniature harvester, a replica of the one his father built.

"If Nathan died a long time ago like Daddy said, then how come I could play with him?" Andrew asked, climbing onto my lap, "and why can't he come back like before?"

"Because it wasn't ordained." Edmund said having overheard. Coming in he took a seat on the edge of Nathan's bed and lifted Andrew onto his lap. "I know how hard this is for you because you're just a little boy, but there is a set purpose behind everything that's happening."

"But Daddy says it's all in our heads."

"Well, you must forgive him that. All you need to know is that he loves you. He's just worried for your safety. Just remember that your dad is not allowed to see what you see. It's only natural he'd think you were making it up."

"But why not?"

"I'm not allowed to say at the moment, so you'll have to trust me."

"Nathan was my best friend," Andrew said.

"Do you think you and I could be best friends?" Edmund asked. I'd really like that." Andrew beamed and threw his arms around Edmund's neck. "Oh, I see you have the harvester I made for Nathan. He wanted you to have it to remember him by." Andrew could hardly contain himself and grabbing the toy ran down to tell Matilda.

I thought Edmund would leave once Andrew had gone, but he stayed where he was and fighting his emotions looked around the room. "It's time we put all this away." He went over and begin rocking Nathen's rocking horse. "I always wanted one of these as a child. Never got one though. Yes, we need to put all this stuff up in the attic. Matilda will help get everything boxed up and then Silas will help carry it up. I'm hoping to move the attic steps further forward so they're not so dangerous." He stopped for a moment then asked, "Julie—isn't it time we talked about what happened the day of the funeral?"

"There's nothing to talk about."

* * *

Suffering from insomnia I tried but failed to fall asleep. Hoping it might help I started down to make a cup of cocoa. Passing Mark's room, I noticed that his normally locked door was slightly ajar, and voices could be heard from inside. So, who was he talking to? I was shocked to discover it was me.

Not only was I in bed with him, we were making love. As his hand slid down my back and over my hips I whispered words of encouragement. It was what he did next that shocked me. But then why should it? None of it was real. I had, some time ago, given up believing that what I was seeing was actually what I saw. Endora had made a fool of me to many times, but no more.

Better I decided to wait and see. If it was her, sooner or later she'd show up to brag and as I waited for the milk to warm she did.

"I told you Mark would give in with a little coaxing," she said, sitting down beside me, "and tonight you witnessed the results. Mark couldn't get enough, poor boy."

"Well, at least he's not going without."

"Is that all you have to say? You see your husband having sex with another woman and you say so what?"

"What I saw was Mark making love to his wife."

"Why must you always ruin everything?"

"The only thing I ruined was your ability to gloat at my expense. And another thing. If Mark can't get enough, shouldn't he be at my door every night begging to be let in? I mean a man who can't get enough doesn't sleep in a separate room behind a locked door. He bangs down his wife's door to get to her."

"Damn you Julie, damn you to hell."

# CHAPTER TWENTY-TWO

Six months after Nathan's passing, Endora began seeing Bunny again. Now however, something was different. Bunny's usual lengthy visits became mere courtesy calls, and on some days, though she waited, he came not at all. By the end of August, Endora had reached the end of her patience.

"Don't walk away from me," she shouted, as Bunny attempted to do so. "I'm, not some chippy you picked up on the street, I'm a Duke's daughter, and you made promises."

"You said Edmund would agree to a divorce once the kid was dead, and he hasn't."

"Give it time, he'll come round—he will." Endora insisted.

"Time is something neither of us have. Now get out of my way."

"You can't leave. Not now."

"Have you forgotten I'm married?"

"Have you forgotten you said you'd wait?"

Bunny stopped and stared up at Endora. "No, I didn't forget, but Edmund will never release you. He'll bind you to him for spite—and spite in the right hands can be a powerful weapon." As Bunny continued down the stairs Endora gave him a shove from behind sending him tumbling down several steps before regaining his balance. Turning around I thought he might strike her. "Try that again and you'll wish you never started this. Have you forgotten who I am?" Endora backed off and appeared frightened, but then her anger broke through.

"You'll pay for this, Bunny Lester. Do you hear me? You'll pay."

"So you say."

Endora ran down the drive to the front gate certain he'd return, but when he didn't she fell to her knees and began to scream. If she hadn't been making such a racket and if the rain hadn't started I might have left her there, but instead I brought her in. "Bunny promised to help me if I brought him back, but he lied."

"And that surprises you? Now let's get you changed and into bed."

"You must wonder why I got involved with him?" I didn't but she continued, "I was staying at a friend's house over the weekend and Bunny was there. He was so commanding. You felt you had to tell him everything, be it for good or evil. Anyway, in a moment of madness I allowed him into my bed and from then on he owned me."

It was all a lie, and we both knew it, but I went along. "No one can own you unless you want to be owned."

"Go on, act holier than thou. But when your turn comes, then we'll see. Now close the curtains and get out."

The hallway clock was striking eleven as the last omnibus of the evening passed under the streetlamp. There would be fog by morning, probably thick. I placed her dressing gown over the chair and was about to leave when she began listing reasons why she was forced to kill her son. It was clear she'd given it a lot of thought for the list, if written down, would be nearly two pages.

I tried to ignore her, but at some point I felt I had to call this pity party to a halt. "Not a single thing you just said is true. And don't tell me you believe it because I know you don't. Everyone knew Nathan hadn't long to live, and that you'd not shed a tear at his passing."

"That's not true. Why are you saying those horrible things?"

"Because someone needs to make you realize that you committed murder for a few hours of peace. Someday, someone will call you to account, and when they do not a single person will stand and say a word in your defense." The color drained from her face leaving her pale and shaken.

"You think you're so clever, that you can see the future," she shot back, "but one day my sins will be yours and no one, not Edmund, not Mark, not even God himself will be able to save you. So go on, preach your little sermons because soon I'll be free and laughing."

\* \* \*

There was no way Endora would allow Bunny to walk away unscathed from what she saw as a betrayal and so, over the following weeks she came up with a plan to destroy him.

That she might also destroy her family's standing in society never crossed her mind. She began with a letter writing campaign that could only be called maniacal. Cruel and vindictive she allowed her venom to drip from her pen like water. It was only natural that the first letter be sent to Rolinda who, regardless how she felt about her husband took no notice other than to say Endora had lost her mind and should be pitied.

Undeterred and infuriated by Rolinda's response, Endora continued her vendetta and sent letters to everyone above the rank of Squire, but several weeks went by before I noticed a subtle change in her mental state. It appeared that her sanity was somehow connected to the ink that marked the page, and with each succeeding letter she grew more unstable. My assumptions were proven right when late one night I found her walking the upstairs corridor. Stopping every few feet she'd press her ear to the wall. "Can you hear him. He's in there somewhere, calling me. Mother . . . Mother . . . I have to make him stop. Somehow I have to make him stop calling me."

Later that week Endora's brother Richard arrived and his anger was palpable. Pushing past Silas, he raced up the stairs and into his sister's bedroom. Still in her dressing gown he demanded she put something on and join him in the sitting room.

"What in the hell is taking her so long?" he asked when I joined him.

"I'll go see." Unmoved by his demands Endora had returned to bed with every intention of staying there. "Yes, stay in bed and make Richard come to you. That's the ticket," I said as she pulled the covers over her head. "Here you are wanting everyone in England to know how Bunny has wrongly used you, yet you refuse to stand up for yourself when your brother arrives. I never took you for a coward."

"How dare you," she yelled from under the covers.

"I dare because that's how your acting. Can't even face your own brother."

"I'll show you who's a coward." Grabbing her kimono, she tied it tight around her. "You'll wish you never said that," she called over her shoulder as she headed down the stairs.

"Do you realize how close to libelous these are?" he demanded, flinging a pile of letters in her face as she entered the living room. "Only yesterday a friend snubbed me on the High Street. So please, don't tell me this is about Rolinda."

"Haven't a clue what you're talking about. Though I wouldn't mind seeing her taken down a peg. She believes herself to be far too important for my liking"

"Oh, for God's sake Endora."

"Mother sent you didn't she?" she asked relaxing down onto the settee.

"Don't start on Mother. She's been wonderful considering the mess you've created."

"I created? I created nothing; Edmund did. He's the cause of all my misery."

"All right, yes you're right, but Edmund didn't write those letters you did, and they're about to ruin not only your family, but the one person who still cares about you."

"Yes, well, why shouldn't he be ruined? When someone makes promises you expect them to be kept. He didn't and now he'll pay."

"Lester had no right promising you anything. You're a married woman whether you like it or not. Besides, Bunny isn't getting any younger and needs an heir. True, Rolinda isn't the brightest sunrise in the world, but she's not malicious or selfish and will make him a good wife."

"Bunny said if I got rid of Nathan, Edmund would free me, and we could be married. I kept my side of the bargain, I got rid of the kid, but now Edmund won't divorce me, and Bunny's gone off and married that bitch."

A look of shocked disbelief crossed Richard's face. "Are you saying—"

Realizing she'd gone too far she became the greatest drama queen in Victorian England and broke down in a flood of tears. "If only you could understand what I've suffered. The cruel way he's treated me. Nathan was in such horrible pain. He couldn't breathe and kept reaching for me. With Edmund gone, Julie refused to help so I had to do something. How can you hate me for wanting to stop his pain?"

"I don't hate you, Richard said, "but to say you killed the child . . . My God Endora, to say something like that when it's not true—what will people think?"

The conversation continued but at some point Endora's darker angel took over and leaping from her chair she physically assaulted her brother. Clawing his face and pounding on his chest it took some time before Silas and I were able to pull her away and return her to her room. Stunned by the fierceness of the attack Richard sat dazed and bloodied on the sofa.

"Is she always like that?" he asked when I returned.

"Afraid so. Now let's get you fixed up and then we can talk."

Taking a seat at the end of the table he took a cigarette from his silver cigarette case, tapped it on the lid, then lighting it took a long draw. "Normally, I wouldn't discuss family issues, but after the spectacle she made of herself I don't seem to have a choice. Something is going on here and I need to know what, if only for the family's sake. So please, tell me what you can."

Since he invited the exchange I described what I knew as fact and refused to speculate. I explained that it was Edmund, not Endora who was the victim of this tragic opera and then explained about Nathan.

"If that's true, and I have no reason to doubt you, why did Edmund take the blame? A man doesn't admit to a thing like that unless he's certain. It would be ruinous otherwise."

"He had no reason to doubt her."

"And you say James Harcourt, my brother-in-law is Nathan's father?" Richard poured himself a drink and then another. "That's crazy."

"James hoped to marry Endora, but he needed Victoria's dowry to pay off his debts and Endora needed someone to take the blame for what James did. They decided on Edmund. They thought it a wonderful joke."

"Not the sort of thing I'd consider funny, he said. But Edmund was—"

"In mourning for Jennifer. True, but Endora can be very persuasive and Edmund was at his lowest ebb. How hard would it have been to coax him into her bed?"

"Father threatened to ruin him if he didn't marry her."

"Your father's a proud man."

"Yes, too proud I sometimes think. I came here once, a stupid thing to do—the man was still on crutches and I accused him of abusing my sister. He should've thrown me out, but not Edmund. He asked how, having been a friend I could believe such a thing? I'm embarrassed to say I thought exactly what they wanted me to think. With his background . . ."

Noting the time, Richard reached for his hat. "Look, I have to go, but if you need me, I'll be at the Hound and Hare in Newmarket till Thursday. After that, at home. And say nothing to Edmund. I'll speak to him when he returns."

# CHAPTER TWENTY-THREE

With each passing day Endora grew more unstable. Edmund home from America would need to be consulted, and once again I was the one chosen for the job. Preoccupied with work he insisted I do whatever I felt best and to stop nagging him about household matters. Things calmed down, order was restored and peace for the most part reigned supreme. Then one early fall afternoon everything came tumbling down. I sent Matilda to refill the coal scuttle in Endora's bedroom. When she got there Endora, out of control, was pacing about the room with a knife in one hand and what looked like a letter in the other.

"What is all this about?" Endora demanded when I answered Matilda's screams.

"All what about?"

"I'm talking about this." She bunched up the paper and threw it at me. Picking it up I gave it a quick glance then threw it away. It was definitely a letter and Bunny's name was on it, but I had little time to read what it said or who it was too. My guess was that it was another parlor trick, but I played along.

"So what about it?" Looking toward the door I saw that Edmund, along with the entire household was gathered in the hall watching.

"I'll tell you what about it. Bunny is mine not yours do you understand? Mine, and if you think you can take him from me you don't know who you're up against."

"Is this about his coming to the funeral to see how I was coping?"

"You're crazy, he wouldn't come and not see me. He wouldn't dare."

"If you didn't know about it that's not my fault. Edmund knew he was here, didn't you Edmund?"

"Yes, I knew," he said staring at his shoes.

"You two faced little bitch. Tell me the truth. The two of you are having an affair."

What no one knew, was that Bunny and I had become friends of a sort. I was sitting alone in the garden when Bunny appeared and asked if he could join me. He soon put me at my ease and explained that he didn't drag me into the basement, Endora did.

"You know she can change her appearance. She just can't stand the fact that our relationship has cooled and that I was concerned for your well-being when Nathan passed. You see," he said becoming more animate, "I'm fascinated by your father's gift of prophecy, and I wanted to learn more about him. So, could we perhaps call a truce?" He seemed sincere and since I saw no reason not to, I agreed. He came several times after that but in secret believing the fewer who knew the better.

"You mean Edmund and I?"

"I mean you and Bunny."

"I don't see where that's any of your business. Now stop all this non-sense and give me the knife."

"Like hell I will. You're going to pay for this."

It was time to end this. Enough was enough. "Fine, then make me pay. There's no time like the present." I moved closer and spread my arms. "I'll even close my eyes." In the hall the servants nervous whispering grew louder.

Having called her bluff, she had only two options. Go through with her threat to kill me, which we both knew she couldn't do, or throw a tantrum.

She chose the latter. Tossing the knife aside she destroyed everything within reach then throwing herself onto the bed beat the pillows till the room was covered in goose feathers. As usual I was left to clean up the mess.

"Seven years bad luck Endora." I held up a piece of broken mirror.

"You poor deluded girl. Do you realize what you've done?"

"What I've done? You're the one that broke the mirror."

"Forget the damn mirror. You just admitted to having an affair with a man the entire household despises."

"No, I didn't."

"Oh, yes you did." By not denying it outright you allowed them to draw their own conclusions. And seeds once planted tend to grow."

Edmund stood waiting by the back stairs. "Is what she said true?" Pushing past him I continued down to the kitchen. "Damn it, Julie—Julie—don't walk away when I'm talking to you." Over by the stove, Clara and Matilda stood silent.

"How dare you use that tone with me. I'm not one of your servants."

"I want to know—"

"Will you can keep wanting because it's none of your business."

"Can we discuss this in private?" he said, nodding toward the servants.

"Whatever."

Once inside his study he closed the door and turned to stare at me. Outside, it was raining. It was always raining. I stood at the window watching the rain splatter mud on the fresh blooms, soiling what was pure.

"So—" he said, "is it true about the affair?"

"You tell me. You seem to know more about this mess than I do."

"All I want is a straight answer."

"If you believe the trash she was selling then you don't deserve a straight answer."

"No, maybe I don't."

"We wouldn't be having this conversation if you hadn't convinced me to stay the day of the funeral. You begged me to stay so I did, and all I got was a lot of nothing for my efforts. For six months I remained in the future and no one even noticed I was gone. Not even you! So, why was that."

"Because when you left everything stopped till you returned. But that isn't what we were talking about. The house was full of people, yet you never screamed. Not even once."

"How do you know what I did?" I asked.

"Because if you had I would've heard you."

"Why, were you listening just in case?"

"Of course not."

"I don't want to do this anymore."

Pushing past him I ran out into the rain and slipping on the wet grass fell, and like the flowers in the garden was splattered with mud. Since no one came to take me in, I remained where I was and wondered how long it would take to be washed out into the street and forgotten. Time passed and night replaced the twilight. Mark arrived and stood looking down at me. After a moment he pulled me to my feet then continued into the house.

"Weren't you supposed to be gone till Friday?" I said, following some distance behind.

"Bob's wife went into labor, so I volunteered to fly back with him. What were you doing out there?"

"Waiting for you to decide we could have another baby like every-one else."

For the next several days I remained in the future and worried what I'd find when I went back. Surely they'd understand I was just trying to get Endora to throw away the knife, but I was wrong. Now they only spoke when spoken to, and the looks and whispered conversations behind my back said they believed the worst. Normally I'd eat lunch in the servants quarters, but when they made it clear they'd prefer I ate somewhere else I carried my lunch out into the garden.

The day being warm Endora's bedroom window was open which allowed me to overhear her conversation. Edmund was still under the impression that it was Bunny he saw at the funeral and was upset because several of his best wines were missing. What moved me to tears was what Edmund said next.

"If Bunny wants to mess around with Julie that's up to him, but I don't want it done here."

\* \* \*

Using outward appearances as an indicator, Endora's erratic behavior now required intervention. Dr. Wood was called in to consult. I wasn't invited so sat on the bottom step of the stairs playing with Andrew's magic slate. Dr. Wood was droning on about Endora becoming a danger to herself. A good doctor and a fine man, but out of his depth where she was concerned. Bored, I went up to help Andrew with his map of the world puzzle. Edmund arrived while we were searching for Spain.

"What do you want?" I asked.

"I came to tell you about Endora."

"Why?"

"I'm not sure," he said, watching Andrew work another piece into the correct space. "Dr. Wood suggested that a Dr. Van Heusen who deals with mental disorders should speak to her. He'll be here tomorrow, and I'd like you to sit in."

"Yes, all right, I'll be there."

Dr. Van Heusen a tall, well-dressed man, with reddish blond hair and deep-set green eyes above a well-trimmed beard seemed a rather pompous man. Like most doctors of the period Van Heusen saw women as emotional slaves to the vagaries of their reproductive organs, and several times during the conversation quoted from Freud's book, *The Psychopathology of Everyday Life*. Most Victorian man without question agreed with his diagnosis, but as a modern woman I considered his theories almost barbaric.

"Edmund please," I interrupted. "there are better ways to do this." Regardless, Edmund stood fast and arranged for the doctor to speak to Endora the following day. Once that was seen to, he would invite Richard over to discuss the matter. Richard coming to Thornwood was difficult proposition at the best of times, but to discuss Endora's mental state was fraught with danger.

"Richard will arrive all fired-up and insist we go into the woods and settle this like gentlemen."

"Perhaps he's changed."

"I can't imagine why he would. It's happened before."

"Did you go into the woods?"

"Do I look the type that would do something that ridiculous?" Richard's carriage coming up the drive sent Edmund hurrying to the window. "My God," he muttered, "what a clotheshorse."

"Julie, how nice to see you," Richard said, as I opened the door.

"Edmund's running a little late. Nervous about the meeting. Could I get you something to drink? Silas is away and I'm standing in."

"You said Edmund's nervous?" I nodded. "Then that makes two of us."

"So, what did he say?" Edmund opened the wardrobe door and began rummaging through his clothes.

"Something about going out in the woods. What are you doing?"

"You saw how he was dressed? If I'm going to be shot, I want to wear something that won't show the blood." I gave him a final once over, and we started down to choose our weapons.

The formalities over, Edmund ushered Richard into the chair near the window and took the one opposite. Both seemed ill at ease, and an uncomfortable silence ensued before Edmund found his voice. "I'd prefer not having to meet under such trying circumstances, but—"

"This won't do. It won't do," interrupted Richard. "We need to get this settled between us." Bounding out of his chair Richard walked about the room stopping every so often to look furtively over at Edmund. Edmund sat stiffly, waiting. "Look here Edmund," said Richard, turning to face him. "Now that I know what's really going on here I believe it's time—" This brought Edmund to his feet with the certainty that Richard wanted a fight.

"I hoped you'd be reasonable, as I have no desire to fight you."

"Fight me? No, I don't want to fight. Bloody hell, we were friends once. What I'm trying to do, and not well is apologize for being an ass about this whole sordid business. Why I couldn't see the truth of it was due to my own blindness." Reaching out his hand, "I hope you'll forgive me for being such a pompous prick." Edmund took his hand and shook it with gusto.

"I don't know what to say," said Edmund looking humbled and surprised. "Please—sit down. Would you care for a drink?"

"Yes, please, a large one. To be honest, your invitation rather surprised me. And those letters—did you see them?"

"I didn't, but a friend did."

"Scandalous. Almost too hot to handle." Richard finished his drink then continued.

"I came here while you were away. Thought maybe I could talk sense to her, but the woman attacked me."

"It won't happen again."

"Then I say thank God. You do realize I'm here because of Julie. She persuaded me to listen and for the first time I was able to see what was really going on. It was very enlightening. Once I was able to see things clearly I had to accept it as truth. What hurt was realizing how badly I had treated you."

"I'm overwhelmed and grateful," Edmund said, his face beaming. "Look, why don't you stay for diner so we can talk over what has to be done. Julie," Edmund called as I passed the door, "if Silas is back, tell him Richard will stay for dinner and you join us." I passed on the message, but Silas now home from his errand, went to Edmund for conformation.

"Excuse me sir, but Miss Julie informs me that his Lordship is staying for dinner. Is that correct?"

"That's what she said, isn't it?"

"Yes. Thank you sir," Silas replied, making a hasty retreat.

"Silas."

"Yes, sir?" he said returning.

"If Julie says to do something, I expect you to carry it out as if the order came from me. Is that understood?"

"Yes, Sir. Of course, Sir." Passing me in the hall Silas left little doubt he was angry. Though not my fault he'd been made to look a fool.

Dinner was being served when I arrived and Richard, waving away the soup course was trying to convince Edmund to have Endora committed. "We can't have her out in society. She's liable to attack someone or make some outrageous comment."

"And how do you propose we do it?" asked Edmund, as Silas served the first course.

"There are several private institutions that would take her. I have a friend—"

Edmund interrupted. "Are you suggesting we lock her away?"

"In a matter of speaking yes. It's the only answer."

"That's rather drastic don't you think?"

"Well, she can't stay with us. Lady Barbara would never allow it. Both women living under the same roof—impossible! Makes me weak in the knees just thinking about it."

"Then Endora will have to remain here. I'll fix up the nursery, new furniture and wall- paper. It's in the back of the house and there's already bars on the windows. That way she'll be out of the way but close to family."

What was Edmund thinking? "You're joking, right?" I interrupted. "You really want to lock her in the room where Nathan died? That's insane. Are you aware that she walks the hall at night pleading with Nathan to stop calling her?"

"Why would I know of that?"

"Because she's your wife. And I'll tell you something else. If you think Endora will stay there without a fight, then you're as mad as she is."

"You suggest something then." So, I did, and by the time I finished Edmund was staring at me as if I'd defamed the Prince and shot the Queen. "Thank you Julie but I think we'll go with my plan. If we redecorate—"

"Didn't you hear what I said? It will still be Nathan's room. You can't put her there. "It's inhuman."

"That's enough, Julie. You're too invested to understand. Why don't you go lie down? You've had a long day."

"Yes, and they won't get any shorter if you carry through with this. And if you do, I'll return to the future and wash my hands of the whole mess." Furious, Edmund escorted me from the room and locked the door behind me. "You'll be sorry Edmund Stanley," I screamed through on the door. "You wait and see."

Edmund came to my room later that evening. "What in the hell is the matter with you? Do you enjoy making a fool of yourself, or does it take practice?"

"I don't know Mark, maybe I do. Besides, you asked my opinion, and I gave it."

"I'm not Mark."

"No, but you sound just like him."

"Didn't you see Richards face?" he asked. "All that stuff you mentioned—and then saying you'd return to the future."

"I am from the future—that's where I live, that's what I know. All that stuff Van Heusen was pushing, it's all rubbish."

"You know nothing about it," he said.

"Pardon me, but I've got a hundred years more knowledge than you, and I'm telling you what he suggested will tip her over the edge. I wish to God you had never brought me here. Now please leave."

# CHAPTER TWENTY-FOUR

Realizing the time, I went to help Endora undress and to hear her thoughts on Dr. Van Heusen. Instead she wanted to talk about Connie. "She doesn't come round much anymore, does she? From what I hear she and Mark are thick as thieves. That would worry me if I were you. Of course I'm not, I could never be that stupid, but it would worry me all the same. It's rumored they're planning to take Andrew if you don't get help—Say why don't you talk to Van Heusen when he comes. Then I won't have to."

"And you're telling me all this because?"

"I figured you'd want to know." She smeared her face with cold cream and climbed into bed."

"And you have proof to back up what you're saying?"

"None at the moment but think about it. Mark drives by her house every night. All she'd have to do is leave the porch light on. If it's on he goes in. If not he comes home."

Endora prattled on, but I was watching the girl standing below me in the driveway. There was fear in her eyes. She didn't like the house and she didn't want to live here. If I were kind, I'd call down and suggest she run away, but I had long since stopped being kind so moved away from the window and let the curtain fall back in place.

Later as I lay alone in the dark I wondered if what Endora said was true or just another lie. She had a knack of making a lie sound like the gospel. What worried me was the part about Andrew. It was a subject that I'd already considered. The question however was would he really take him, and how could I stop it?

Hearing the front door creek open I went to see who came in. Straining to see through the darkness I was leaning out over the banister when something warm splashed onto my hand. Blood was dripping from the chandelier hook covering everything. Dipping my finger into it I rubbed it across my lips. *"It's an acquired taste Julie."* Below me Mark hurried toward the front door with Andrew in his arms. Connie followed with a bag of clothing.

"Mommy, Mommy," Andrew cried. "Don't let them take me, I want to stay with you—Mommy, please—help me."

I tried to go after them, but the stairs were awash with the thick sticky liquid and I was unable to move. "Curse you for what you're doing." I called after them. "As God is my witness, I'll get him back, I swear I will."

"Mommy! Mommy! Stop, you're scaring me," Andrew kneeling beside me on the bed shook me awake. "You had a bad dream. I was afraid," he said his cheeks awash with tears.

"Andrew— I'm sorry. I'm so sorry. I didn't mean to scare you."

"It's okay, now that you're awake."

"I want you to listen to me Andrew." I pulled him into my arms and wipes his tears. "There may come a time when they'll take you away from me. They'll say their afraid I might hurt you. But that's a lie. I could never hurt you. Never. If that happens and they take you away I'll come and get you back. Do you understand? I'll come and get you no matter how long it takes."

"I'll remember Mom, I promise."

As dawn broke, and the room grew light, a vague plan took shape in my mind. Nothing concrete, but a plan, nonetheless. First, I had to discover for myself if what Endora said was true. I called and invited Connie to lunch. She didn't seem very enthusiastic, but she came.

"What do you plan to do while Charlie's away?"

"I was going to ask if you and Andrew would like to go to the circus down in London? I've got tickets and we'd have a great time. We could go early and let the kids ride the rides. What do you think?"

"I don't like the circus. The clowns scare me."

"Then how about we go up to Great Yarmouth for a few days. There's a wonderful hotel right on the promenade that's reasonable. The kids would love it and we could lay out on the beach and talk."

"No, I can't."

"Why not?" Connie asked, "You never want to do anything anymore."

"I have too much to do here."

She looked around the kitchen. "It doesn't appear you've done anything for months. I'm not sure what you're trying to prove but have you looked in the mirror lately. You've lost weight, your clothes hang on you, there are dark circles under your eyes, and your hairs a mess."

"What do you care how I look?"

"I just thought—"

"Why aren't you eating?" She didn't answer. "Not good enough for you?" I opened the frig and took out a salad I'd made several days earlier. "Here maybe this will suit you."

"We can't eat that. It's all moldy. It needs to be thrown away," she said pushing it aside. "What else have you got in there?" she said elbowing me aside. "Good grief Julie." She didn't ask, she just started dumping everything in the trash. "It's a wonder you haven't gotten food poisoning."

"There was nothing wrong with it when I made it."

Connie cleared away the mess and came back to the table. "We need to talk."

"You mean about your affair with my husband?"

"What!" she asked.

"I thought I made myself perfectly clear. Why are you sleeping with my husband?"

Enraged that I would suggest such a thing Connie reached for her purse and headed for the door. "There's something very wrong with you Julie, and if you don't get away from here and soon, you'll lose everything. I'm really worried about you?"

"Yeah, than why are you sleeping with Mark."

"I thought I could talk to you. Try to make you see what you're doing, but it's hopeless. You need to get help."

When I was sure she was gone I went down to the wine cellar to get a bottle of wine. "You need to get help Julie. Blah, blah, blah . . ."

"How'd it go?" Endora asked joining me.

"Knowing your situation, I'd think being underground would be unsettling."

"Hilarious, but her denial was rather weak. How convenient that Charlie leaves the day before Mark. Perhaps he'll invite her to go along. She wanted to go to the beach. You should drive up and check it out. It's not that far."

"I would but I have to be here when Van Heusen comes tomorrow." Endora shrugged and returned to her room.

The doctor arrived on time, but Richard was late due to his horse throwing a shoe. Everyone gathered in Edmund's study for a glass of port and a cigar. Van Heusen drank the port, refused the cigar, and began the discussion after clearing his throat.

"Endora, since the death of her son, has been suffering from what I believe is extreme emotional fatigue." I wanted to laugh out loud but restrained myself. "If the situation doesn't soon improve her mental state will deteriorate and a complete breakdown is possible."

"That's all well and good," Richard said, "but the woman attacked me. My sister's a menace to anyone who goes near her. Surely, you're not suggesting we allow her to roam free and attack people willy-nilly?"

"That was never my intention, but perhaps a private institution—"

Edmund interrupted. "Endora will stay here. I'll redecorate the nursery and she'll be fine."

"Yes, that might be for the best. That way she can be surrounded by her loved ones."

"The best? Locking her away in the room where her son died? How could that possibly be for the best? Unless of course you really want her to go mad. Besides, how can you surround yourself?" Immediately ordered from the room I went to give Endora the bad news.

"What do you want?" Endora asked, coming up behind me.

"Van Heusen's going to put you in the nursery, so you'll be closer to your loved ones."

"I don't have loved ones."

"Exactly what I said. Richard says you're a menace."

"Richard's an idiot. I'm not dangerous, I'm mentally fatigued."

"Come on Endora, I wasn't born yesterday—wait a minute—I haven't been born at all. Imagine being alive before your parents . . . No wonder I appear so young."

"Julie! Stop being stupid."

"Anyway, that's what Edmund agreed to."

"Julie," she said, reaching for me, "when I'm in that room, when I'm locked away—you'll come won't you? You won't let me be there alone . . . Not all the time anyway?" As the defused light from the stained-glass window fell across her face, her expression was one of dread. I needed to have this out with Edmund.

"Well, there she is, little miss smart remarks."

"We need to talk about Endora. About putting her in that room."

"I don't wish to discuss it," Edmund said studying the blueprints for the new mill.

"This is your way of getting even, isn't it? That's what this is all about. Getting even."

"It's nothing of the sort." He threw his pencil aside and studied me. "As bad as she's been to you why do you take her side?"

"I don't know. Maybe because like me, she has no one else."

Edmund started to say something but instead returned to his work. It was clear he'd never see the point of what I was saying so I turned to leave. Almost out the door he called after me. "Thanks for speaking to Richard. I'm in your debt."

"I did it because it had to be done. Not for any other reason."

* * *

On Sunday Mark left for Skegness, and the urge to follow was overpowering. By lunchtime my anger and jealousy were driving me to distraction. Picking up the phone I called Connie. No one answered. In fact, no one answered for the next five days. Then on the day of Mark's return she answered. I hung up.

I waited till Mark was in the shower then searched his car. It didn't take long to find something. Scrunched down between the seats was her headscarf and comb. By bedtime I was seeking solace in a bottle of wine.

"Don't you think you have enough?" Mark asked when I poured another glass.

"Did you and Connie have a good time?" I threw the scarf and comb on the table in front of him.

"Find your own answer, you'll like it better." Pushing past me Mark continued up to bed.

"So, tell me," I asked next morning, "why don't you ever take me any place?"

"Maybe because I'm ashamed to be seen with you."

"Still quick with a compliment," I called out as he drove away.

# CHAPTER TWENTY-FIVE

I was finishing the dishes when Edmund came in, poured a cup of tea and took a seat at the table. I knew what he wanted, but the answer was still no.

"But you're better with her than I am. She'll listen to you," he said with a voice dripping with charm.

"If you need help, ask the servants."

"Endora doesn't like them." He rinsed out his cup and sat it on the drain.

"All right. Fine. I'll do your dirty work, but the servants have to help. I can't do it all on my own. When do you want it done?"

"Tomorrow—if possible. And I'll see to it that they help."

So next day we moved Endora. It wasn't pretty. First because I was in charge, and second because it meant extra work for them. I warned against it, but when Endora refused to move Clara insisted on using force. This resulted in Clara being bitten and punched in the face. When Silas stepped in she tore his jacket, and a quick kick in the crouch sent him to his knees in tears. In the end I calmed her down, the deed was done, and no one was happy.

With the room in order and Endora safely locked away I gathered everyone together and informed them that Edmund insisted we all share in Endora's care. She was still the lady of the house regardless her current situation and all were to respect her position. Clara bruised, but not broken spoke for the others.

"I'm a cook, not a nursemaid. I cared for Nathan because he was the Master's child, and I loved the little mite, but Endora—she can rot for all I care. If you want her seen to, do it yourself." Getting down a pot she filled it with water and put it on to boil.

"But, Clara, I can't do everything—I have other duties."

"What other duties? All I see is you being in the way of those that hav'em."

"Clara—"

"Look, Madam doesn't like me, never has, and that's fine, because I don't care much for her either. She likes you well enough, so let that be an end to it." Picking up several potatoes she dropped them into the boiling water.

"Try to understand."

"It's not my job to understand. My job is to cook the Master's meals and keep his kitchen in order. I'm not here to cater to the likes of her or you, for that matter. If you don't fancy the job, talk to the Master."

"But Edmund wants us both to see to her."

"Well, I'm sorry about that, but the answers no."

"Can't we try to get along?"

Clara stopped clearing away the potato skins and stared at me. "I saw the Master's face. The hurt in his eyes. But we knew my girl. Silas told us how every time that fancy man of hers came round he sought you out first. We figured Lester was just trying to upset Madam but now we know."

\* \* \*

During the first week of Endora's imprisonment she spent her time screaming and pounding on the door for someone to come let her out. When that failed she began destroying things. Furniture, clothing, even the curtains would become victims of her wrath. In the end she sat by the door sobbing and mumbling to herself. No one seemed to care but me, and if Edmund didn't do something, I'd go mad.

"No! You're not to give in. It will only make matters worse." Edmund turned so Silas could help him off with his jacket.

"But I can't take—"

"The answer is no," he interrupted. "Silas, is it possible to get something to eat at this late hour?"

"But I have problems of my own. I can't deal with much more."

"I believe Clara left a plate, sir."

"Thank you, Silas, I'll eat in my study. Now please Julie, I've had a hard day, and I'd like some peace."

"There is no peace at Thornwood," I shouted down to him as I made my way upstairs.

"Julie please," Edmund called up to me, "leave it alone. This is how it has to be."

"That's your answer for everything." Returning to the future I tried to find rest, but there was none for Endora's heart breaking sobs echoed through time to haunt me.

"I told her straight out," Clara was saying when I returned next morning, "Madam is her problem not ours, so what does she do? She goes running to the Master and when he won't listen, she walks out on him. Now can you imagine?"

"Did you notice," Matilda said, scrubbing down the table, "even the Master avoids her now. Quiet, she's coming."

I said good morning, but receiving no reply went about the business of preparing Endora's breakfast. Once again her room was a disaster. All her clothes were on the floor and pieces of broken water pitcher lay scattered on the carpet.

"Did you know Mark's in a great deal of trouble at work?"

"How would I know that?"

"Everyone's noticing how preoccupied he is, and they blame you and your crazy antics. He's making mistakes that could get someone killed. Colonel James warned that if Mark's evaluations didn't improve something would have to be done or he'd be grounded. Both agreed that you're a situation that needs fixing."

Refusing to play her games I left her room as I found it. She could clean it up.

# CHAPTER TWENTY-SIX

It was Andrew's first report card and his grades were cause for celebration. I suggested going to his favorite restaurant and afterward perhaps a trip to the toy store, but unable to find my keys went to find them. Coming in from the kitchen I heard Andrew talking to his father on the phone. At first he denied it but breaking into tears finally confessed.

"Dad said when we go out I have to call him, so he knows where I am." His statement took my breath away. What did Mark think I was going to do with Andrew? Throw him off a bridge or something? Though I was beyond angry I did my best to explain that what his father did was wrong. That I was his mom and we could go wherever we wanted. I thought it a cruel thing to do to a little boy, but we put it aside and continued with our celebrations. Andrew was picking out a toy when Connie arrived. Pretending surprise, she insisted on joining us, but I refused and headed for the car.

"Julie, wait up, I want to talk to you. Julie—for God's sake—stop a minute!" I ignored her and got Andrew into the car. "Don't be like that."

"How should I be when you're here to spy on us?"

"Why would I do that?"

"Because Mark sent you. And don't say he didn't because how else would you know where we were? Now get out of the way I want to get in the car." When she refused, I pushed her aside, and she fell.

"You should've seen her face when I said Mark was using Andrew as a spy," I told Endora when I got back.

"Please, I'm losing count of how many jacks I have to pick up."

"Forget the jacks, what do you think I should do?" Endora smiled up at me but said nothing.

"I'm the kid's mother. I'll take him wherever I damn well please."

"Now don't get yourself all upset, you know how he is about Andrew."

Unable to pick up all twelve jacks at once she threw them across the room. "You need to make a plan. Now, before things fall apart—and they will, trust me. Oh, and could I be allowed out once in a while? This is such a dreary place and I'm bored." With problems of my own I didn't need hers, so without thinking I agreed.

By mid-afternoon my mood had grown darker and by the time Andrew went to bed, I wasn't fit to be around. I opened a bottle of rather indifferent wine and sat down to drink it. Funny thing was, I didn't like wine. Never had and never would. I drank because it was there.

"Where's Andrew?" Mark threw his jacket toward the chair but missed.

"Where he always is at this hour. In bed. So why the sudden interest?"

"Because he's here with you." I took a long drink of wine, and then another.

"Drinking won't help."

"Want to make a bet?"

"Connie said you knocked her down in the parking lot?"

"Then don't send her to spy on us."

"You're disgusting, you know that." Mark said.

"But at least I'm not screwing my best friends wife."

That quick, he reached out and slapped me hard across the face splitting my lip and knocking the glass from my hand. "If there was any way—any way at all, to keep people from knowing you were mine I'd do it in a heartbeat."

"Then damn it, there's the door—leave." This was madness, and I needed to stop, to walk away, but I couldn't. "I know about your meeting with Colonel James. About my being a situation that needs fixing. Is that what I am to you, a situation?"

Mark walked away but stopped and came back. "How did you—? That was a private conversation."

"Yeah, about me."

"Who told you?"

"Then it's true. I'm nothing more than a situation."

"You know what? I'm sick to death of your games and I'm sick to death of you."

"Games? You think this is a game? I love games. What shall we play?" I said.

"Your insane Julie and need to get help."

Out of control I began hammering him with my fist. Picking me up he carried me into the bedroom and ripped my clothes away.

"You're hurting me. Stop it—"

"You said that's how you liked it, remember?"

"No, that wasn't me, I never said that."

Mark stopped and appeared to be waking from a bad dream. "No—this is all wrong . . ." Dressing quickly, Mark told me it was over. He was leaving. "And if I can get Andrew away from this madhouse, I'll do it." He didn't say goodbye. He didn't slam the door. He just walked away.

I tried not to think about what Mark said, but the imagine of my son being pulled from my arms keep playing over and over in my head.

* * *

Sitting out on the front porch I watched as a mist formed over the wheat fields across the street. In the distance could be heard the short shrill shriek of a fox. I had never felt so alone or unwanted.

"So why do you insist on provoking him?" Endora asked sitting down beside me.

"He started it, not me. I just asked a question."

Picking up a twig she began scribbling in the dirt. "Yes, but then you started in about your being a situation."

"I needed to know."

Endora threw the stick away, sighed, and returned to her room. A chilled wind blew the leaves across the yard and scattered the mist. Fall was coming. Before going in I read what she wrote. October 31, going back. I shivered. Had someone walked over my grave?

# CHAPTER TWENTY-SEVEN

Edmund said not to take anything Mark said in anger personally, but when I asked why it didn't work both ways his answer was rather ambiguous. Angered by his avoiding of the question I let it be known that if Mark thought he could take my child from me he'd be signing Andrew's death warrant because I'd kill Andrew and myself before I'd let Mark have him.

"How could you even think that?" Edmund said horrified at the thought. "You would rather see Andrew dead then with his father? The idea is too horrific to even contemplate."

"Andrew's my son not Mark's, and if that's what has to be done to keep him with me I'll do it. I won't let Mark take the only thing I have left."

* * *

Tuesday morning, I received an alarming call from Amelia Goodfellow, Andrew's teacher. Andrew wasn't at school and she worried that he was ill. Taken unawares I stumbled through an answer, thanked her for her concern and hung up.

"That bastard." I said heading for the car. "If he thinks he can just waltz in and take my son he's sadly mistaken. Driving out to the base my anger grew with each passing mile. If this is how he wants to play it, fine. By the time I reached the squadron I was out of control. My anger was driving my every action. I didn't stop at the duty desk. Instead I began screaming Mark's name at the top of my lungs along with several other colorful adjectives.

"Come out and face me you coward. You took my son without permission and I want him back. Do you hear me Mark. I want him back!"

Everyone was watching; no one tried to stop me. I found Andrew watching cartoons in the Rec-room. On my way out the duty officer tried to hand me the phone saying Mark wanted to talk to me, but I told him to tell Mark to go to hell and left. Halfway home my nerves kicked in, and I thought I'd be sick. I'd burnt my bridges and there'd be no road back.

For the next several days I tried to decide what to do. Andrew loved school, but I couldn't risk Mark taking him again. In the end I called the school, said we'd gotten notice that a house was available on base and we'd be moving at the end of the week. I was sorry for the short notice, but it all came up unexpectedly. It broke my heart to do it, but I had to keep him safe.

* * *

Edmund's leg had grown increasingly more painful and walking was becoming impossible. Everyone knew he needed surgery, but he steadfastly refused. In an act of desperation, I sent word to his father to come and talk some sense into him. After a rather heated argument Sir Owen came down for a cup of tea, and a chance to calm his nerves. "The boy is incorrigible. Has been since a youth. Takes after his mother. Regardless, it needs seeing to or else in time he'll lose it all together."

"You don't have to convince me," I said serving tea.

"Tell me, how are things concerning Endora. A bad business that. Bad for everyone involved." I explained the situation and mentioned the servant's refusal to help. "Has Edmund no control over these people?" he interrupted. "Demand they help or fire them. Insubordination can't be allowed, or they'll take advantage. Well, it's getting late and I must go and try one last time to talk sense into the boy."

A shouting match ensued before Sir Owen gave up and made his way back downstairs. It surprised me that after such a heated conversation his manner would be so subdued.

"Did things go badly up there?" I asked.

"I was just remembering a promise I made some years ago and how hard it's been to keep," he sighed. "It's just taking so damn long. Well, must be off or I'll miss my train."

"So what did Sir Owen want?" Endora asked when I went to get her settled for the night. "He's worried about Edmund's leg. It's getting worse."

"Well, never mind, I've got news of my own. That little show you put on at the squadron had everyone talking and Colonel James is furious. If Mark doesn't get you under control, you'll be sent home and that would be a disaster all round."

I figured it wouldn't go over very well, why would it? I finished turning her bed down and returned to Edmund's room. He was working from bed and managed to spill most of his papers on the floor.

"If you'd do what your father asked—" I got down, collected the ones that wound up under the bed and laid them on his lap.

"Stop nagging."

"I'm not nagging. I want to ask a question. "Do you think Mark will try and take Andrew again?"

"I don't know. He's rather unhappy with things at the moment."

"Gosh, Mark isn't happy. That makes two of us. Maybe it's because you refuse to show yourself to him so he can see I'm not out of my mind insane. Thanks to you I'm about to lose my son."

"I'll tell you what I can." The reason we can't allow Mark to see what you do is because if he did, he'd move you elsewhere, and nothing here would change."

"In other words, I'm the fatted calf being led to the slaughter to satisfied Endora's desires."

"No, it has nothing to do with what Endora wants. In time you'll come to understand that. You have to trust that I—"

"Trust? Like in depend upon, have confidence in, pin one's hopes on, that kind of trust?"

"You trust Endora. In fact you hang on her every word," he said. "That's where all this nonsense about killing yourself and Andrew came from. It came from her."

"No, Endora had nothing to do with it. And I don't trust her, but that doesn't mean I can't care about her."

Edmund threw off the covers and struggled to get to his feet. "I have to go out."

"You're not fit to go anywhere. If you not careful you'll fall."

"You can't expect me to lay here and do nothing while you make the biggest mistake of your life?"

"No, the biggest mistake of my life was being born. I was eight years old when Father said I was born under a dark cloud, eight years, pretty young to hear you'll have to die to save yourself, but that's what he told me. Even Aunt Bertha, "if it wasn't for you your parents would be alive today." I lost my baby, I'm about to lose Andrew and my first and now second marriage is in ruins. My life is spinning out of control and you tell me I'm making a big mistake." I started to laugh. "Can you think of a bigger mistake than me?"

\* \* \*

The first treacherous storm of the season had arrived. High winds and rain mixed with sleet, lashed the house. Worried Andrew might need another blanket I went to check but found his bed empty. Looking down into the stairwell I saw Mark holding a dead child in his arms.

"You did this," he called up to me. "You pushed him over the railing."

"No! that's not true. I wouldn't . . ." But hadn't I threatened? No—I'm a good mother. Good mothers don't kill their children. But Mark said I did, and Mark never lies . . .

Waking, I ran out onto the landing and looked down into the stairwell. A dream—another horrible dream. But then I heard that familiar cackling laughter and the sound of breaking glass. Racing down the stairs I headed for the dining room. Over by the fireplace Edmund, covered in blood lay help-less on the floor. Endora, scissors in hand prepared to strike the final blow. Screaming her name, I rushed forward and taking hold of her arm managed to wrestle the weapon away from her. Moments later Silas joined the fray and together we forced her from the room and back up the stairs. It only lasted a few minutes, but they were minutes that could cost Edmund his life.

"Merciful heaven's, Julie. What's happened?" Clara's frightened voice called out.

"Phone Dr. Wood." But Clara also called the police.

While Silas cradled Edmund's head in his lap, I did what I could to keep him alive. Endora's part in this had to remain secret, and though the servants were angered by my decision, I refused to give way. The police and Dr. Wood arrived simultaneously and took charge. Questions were asked and answered given. Edmund was safely on his way to hospital and I stood, dizzy and lightheaded against the door frame.

"Why didn't you say you were hurt?" Dr Wood said, noticing blood dripping down my arm. "Here let me get you into a chair so I can look at that arm. Now tell me what really happened. Do you realize what you've done, and where you'll wind up if the police find you lied?"

"What choice did I have? Tell them Endora did it?"

"Yes, well—you have a point. But an intruder? Have you forgotten Edmund's position in the community? Every paper in the area will have this as their lead story. They'll launch a manhunt. Everyone will expect Endora to visit the hospital, and when she doesn't they'll assume the worst."

"Then I'll have to make something up. Will Edmund be all right?"

"He's lost a great deal of blood—I've got Dr. Keaton seeing to him, and he's the best there is. Excellent fellow." He wrote out instructions for me to follow then in a stern voice said, "We don't want that getting septic. I'll call by later. Now try to rest, it's the best medicine." True to his word, he returned mid-morning. Though many of Edmund's wounds were deep, none were life threatening. Edmund would recover, but it would take time.

"Have you seen the papers?"

"Not yet."

"Let Silas get one for you."

At the top of the front page in bold print, the shocking headlines. *"Stanley Manufacturing Owner, Struck Down by Intruder."* It was all there; quotes from the servants, my statement to the police, and plenty of speculation concerning who the culprit might be. It listed Edmund's philanthropic pursuits, then a word about his work for the local Children's' Preservation League for the Homeless and Orphaned. At the bottom, it mentioned his military service and added a hearty wish for a speedy recovery.

\* \* \*

After the attack the servants began an insinuations campaign. Did I want this to happen? Did I leave the door unlocked on purpose? Why didn't I go to visit him? The reason was simple, but I couldn't tell them. While in the past going beyond the gate was impossible.

It was a month before Edmund came home and with his arrival Endora lost the well to fight. Her appetite waned, her tantrums ceased, and she became quiet and introspective. An air of melancholy surrounded her and fearful of being alone, she sought my company at every opportunity.

"Can you believe the time she spends up there? And after what that witch did to the Master," said Clara, pounding the bread dough extra hard.

"I'd let her starve if it were me," answered Matilda.

"Julie doesn't see it that way," Clara said. Taking a handful of flour, she scattered it over the dough board. "Well, they're cut from the same cloth."

It saddened me to hear them speak that way, but several days later, as I carried cocoa up to her room the hall grew dark and a presence unseen, yet felt, entwined itself about me. "Continue in your kindness and all will be well," it whispered, and so I did, and found a kind of peace in the doing.

"I have something I need to tell you." Endora took a seat on the bed and waited while I put away her clothes. "Soon a letter will arrive from Dr. Connelly stating that charges have been made concerning your ability to care for your son."

"I won't give him up Endora. I won't."

Reaching for her cocoa she managed to spill it down the front of her dress. "Now look what I've done." Starting to cry she tried to wipe the worst away. "I'm so sorry." I stopped and looked at her. She was sorry?

"It was just an accident. Nothing to fret about. I'll get you something else to put on."

"Tomorrow's All Hollow's Eve. I dread that night."

"I've always thought it rather fun."

"People like to play at spiritualism. Even the old Queen. They consider it a harmless game—but it's not. Everyone's sitting around the Ouija Board, their hand going this way and that. It hints about something, and then it happens. You think you have the power, that you can control it, so you ask for more and you get it. Not satisfied you continue on until one day it reaches out and devours you."

"My father said evil comes in through the cracks in the door. You don't know it till you feel it on the back of your neck."

"Your father was a wise man." She said no more till I was about to leave. "Julie—don't blame yourself for what happened to Edmund. It wasn't your fault. Locks are not a boundary. I'm in this room because I have to be. It's part of my—" but she stopped and unwilling to continue said she wanted to be alone. So different was her behavior that I grew afraid for her. Never had Endora spoken with such emotion or honesty. She knew what was coming and dreaded it.

* * *

That evening as I made my way up the stairs everything changed, and I found myself in the middle of a dense forest. Two paths lay before. One narrow, one wide. Which should I take? The wide path was smooth and well-marked, but the narrow was rocky and overgrown. Remembering a passage from the Bible about the wide and narrow paths, I choose the narrow, and though the way was difficult in time the forest gave way to lush pastures and the dim light of a setting sun desperate to stay. Jealous of the approaching darkness, its rays clung tenaciously to the few remaining wispy clouds that crisscrossed the evening sky. Fighting to hold on, its colors changed from brilliant pink, to a paler purple and then, too weak to continue, faded to grey and disappeared.

The moon, occasionally hidden by passing clouds made remaining on the path difficult as the momentary darkness was intense. Still, I refused to linger and in time arrived at what appeared to be a vast ocean. What was I to do? How was I to proceed? My fears grew out of all proportion as the sound of a roaring lion echoed out over the water and caused the moon and stars to abandon the sky.

With no light to see by I was forced to feel my way along. Growing desperate and weary from the journal I thought myself lucky to find a tree to shelter under for the night. Resting against its trunk I fell quickly to sleep but woke abruptly when I became ensnarled in it branches. The more I struggled to free myself the more entangled I became.

It was then that I realized how close I was to the water. At first the waves barely touched me, but with each subsequent wave the water came in faster and receded more slowly until in time it reached my shoulders. A few more incoming waves and I would drown.

With all hope gone a light appeared in the distance. Not bright, but a light all the same. Straining to keep my head above the waves I saw that the light wasn't a single light but twelve glowing lanterns each held by a man in dazzling white. Approaching, they gave a mighty shout and instantly the tide receded, the trees branches fell away and the heavens were again filled with light. Lifted up, I was carried to a place of safety and calm. At peace, I fell asleep to the soft murmurings of their prayers and chants.

*Pulled from the water, saved from the waves*
*the one that died, will come to reclaim.*
*Love that was stolen will soon be restored,*
*while love that endures will find its reward.*
*Hearts that were broken, are hearts that will mend,*
*evils defeated, when love defends.*
*Peace will be granted, the truth will be told,*
*All in the fullness of time.*
*Amen*

# CHAPTER TWENTY-EIGHT

Andrew, eager to get the pumpkin carved woke me earlier than usual. "Come on mom, let's get started," he called out as he hurried down the stairs. It was a huge pumpkin by any standard and though we made several false starts we managed what Andrew proclaimed a masterpiece. He said it was a goblin, but I had my doubts. It looked nothing like Endora. Delighted he somehow managed to carry it back so he could show the servants. I went up to Edmund's room.

"What's Clara trying to do, fatten me for the slaughter?" Edmund asked nodding toward his plate. "How can I possible eat all this?"

"I'll help." I reached for a piece of bacon and he slapped my hand. "I have something weird to tell you." I said.

"It's Halloween, things are supposed to be weird. But go ahead I'm listening."

He turned his attention back to his plate while I took a seat and began. "Maybe you can explain it because it makes no sense to me. I was going up to bed when suddenly I found myself in a dense forest." Continuing, Edmund's smile disappeared, and his expression turned serious.

"What you saw was the story of your life here at Thornwood. How in the beginning you seemed confused and unsure whether to stay or go. Hence the wide and narrow paths. Choosing the narrow path was your decision to stay regardless the problems you might face." Edmund's voice grew soft and full of wonder. "The Sun fighting to hold on, was your desire to rebuild your marriage and to cling to the love you have for Mark. The intense darkness—your soul in turmoil, overwhelmed by fears and doubts. I realize this is difficult to understand—"

"But what about the stars and moon returning and the tides ebbing? And the prayer if that is what it was. What about that?"

"All that is yet to be revealed." Edmund's expression changed from wonder to worry. His eyes darkened and his voice took on an air of urgency. "You're right, it was a prayer, but also a defense against the evil that surrounds you. Tell no one, especially not Endora. I can see by your expression you doubt me, but please, hold off on judging me until all is revealed."

There was so much I needed to know, so much I wanted to ask, but his strength failed him, so I went to prepare Endora's breakfast.

Approaching her room, a sense of dread overcame me. My hands grew clammy and my heart pounded against my chest. Reaching her door, I considered turning back, but gaining courage forced myself to enter. Unable to see through the eerie darkness I placed the tray on the floor and felt my way toward the window hoping to let in some light, but nearly there something blocked my way. It was Endora, hanging from a rope thrown over the closet door and tied to the knob on the other side. A chair lay on its side nearby.

At first I thought it a Halloween prank, a trick she devised to frighten me, but the idea quickly passed. This was no prank. Endora had committed suicide knowing full well that I would be the one to find her. Without thinking I picked up the shoe that had fallen from her foot and eased it back onto her foot. Why would she do such a dreadful thing? I needed to get away from her, to get out of the room and back to Edmund but I couldn't find the door. Someone had taken it. In a panic I ran my hands over where the door had been and finding nothing searched the entire wall but there was no way out.

"Oh God, help me find the door, don't leave me in here alone with her," I prayed. Feeling my way to the window I pulled back the drapes to allow in some light, but the room remained in darkness.

"Remember Julie, your life will mirror mine. My future will be yours," she whispered.

Losing control, I began banging on the wall. "Let me out" I shouted. "Let me out—please. Don't leave me here with her—please, I'll go mad." Tears overflowed my eyes as I tried to understand why no one would come. Did the hate me that much? Please," I screamed, "I need to get away from here I need to get out of this room." Behind me Endora's familiar high-pitched cackle filled the room like the crack of lightening and I held my ears against it.

"Mommy, what's wrong? Mommy stop." Andrew called out running down the hall toward me. "It's okay Mom honest, I'll help you. You're in the hallway."

"The door. Someone hid the door—I couldn't get out?"

"The doors here Mom," Andrew said. "See, I'll open it for you."

"No—Andrew don't! Find Silas—tell him to come to Uncle Edmund's room. You stay with Clara. Stay with Clara!"

"I can't do this anymore, I can't." I said bursting into Edmund's room.

"Can't do what?" Edmund asked, laying aside his papers.

"Endora. Her shoe—I can't do this anymore, I can't. You have to make it stop before I go mad."

"Julie, my love—"

"No," I said pushing his hand away. "Your love is hanging dead in her room. You sat there listening to my dream and all the while knew what was waiting for me a few doors away. Why would you do that? Tell me! I can't go back in there. Not with her like that."

Silas arrived and Edmund explained what needed doing, but Silas steadfastly refused. "Julie is responsible for Madam, and if she needs taking down, Julie will have to help me do it."

Edmund's face went red with rage. "Who in the hell do you think you're talking to? I'm the Master of this house and when I give an order I expect it to be obeyed."

"I'm sorry Sir but this time I must say no. I cannot take her down by myself, so Julie will have to help if I'm to move her."

"Then she'll remain where she is till the doctor arrives. When he does you will help to get her down or look elsewhere for work. I won't have people in my household telling me no. Is that understood?"

"Yes Sir, I understand." He withdrew from the room and returned to the kitchen. Silas had never used that tone with Edmund, and I was shocked that he would do so.

"It's me they dislike. They have it in their heads that because I cared for her I was on her side. That's why he wouldn't do it."

A telegram was sent to her family and Richard arrived several hours later with rather shocking news. Since Endora had publicly disgraced her family she would not be buried at Castlegate. Rather, she would be interred at Bedford Manor. Also, if Edmund would agree the service would be for family only here at Thornwood, and afterward since Edmund was still healing Richard would escort the body north.

Endora wouldn't be pleased with the arrangements but she brought it on herself. The funeral was a sad affair, with few attending and those that did whispered that Edmund was the one responsible for her untimely death. If he had treated her better . . .

The service over Silas and I helped Edmund back into bed. I planned to return to the future, but Edmund relaxing back against the pillows asked me to remain.

"I stayed before and look what it got me."

"Julie, please . . . Listen to me. I know this all seems vastly unfair, but you have to understand. The Council favored you. That means they hold you in the highest regard. Here, take this." Edmund placed a small gold locket in the palm of my hand. "Father gave it to Mother before leaving for the continent."

"Edmund, I can't."

"You must. Watch—turn the side with the heart to the left and it will form a key. A key that will open a book that comes unexpectedly into your possession. It's important that you remember."

* * *

Six months had passed since Endora's death and though Bunny came several times to discuss my father's gifts of prophecy and to ask how I was coping, I had to admit that I missed her more than I thought possible. I waited each day for the letter she said would arrive, but when it didn't come I assumed it was another of her cruel jokes. Father always said, "*when things expected don't appear it portends trouble,*" and on most occasions he was right.

In early January my physical and mental health began to deteriorate. My insomnia had increased to the point that going to bed was a waste of time. I was losing weight I couldn't afford to lose, and the simplest tasked became more than I could physically handle.

On one particular evening I was feeling so unwell I left Andrew with Edmund while I went home and fell into bed. Over by the window a small beam of light appeared. Growing larger and more vaporous it moved about the room as if unable to settle. I lifted myself up on one elbow and watched as it came to rest at the foot of the bed. Ice formed on the mantel, the windows frosted over, and the air turned frigid. I closed my eyes against the growing brightness and when I looked again, there stood Endora.

"The room will warm once I've gone." she said. "It takes time for the body to return to normal temperature and until then wherever I go the cold goes with me. Annoying, but necessary. So, did you miss me?"

"If you're waiting for me to say yes, you can keep waiting. Why did you put me through all that if you knew you'd be back?"

"It wasn't my call to make." She smiled and took a seat on the bed. "I'd explain but being complicated you wouldn't understand. What matters is I'm back!"

"What do you mean no choice?"

"It's part of my punishment."

"If you're being punished I sure don't see it."

"Well I am whether you can see it or not. So, tell me about the letter. What did it say?" Taking a seat on the bed, her expression was one of excited anticipation. When I said it never arrived, she exploded in anger. "Of course, it arrived. When was the last time you checked your mailbox?"

"Mailbox? I assumed it would come here."

"You idiot. First thing tomorrow, go get it. And you'd better pray it's there. Damn Julie, sometimes you can be such a dolt."

Next morning, though I was still ill, I drove out to the base post office. A note in the mailbox said, 'see clerk' and my heart sank. "You're supposed to empty the box at least once a week. You're lucky we didn't send it back as undeliverable."

I apologized for not following procedures and raced home with a large box of mail sitting beside me. Dumping everything on the table I made a frantic search for the one letter that had the power to destroy my life, and there it was, hidden under a pile of magazines. I was surprised by how ordinary it looked. There was nothing official looking about it, and even the enclosed letter left a lot to be desired. I mean if you're going to take someone's child away you should at least write more than a page to explain why. It was rather unkind of Mark to say he thought me unstable. How stable would he be in my situation?

According to the closing paragraph I was allowed to bring two-character witnesses. I laughed at that. Even worse, I had only five days to get it all done. "Five days," I said aloud.

"It's your fault for letting it go so long," Endora said joining me. "Perhaps it's time to carry out your threat. You know, the one where you kill Andrew and yourself."

"What are you saying?"

"I'm only repeating what you told Edmund. You did say that didn't you?"

"Yes, I said it, but—"

"You're not getting cold feet are you?" she interrupted.

"I just need time to think. I need time."

If I could prove the truth of what I was saying there'd be no need for Dr. Connelly and his hearing. It would have to be something they could see. Something tangible, but what? Andrew and I racked our brains but then we had it. The old attic steps. I'd have to tear down a wall, but so what? I found a sledgehammer in the basement and got to work. Andrew, always helpful sweep up some of the mess. By four the next morning our task was accomplished. The wall was down, and the steps were visible. We went to our beds believing that finally we had proof positive.

# CHAPTER TWENTY-NINE

Mark showed up the following afternoon to collect his things. He didn't tell me he was coming and didn't announce that he had arrived. He simply marched upstairs and began clearing out his stuff.

"Not brave enough to face me?" I asked leaning against the door frame.

"I came to get my things. I would've come sooner but I was in Spain."

"Yes, always best to get it done as quickly as possible. No sense hanging about. Bet you don't know where I was last week? I was here celebrating Andrew's eighth birthday and trying to explain why you didn't bother to call or send anything. But you brought him a gift, right? No? Guess you were too busy being a good parent."

"Give it a break Julie."

"I have something to show you," I said directing him down the hall. "It will prove I'm telling the truth."

"And I helped Dad. Wait till you see it. Mom did great." Andrew said pushing Mark along. Only there was nothing to see. The wall had been rebuilt. Andrew ran his hands over where the opening had been. "They were here Dad, honest." I tried to explain, to get Mark to help us take it back down, but he pushed me aside and returned to his packing.

I sent Andrew out to play but instead he lingered on the stairs listening. For the first time since we were married I actually hated Mark. Shoving him aside I opened the wardrobe and threw his clothes out on the floor. "Take everything. Leave nothing behind to remind me you were ever here. You don't want to be seen with me? Will fine, now you don't have to. You talk so high and mighty about how concerned you are for Andrew, but when was the last time you were here for his birthday or parent-teacher meetings? You couldn't even visit him in the hospital. He wanted you to take down the wall, but you wouldn't even do that."

"I'm not going to tear down walls in a house that isn't mine, that would be stupid."

"Why is everything we went stupid?" Andrew asked joining us in the bedroom.

"I didn't mean—"

"Yes you did. What mom said is true. You just don't want to believe us. All you do is yell at her. You never listen." Andrew stood in the doorway crying. Mark tried to explain but Andrew was beyond reasoning. All he understood was his father didn't care enough to make an effort. When he drove away Andrew chased after him and waited by the gate, but when Mark didn't return, it was Edmund he ran to.

"What's going on?" Edmund asked when I joined them. Unable to find the words I returned to the future where Edmund was waiting. "Julie, come on—talk to me."

"And say what? That Mark's gone and Andrew's heart is broken. Why couldn't he help us take down the wall? Was it too much to ask that he try and see that I was telling the truth? Tomorrow I have to testify why I shouldn't lose custody of my son. Why I'm not the danger Mark says I am. They say I can bring someone willing to testify on my behalf, but there is no one. No one at all."

"There must be someone—?" Edmund said.

"I figured if Mark saw the stairs— It's like you deliberately want to destroy us. I just wish I knew why everything I've ever loved is being taken from me. Now please, go away and leave me alone."

\* \* \*

Today was the day. It was seven-thirty and the hearing started at ten. I fixed Andrew's breakfast, then sent him to stay with Edmund while I went in search of something decent to wear. Something that didn't hang on me or make me look crazy. There was little to choose from. I tried the brown one but no, then tried the pale green. That wasn't much better but at least I looked alive. How had I come to this? Twenty-seven going on ninety. My eyes were blood shot and ringed with dark circles. My skin was pale and lifeless and even my hair had lost its luster. At least now I knew why Mark didn't want to be seen with me. I wouldn't want to be seen with me either and I started to cry.

"Bunny appeared and coming over to where I was standing put his arm around me. "You look as you do because of what they've put you through." He took my hand and smiled.

"So why are you here?"

"I thought you might need someone who cares. And didn't your father say—?"

"He said a lot of things." Something about Bunny was different. The softness of his tone—the tenderness in his eyes . . . Had I misjudged him? I could use a friend right now.

"They won't give Andrew back Julie. They'll say you live in a fantasy world. That you're losing your mind. They want to destroy you, and this is how they'll do it. Come with me Julie and perhaps together we can figure something out."

Yes, maybe we could. The longer we talked the surer I became that he was my only hope. When he offered his hand, I took it without reservation and together we traveled back through time. At first it seemed as if I were dreaming, but then his voice broke through the fog and I realized my dream was a nightmare. Chained hand and foot to a stone slab I struggled to break free without success. "You said you'd take care of me."

"And I will."

This wasn't the Bunny I met at Thornwood. This Bunny was the one Endora craved. The one that wore a crimson cape trimmed in fur and flared out behind as he moved about the room. His hair, no longer greying was the color of pitch, combed back and falling over his shoulders. A picture of Satan before the fall crossed my mind.

"Perhaps now you'll admit that I'm far more handsome than either Mark or Edmund."

"I can't admit to what isn't true."

"Oh, Julie, what a foolish child you are." Leaning down he stroked my cheek. "If you want me to be kind, you must learn to be more circumspect. Before we start, let me assure you Andrew is with Mark, which, under the current circumstances is for the best."

"How long have I been here?"

"Julie, Julie, Julie. The question isn't how long have you been, but rather, how long will you be, and that's unknown. Everything depends on when I get bored or you beg to die." In the corner a large table stood overflowing with jars and vials. "All for you," Bunny said as he mixed and measured, and mumble and stirred.

"I assume you've already guessed that Bunny isn't my real name, he said over his shoulder. I have many others and my following is legion. It's not the name you see, but the power behind it." He returned to his potions and when satisfied came and stood looking down at me. "Do you remember what your father said about a dark cloud? We spoke of it often after Endora's dramatic exit. I am that dark cloud Julie, the one who will see you into the next world.

I am all and none of those people. But I tell you now I am the one that will see to Endora's destruction and do it with pleasure."

And so, it began. One day melting into the next, and all a nightmare from which I couldn't escape. No longer did I experience pain, I was pain; intense and growing. I lived it, breathed it, smelled it, and cried out in agony because of it. Time, my enemy, became the means by which I measured the intervals between one torment and the next.

"Endora had plans Julie. Big plans," Bunny said, while working, "but because of her betrayal, it will all come to nothing. Endora always underestimated her stupidity. She failed to recognize that I neither forgive nor forget, and so like the fool she is, she insisted that the Council call me back. She wasn't aware that I'd been watching you since birth, waiting for the moment she would try to use you to destroy Edmund. Now her plans to save herself will come to nothing."

What I longed for was for Bunny to stop talking, to take a breath if only for a moment, but like the dripping water he kept on until his voice became a tool that created as much pain as his instruments.

"Can you imagine Endora assuming she could outmaneuver me?" He stopped and wrote something in his notebook. "You know, I've given a great deal of thought to your demise and find it a perplexing question."

A sudden white-hot heat snaked through my body. I was on fire, and though you couldn't see the flames I could feel them. Then came the rain, flowing from my fingertips in dark red torrents to end in a pool of blood on the floor. Picking up his notebook he wrote feverishly then throwing it aside left the room. For a few blissful minutes there was total silence. Upon his return the old Bunny stood before me.

"Business has laid claim upon my time unfortunately, but it can't be helped. Work before pleasure I'm afraid. This will give you time to rest and prepare."

Did it never occur to him that I'd been preparing for this for months? They were taking my son and declaring me unfit. But what had I done? What wrong had I committed to earn such a punishment? With no answer to give I allowed the pain to wipe away all other thoughts.

On his return, Bunny spoke of nothing but death and dying. He hoped to terrify me with his words, but they had long since lost their power. No one wants to die, even those that commit suicide hesitate. Some out of fear that no one will stop them—others that someone will. I held onto life not because I wanted to live, but because I wanted to deny Bunny the pleasure of destroying Endora through me. He knew what my death would cost her and salivated at the idea, but in time the pain grew beyond my power to endure and my only thought was how to make it end.

"Then you're ready?" Bunny asked as if speaking of an erotic experience. "Dying is an art," he said as he carried me to the sight of my execution. "To be savored like fine wine. Do you see the bag of sand? In a moment I'll tear it open and its contents will flow down the chute and into the bucket. As you can see the bucket is connected to the rope around your neck. As the bucket fills, its weight will tighten the rope and lift you off the floor. I estimate about four hours from start to finish. Rather ingenious, wouldn't you say?" After making several minor adjustments, Bunny stood back and admired his work. "I'll leave you now, but never fear, when the end is near, I'll return to see you on your way."

As I stood waiting, I could feel the rope tightening. Blood from several wounds was pooling below me while my fascination with the sand grew out of all proportion. I could think of nothing else. How much more would have to fall before the rope cut off my air and my feet left the ground? For a moment I thought Mark was standing in front of me. I tried to whisper goodbye, but breathing was becoming difficult. My one concern was how much more sand was needed.

"How are things coming along?" Bunny asked, returning. "Fifteen minutes more should do the trick."

For all my brave talk, I was giving Bunny what he wanted most. My death would secure his victory over Endora and having done so would let him experience a climax far greater than any sexual act could afford.

And so, we waited, and when the last grains of sand slipped from the bag and my feet no longer touched the ground Bunny threw his notebook aside and hurried from the room leaving me to die alone.

# CHAPTER THIRTY

Having lost everything, death was a blessing. The pain ended, my fears fell away, and for the first time ever I was at peace. But then there was this woman. Battered beyond recognition, and hanging lifeless in a cold, dank, empty room. What was she doing there and why had she been so brutally abused? Distant voices beckoned but how could I leave her? To go would be unforgiveable.

A door at the far end of the room creaked open and two men appeared. For a time neither moved, and I could see uncertainty written on their faces, then seeing the woman they rushed forward. One held her, while the other cut her down and laid her on a blanket spread out on the ground. The woman was known to them for both called her by name. The taller of the two, the one most distressed knelt and began to pray over her body. As his words became more fervent, I could feel myself being pulled toward the scene. Why was this happening? I had nothing to do with that woman, so why was my soul beginning to stir, and my heart beginning to beat? A sudden burst of air filled my lungs and once again I rejoined the living. I was wrapped in the blanket and carried from the room.

"She'll never survive Edmund. There's barely anything left of her."

"She'll survive. She has to."

"We can't even be sure it's her."

That was the last I heard before falling away into the hellish world of ghostly apparitions and nightmarish horrors. For three months I remained in a state of limbo, neither dead not alive, but slowly reviving then fading away. When the darkness began to pass, I found myself in an unfamiliar house surrounded by strangers. Everyone appeared to know me, but I recognized no one.

Two women saw to me, neither willing to do so, and each day made it clear that I didn't belong. "Why we have to spend our time caring for the likes of her is beyond me."

"And when you think of all the trouble she's caused."

"A woman of her sort doesn't belong in polite society. There's places for people like her."

"She seemed so nice in the beginning, but then you never know, do you."

"I just don't see why they can't put her someplace else. In one of them homes for woman of the street."

"But then no one asked us."

"No, they didn't." I couldn't see him, but they could, and fear flashed across their faces. It was the voice of the man that found me. "And if I ever hear talk like that again either here or below stairs you'll both be out on your ear without a reference."

There was no doubting his anger, and neither woman dared look at him. "I never thought I'd be ashamed of you, but I am now. This poor girl never said an unkind word to either of you the entire time she lived here, and to have you disparage her in this manner after all she's been through is unforgivable. Now get below stairs and out of my sight."

"The older woman managed a whispered 'yes sir,' then after a quick curtsy both hurried from the room.

"They don't understand," he said sitting down beside me, "Maybe it's time they knew the truth." In a voice almost pleading he asked, "Give me some sign Julie, anything to give me hope you'll come back to me." Sadly, hope was something I knew nothing about.

I was cared for by two doctors, but it took some time to actually become aware of their presence. The one called Dr. Wood, saw to my body while the other, a Dr. Van Heusen was more concerned with my mind. Continually asking questions which I saw no reason to answer they argued as to what should be done. Both agreed that all mirrors and shiny object s be removed from the room.

On sunny days the man called Edmund would carry me over to the chaise lounge by the window so I could watch a world I no longer felt connected to pass below my window. Twice every afternoon an over-loaded Omnibus would chug by and afterward a handful of children would hurry past on their way home from school. One day a young boy climbed the gate and running up the drive called out to me. "Mommy, Mommy, I want to come home. Please, you promised."

Why was he saying that? What did that child have to do with me? I needed to talk to him. To find out why he called me Mommy and asked me to come get him. With difficulty I stood and took a step, but only one before I fell and tipped over the end table.

"Oh, dear God Julie, what's happened?" Edmund asked rushing over to me. Carrying me back to bed he went and close the curtains. I thought he would say something. Perhaps explain why the boy climbed the gate, and why he called out to me, but he made no mention of it and called Matilda to come clean up the mess.

Over the next few weeks Dr. Van Heusen worked at bringing me out of the mist and into the sunlight. Concerned that I had yet to speak he blamed the damage done to my throat, but the real reason was having nothing to say that was worth saying.

In time I began to recognize the people around me, but I also began to understand the burden my care placed upon them. On this particular day it was Clara's turn, and though she was with me for over an hour she never spoke. A sudden anger overtook me, and I wondered what I had done that could make them hate me so.

"I know I'm a burden," I said as she started for the door, "you told me as much, but I don't understand why you hate me. Have I hurt you in some way?"

Clara stopped and her eyes filled with tears. "Oh Miss Julie, we don't hate you. I didn't speak because I was too ashamed to do so. I said some horrible things I should never have said, and in your condition I wasn't sure you'd understand if I tried to say I was sorry. I must fetch the Master."

At once Clara ran to the door and shouted for Silas. "Go fetch the Master. He's out in the back. Tell him to come at once." Edmund arrived before Silas had all the words out. The joy I saw in his eyes when he arrived overwhelmed me and tears ran unhindered down my checks.

"My darling girl," he kept saying. "You have come back to me."

"I'm sorry for the trouble I've caused you. I never meant—"

But he wouldn't let me finish. "There's nothing to be sorry for. None of this was your fault."

Silas handed Edmund a note. "You're needed at the mill sir. I've saddled your horse."

"Tell them I'll be there in a moment. Clara, let's get Julie into her chair and then I must be away."

"Might I have a word?" Clara asked once we were alone. "It's like I said. We don't hate you Miss Julie, we love you. We just didn't understand all that was happening. When the Master finally told us, we could hardly believe the things he was saying. And when he said you came from years in the future we all laughed out loud. From the future indeed, but then he showed us how it was done, and mentioned some of the things you would say. Suddenly all that odd stuff made sense. We couldn't take it in. Still can't to be honest. Well, you need to rest, so I'll leave you for now. But I'll come back later for a visit if you like."

That evening Edmund came and helped me eat dinner as I had trouble holding my knife and fork. It was kind of him though I felt rather embarrassed not being able to do such a simple task myself.

"I need to tell you something," I said when finished, "at the end—when I died, I could see everything but at a distance. Voices called for me to come away, but then there was this woman hanging from a rope in the room below me. I couldn't leave her there alone. I had no idea it was me until you began to pray. As you went along saying words I couldn't understand I felt a force pulling me toward her. I admit I struggled against it, but the force was too strong. Then suddenly the woman and I were one again. The pain returned, the anxiety, even my father's words, *"I fear you'll have to die in order to live."*

\* \* \*

A woman's voice echoed outside my door. Then a sort of scuffle and arguing. "Come on—I read his journal. I witnessed what he did."

"What do you expect me to do? Break down in tears. I simply have to keep a tighter rein on things."

"A tighter rein? He was inches away from destroying your last chance at redemption?"

"Stop being so melodramatic. Bunny knows what will happen if he crosses me."

"Does he? Because it doesn't look that way to me."

"Am I supposed to care what you think? Because I don't and never have."

"I'm well aware of what you think, but the Council has had enough. They've decided their agreement with you is no longer in force."

A moments silence ensued as she tried to grasp what Edmund said. "They wouldn't dare. I'll go to a higher power. We had an agreement."

"He won't see you. It's done."

"Damn them all to hell," Endora shouted.

"Being damned to hell is what started all this. They gave you ample warning that this would happen, but you refused to listen. They said your actions amounted to a foolhardiness bordering on irrational recklessness."

"If they think I'll let them get away—"

Edmund interrupted. "Do you hear what you're saying?"

"I hear."

"You're delusional Endora, completely delusional."

Now fully awake, I picked up the tablet Edmund had left behind on the nightstand. Most of it concerned his business dealings, but around page twenty he began mentioning me. How I responded to things, my care of Nathan. Then several pages further on he spoke about my disappearance.

"Is something wrong Julie?" Edmund asked from the doorway. "I noticed your light and wondered if you needed something."

"No, I'm find, just not sleepy. I hope you don't mind but I read what you wrote about my disappearance. Why did you keep all this from me?"

"I wasn't trying to hold anything back, but I wasn't sure you could handle anymore at the moment. If you think you're up to it I'll tell you whatever you want to know. And so, he began. He told me about Andrew and Mark, about Thornwood and Endora.

"So where was I going that day? What was happening?"

"I'm not sure—"

"Tell me." I insisted, and so he did, and I began to wish he'd never found me. "Was I such a threat that my husband thought Andrew was in danger?" Mark assured me the answer was no, but it was the expression on his face that told me otherwise. Giving me no time to question him further he insisted I turn out my light and get some rest. But rest wasn't what I needed. I needed answers to fill in the gaps he left open.

I couldn't get past the idea that no one seemed to care that my life, our life had been destroyed. That Mark and I had loved each other and only wanted to be left in peace. What right did they have to destroy us for their own purposes? Have I lost Mark forever? Have I lost Andrew? I wanted to scream out my frustration and demand they give back what they took, but it would be a useless effort. Our lives were no longer our own and how it would end was anyone's guess.

As usual Edmund came directly to my room after work the following day, but I was in no fit state to welcome him. I asked him the same questions I had asked myself, and when I heard the answers I could barely control myself. "So thanks to you and Endora everything I love is gone. My husband, my son, even how I look—

"No, that's not true."

"It is and you know it."

"But that's why I didn't say anything. I didn't want you to give up and fade away which I knew you would. I do believe you can get him back, that things will work out, but it will take time."

"And what about Mark? Will I get him back? Everyone saw what Mark went through, they saw it with their own eyes. Every person in Mark's squadron saw how unstable I was and heard me talking about seeing dead people and traveling through time. They see their top navigator falling apart because of his wife— How do I overcome that? I made him look a fool in front of his fellow officers. That's not something you get over easily. As for Andrew, if I want him back I'll have to steal him." Not wanting an argument I changed the subject. "So how did you know where I was?"

"You can thank Richard for that. He had a friend staying that mentioned wanting to breed his mare to Lester's stud. Over dinner Richard casually asked how he came to know Bunny. It turned out that they were at Cambridge together.

"Anyway, this friend said that Hellborn sat atop what was once the Abby of Saint Steven, which was partially destroyed during the dissolution by Henry VIII. Below the Abby there's a labyrinth of passages and secret chambers where the Monk's would hide from Henry's men. Richard and I decided to take a look.

"Words can't describe what we found. Doors with no rooms behind them, hallways that led nowhere. Stairs that went down into caverns and ended halfway up the wall. It was only by sheer dumb luck we found you. A few minutes longer . . ."

"Yes, a few minutes longer . . ."

# CHAPTER THIRTY-ONE

It was late afternoon when Richard arrived unannounced and went directly into Edmund's study. For two long hours they remained locked away. When they finally emerged, Edmund shouted for Silas to help him pack. The two men were going to Paris with no idea when they'd be back. Packed and ready he grabbed his cane and hurried to meet Richard waiting in his carriage. What caused them to leave in such a hurry was the main topic of conversation below stairs for almost a week. Everyone had a theory, but none seems plausible.

During Edmund's absence, Dr. Wood thought I should start walking again. My feet had healed sufficiently, and my legs were growing stronger. At first I thought I'd never succeed but with everyone's encouragement and help I soldiered on. It was my reflection in the hall mirror that sickened me. How would I ever explain the changes to my appearance?

It was my mind however that gave the most trouble. I found it impossible to concentration, suffered blackouts, and migraines, and had large gaps in my memory. Fearing it would keep me from returning to the future I did my best to pretend that everything was fine.

Three weeks later Edmund returned from France and though I pestered him continually to say why he went, he refused and acted as if the whole thing was of little importance.

What amazed and overwhelmed me was the care and concern his family and Richard's showed me. Lady Barbara came weekly and brought the boys who had no end of stories to share and games to play. Lord Owen and Lady Beatrice couldn't do enough. Then, before we realized, Christmas was upon us and the pain of not having our boys made the season difficult.

"You're thinking too much, my girl, and it will only drag you down," Clara said rolling out the cookie dough. "You need something to keep your mind from wandering."

"Maybe I should go back and turn myself in."

"Now you listen here, I'll not allow any more of that talk in my kitchen. Talk like that is nothing but foolishness. Here, get busy on that lot." Clara pointed toward the small finger cakes that needed decorating. "I'll get you a stool, so you won't have to stand." Resigned, I started on the cookies.

On Christmas Eve, Edmund brought in a tree, the family came, and everyone helped with the decorations. Afterward, we drank mulled cider and sang Christmas carols. As the evening wore down, and people drifted off to bed, Edmund and I remained behind to watch the first snowfall of the season cover the yard with white and remember other Christmas's of happier times.

The servants joined us on Boxing Day to share a bowl of Christmas cheer, then surprised me with a gift for Andrew. "I won't open it," I told them, "Andrew can do it once he's home."

"And now, it's your turn to receive." Edmund gave each an envelope containing a five-pound note and a small personal gift from me. Embarrassed but pleased, they returned to the servants' quarters believing Master Edmund was the best in all of England.

In March, Dr. Wood released me from his care with a warning not to overdo. "Inform me at once if a problem arises. Dr. Van Heusen cut his visits back to twice a week as there was little more he could do for me. With nothing to hold me back I began making plans to return to the future and retrieve my son.

"Edmund, I need to ask a question. When I go back how will I explain how different I look?"

"You won't. Remember when you told Mark how bruised you were, and thought you'd been in an accident?" I nodded. "Well, Mark didn't see anything did he? Not even a scratch. It will be the same when you go back."

"But how?"

"Because you can't be injured if you weren't born yet. You will look exactly as you always did and still do—beautiful. But I wish you'd consider staying at least until after my surgery." Sitting down beside me he eased his leg into a more comfortable position. "I feel like I'm being abandoned."

"No, you're not. Once your home, I'll come back. Beside I couldn't get to the hospital anyway."

"And what if you can't come back? Or something unforeseen happens? What then?"

"We'll just have to deal with it, but I promised Andrew I'd come and that's what I'm going to do."

"But what if he's happy being with Mark?"

"Why would he be?"

"I don't know. I'm only asking. But is it fair to ask a child of nine to choose which parent he prefers? You might as well cut his heart out. Mark's many things, but he loves Andrew, and he'll fight to do what's best for him." Going over to the fire Edmund poked at the dying embers.

"What do you want me to say—that I'll give him up without a fight? Getting him back is what's kept me going and nothing is going to stop me." My temper getting the best of me I got up to leave.

"No, you don't, you'll stay here and hear me out. I understand how you feel, but it's possible that what you intend will cause more harm than good."

"Then I'm the one that will have to live with it."

"No, Andrew will as well."

"Edmund, please, I don't have a choice."

"Damn it, Julie, you do. You're the one in control now. Whatever happens from here on out is down to you. If you make the wrong choices it will damn us all, and Endora will go free." The force of his words left me with no response. Never had Edmund stated with such passion his deep concerns over the actions I might take. "I appreciate all you've said, and the reasons behind it. You think I'm siding with Mark, I'm not. Suppose Andrew wants to be with you, and they won't allow it? What happens then?"

"I'll wait till I get a chance and then take him. Once that's done we'll come here."

"You can't come here. Not forever at least."

"Why not?" I asked surprised.

"Because no one can live before they're born. The Council made a temporary exception in your case, but once their reason for your being here is over, they'll not allow either of you to return."

"But the Council's supposed to be on our side—"

"They don't take sides."

\* \* \*

Regardless my mental state I returned to the future the following month and found the house empty of everything but my personal belongings which were stuffed into several large cardboard boxes. That my car was still there and in working order surprised me, and it made me wonder if Mark thought I'd come back in time.

I'd need money, so scrounged through every pocket and purse I possessed, until I found what I thought would be enough to see me through. Next, I'd need coal to make a fire so headed down to the basement to see if I could find enough in the bin to do me. With everything in order, I pulled a pillow out of the box and sat down to rest. For the first time in over a year, I was blissfully alone. No one to answer to, argue with, or obey—and then Endora showed up.

"Mark didn't leave much behind, did he?" she said surveying the room.

"What are you doing here?" She stacked up the two remaining pillows and sat down uninvited.

"Just checking to see if everything's all right. No harm in that."

"Since you're here, I want to ask a question. You knew what Bunny was going to do didn't you?" She started to protest but I cut her off. "Don't lie, I felt you in the room. Weren't you afraid he'd go too far?"

"No because Edmund came to the rescue. He enjoys being heroic."

"He was a little late if you ask me."

"But late is better than never, don't you think? I do have to say you lasted longer than I expected."

"I wish they'd never found me."

"Do you know why they went to Paris?"

"He never said."

"They went to kill Bunny. Richard discovered he had a place there and the two of them decided to give Bunny a taste of his own medicine. Unfortunately killing Bunny is impossible. A much higher power will have that pleasure," Endora said looking toward heaven. "They weren't to know that but in the end, all they managed was to make Bunny angry, and that's never a good thing. Now he'll return more dangerous than ever."

Next morning, I tried to build a fire, but unable to keep it lit turned my attention to more important matters. First, I needed to find out where Andrew was. Connie's place seemed the most likely, but after two days of unproductive surveillance, I decided that regardless the risk, I'd have to drive out to the base and try to follow Mark home.

I located a place to park where I could watch unobserved and waited. Several nervous hours dragged by before four planes in tight formation approached from the West. Each broke away, circled round and forming a single line, eased themselves back onto terra firma. Racing down the runway with tires smoking and drag chutes open, they slowed to an earthly pace, turned, and taxied back to their designated parking spots. Mark's plane was the third in line, and while the ground crew attached the ladder, he gathered his things and climbed down. In less than ten minutes, all eight crew members were heading into the squadron to debrief.

I told myself I was over him, that any love we had for each other was long gone, but I experienced such a rush of conflicting emotions I had to remind myself this wasn't about Mark. No matter my feelings, things could become very complicated if Mark discovered I was back.

An hour passed before he left the squadron, loaded his gear in the trunk and headed for home. I followed at a discreet distance. We hadn't gone far when he pulled off the A12 and into the driveway of a rather pretty cottage on the outskirts of Saxmundham. The front door opened, and Andrew came running out to greet him. The urge to go to him was overpowering and took all my strength to resist. I had to keep control of myself.

A few moments later an older woman appeared. I assumed it was the housekeeper. Mark asked if she could come an hour earlier on Wednesday to get Andrew off to school. She agreed then walked down the road to the bus stop.

I should've been elated that he looked so well and happy but all I could think about was getting him back. Returning to Thornwood I went back to the warmth of Clara's kitchen, where before I could say hello she had a plate of food sitting in front of me.

"So, did you find Mark?" Edmund hung his cane over the chair back and took a seat.

"I would've come up after I ate."

"I couldn't wait. What about Andrew?"

"I only saw him for a moment, but he seems fine."

"So, do you still intend—"

"Yes, I do. Clara, this is delicious. Thank you. Mark has a cottage off the A12 in Saxmundham. Oh, and Endora showed up the other day."

Edmund looked anxious but not surprised. "Did she say anything?" When I didn't answer he reached over and shook my arm. "Julie, where are you? Come back."

I pointed my fork at him for emphasis, "Mark seems well on his way to being over me. In fact, it's the happiest he's been since we got here. He was laughing and joking. I can't remember the last time he did that with me."

"And Andrew? How did he seem?"

"I know what you're trying to do. All right, he seemed well cared for and happy. But so what? He's still my son."

"You said one of the reasons you married Mark was because he accepted Andrew as his own. Now he wants to take care of him and you're still not happy."

"I wanted him to *care* about Andrew, not *take* him."

He reached over and touched my arm. "Julie—your minds wondering. Look at me." I re-focused, and he continued, but I'd had enough.

"I'm not changing my mind Edmund so stop trying. I'm going home."

For the next few days I sat outside Mark's house and learned his routine. I also visited the chemist on the corner and striking up a casual conversation discovered that Mrs. Gilbert, Mark's housekeeper, came in every Wednesday around one to pick up her copy of *News of the World*. Several nights later I walked the distance between the shop and his home. Aware that she never tarried, it would give me a little more than half an hour to get Andrew and be gone.

# CHAPTER THIRTY-TWO

I picked up my notebook and studied the information I had gathered, but thanks to the workings of a damaged mind each entry was little more than a jumble of disjointed indecipherable words. Doctor Wood and Van Heusen were less than pleased.

"And you waited till now to tell us? What other problems have you kept from us? Van Heusen demanded.

"Confusion, disorientation, and terrifying hallucinations," I said without looking at him.

"My dear girl, you must see someone in the future. Someone modern. A person far more knowledgeable than the two of us. I know you feel it's too dangerous to do so, but it's the best advice we can give," said Van Heusen.

"He's right I'm afraid. The medicines we have might do you more harm than good, especially with you traveling back and forth through time. You must try to find someone who can deal with your issues properly," Dr. Wood said.

I argued the point but got nowhere. "What if I wasn't from the future?"

"But you are," Dr. Wood insisted, "and that's the point."

Their inability to make me better was understandable but unhelpful since I needed to call the squadron to get Mark's schedule. If I messed that up the consequences would be too dreadful to contemplate.

The best thing to do was to write everything down and read it, but once again the words were nothing but gibberish. I needed to think, to decide what to do, but those hideous black bugs with the grotesque yellow eyes and spiderlike legs ran off with my paper and pen. When they refused to give them back, I smashed one with my foot, but it split in two and ran into the fire. So why was I writing a note? I held my head and tried to think. A bug ran out of the fire and pointed to the phone, but the phone was so large and heavy I couldn't lift the receiver.

Next morning, I woke with a clear head and thankfully the bugs had disappeared. Since I had no idea how long my mind would function properly I wrote down what I wanted to say and made the call. I told the duty officer I was Mrs. Gilbert, Captain Hammond's housekeeper. I needed to make a doctor's appointment but didn't have a copy of his schedule. He told me to hold, then came back and said Mark would leave on Wednesday for Spain and would be gone for two weeks. Otherwise he'd be flying a normal schedule. I thanked him for his time, hung up and danced around the living room. Mark was leaving on Wednesday for Spain.

So, when exactly was Wednesday? Stopping by the newsstand I checked the date. Today was Friday. Five days before Wednesday. The number of days before the hearing. No, Bunny went to the hearing—or did I? I sat on the floor and rocked back and forth. The bugs were back and bigger than before. Now standing upright they waved at me and demanded I make more space for them. Wednesday—I repeated the word aloud. The day Mrs. Gilbert goes for her magazine.

Unsure how things would go, I returned to the past to say my goodbyes. A sad affair, but one that needed doing. Edmund, back from the hospital was resting in bed.

"So, home at last?" I said, forcing a smile. "You're looking better already."

He studied me for a moment then reached for my hand. "I'm fine, it's you I'm worried about."

"Well don't. You concentrate on getting better."

"Dr. Wood says your hallucinations and headaches are getting worse."

"Dr. Wood talks too much."

"No, I don't," said the doctor as he joined us. "Now come, we need to talk." He ushered me out the door and down to the living room where he called for Clara to bring tea and anything they had on hand to eat. "Now, tell me how you're doing. You look exhausted."

"I'm not sleeping—"

"Julie, you must see someone." Clara brought a tray with salmon and cucumber sandwiches, some sliced meats, cheese and jam tarts. "Now eat." I brushed the bugs away and began.

"What about Edmund?" I asked licking the jam off my fingers.

"He had a rather large piece of shrapnel embedded against his thigh. The pain must have been unbearable. I asked if he would still need a cane, but his answer was tentative. He just couldn't say for sure, but at least he'd have far less pain to deal with. Noting the time, we said our goodbyes then I went back to the kitchen for another painful parting. Everyone tried to put a brave face on it but underneath we were all crying.

"So," I said returning to Edmund's room, "it looks like you'll be right as rain in a few months. Hopefully you won't need that stupid old stick anymore."

"Julie please, I know how much you love Andrew and want him back, but this isn't the way to go about it."

"Then tell me how it's to be done? Do you think there's a hope in heaven they'll give him back simply because I want them to—because if you do you're living in dreamland. I'll be lucky if they let me see him on his eighteenth birthday."

"But maybe Mark has changed—maybe he's willing to listen now."

"If that's what you want to think—but I didn't come to talk about Mark, I'm here to say goodbye, not to argue." Now the tears came, and I fell into his arms.

"Oh, my darling girl, I am so afraid for you. There is so much as stake. Please take care—no, better stop while I still can." I could see he was exhausted, so I left him there and returned to the future.

I was full of confidence when I went back to say goodbye, but Edmund's words haunted me. Doubts were creeping into my will laid plans and I had to fight to keep my fears at bay. If only there weren't so many ways for things to go wrong. I made myself a cup of tea and rebuilt the fire. The coal was running out—but then so was time. Later Endora showed up to ask where I'd been.

"I was meeting a woman that wasn't there."

"How can you do that?"

"Ask Bunny, he knows."

"It's cold in here. Can't you add more coal?"

"There isn't any more."

"You went back didn't you? No, don't lie. I know you did. The question is why?"

"To say goodbye of course. They're my friends."

"Friends understand what you're feeling, and it's clear they don't. Otherwise they wouldn't try to talk you out of it."

"They didn't try because they couldn't."

"But you've allowed him to put doubt in your mind. We both know that Andrew's place is with you, not Mark. You've been strong up to this point now don't lose your nerve."

\* \* \*

Wednesday morning, I drove out to Mark's and began my vigil. At eleven fifteen Mrs. Gilbert arrived, came out, swept the front steps, shook the mat, and returned to the house. Mark left at eleven thirty. Andrew's bus arrived at noon. An hour later Mrs. Gilbert walked down to the news stand.

*"What if Andrew wants to stay with Mark?"* I entered through the back garden and forced the lock.

"Andrew," I called out. "It's Mother?" At first I received no answer, then I heard him shout Mom as he raced down the hall and into my arms.

"I knew you'd come. I knew it." With no time to spare, we gathered his things, and headed for the car.

"Help me get those bugs off the seat."

"What bugs, Mom?"

"Over there, on the seat."

"Mom—lets go home."

By the time I pulled onto the motorway, the bugs had taken over and driving was impossible. When a rather large multi-colored one tried to put on the flasher lights I pulled off the highway and demanded they get out. How can I drive with bugs crawling all over me?

"Mom, really. There aren't any bugs, honest. They all got out."

"But they'll be back, you mark my word. They'll be back."

"Come on Mom, we need to go home so you can rest." As I pulled back onto the road he moved closer and laid his head on my arm. "I love you mom."

# CHAPTER THIRTY-THREE

The house was dark when we arrived, and I shivered remembering the first time I saw this horrible place. If I had followed my instincts we wouldn't be here now. We'd be in some nice little cottage closer to the base and our family would be intact. I sighed. So many regrets.

Eager to see his friends Andrew bolted out of the car and raced up the steps and into the house shouting Matilda's name as he went. He returned disappointed. "No one's here Mom. I tried to go back but couldn't. Why aren't they here?"

"I'm here," Edmund called down from the second-floor landing.

"Uncle Edmund," Andrew yelled racing up to him.

"What's going on, Edmund?"

"Mom came and got me," Andrew said giving Edmund a hug. "I tried to go back, but it didn't work."

"It's not the time for going back right now. That's why I came to you."

"Edmund, I asked you a question. Why are you here?"

"You need to ask?" Edmund said lifting Andrew into his arms. "Please, I beg you. Don't do this. Don't give her the victory."

"This isn't about Endora Edmund it's about me. He's all I've got left. Now please, leave me in peace."

The distant thunder give way to the rain, and it poured down as if all the angels in heaven were crying. Andrew, asleep on my lap woke for a moment, looked to see that I was there, then returned to his slumbers. Shifting him onto the blanket I picked up the phone. I needed to talk, to explain, but the only one I knew to call was Connie. We'd been friends in another life.

"Where are you? Mrs. Gilbert is sick with worry. You had no right—"

"No right! I had every right. I'm his mother."

"Tell me where you are, and I promise I won't bring the police." I said no, and she turned hostile. "Do you know how much trouble you're in?"

"Why should I be in trouble for taking what's mine?"

"Oh, for God's sake Julie—stop it. We need to get this sorted before Mark gets home."

"Mark's coming home?"

"Yes, he's coming home. You kidnaped his son."

All I wanted was to talk, to make someone, anyone, understand, but she won't listen. No one ever listens. "I'm not crazy like everyone thinks. I just want to have my son with me. Is that too much to ask for? I love him and would never hurt him. Can't Mark see this is destroying me?"

"Destroying you? What about Mark and Andrew? Do you know what you've done to them?"

"What I've done? I've done nothing—oh the hell with it." I slammed down the receiver and returned to my son.

"Connie's rather unhappy with you at the moment," Endora said joining me.

"Go to hell."

Just after midnight I woke Andrew and led him up the stairs. As we went I shared my father's poem. *"When I was going up the stairs I met a woman that wasn't there."* Andrew laughed and smiled up at me. *"She wasn't there again today. I wish, I wish . . .* but wishes were for children. I climbed over the railing then lifted Andrew over. Frightened he held on to me and I could feel him shaking. The ledge wasn't wide, maybe four inches, and if not careful we might fall. Below me I thought I heard someone moving about.

"Julie! It's Connie—where are you?" Fearing Andrew would call out to her, I motioned for him to be still. "Julie, where are you? Answer me." When she started up the stairs I shouted for her to go back.

"Oh my God!" Connie's eyes widened in horror. "Julie, is that you?"

"Stay away from me."

"Please, I beg you, don't do this."

Endora watching whispered, "She's only here for Andrew. It's Andrew she cares about. Taking advantage of my inattention Connie move further up the steps.

"Get back, or I swear I'll jump."

"No, Mommy don't!" Andrew screamed his arms tight around my waist.

"Andrew," Connie called out, "it's all right—be still. Be very still."

"You have no right to tell him anything."

"I don't want—"

"To hell with what you want." My mind was in turmoil. Maybe if Bunny would untie me, my head would stop hurting, and I'd remember why I was standing on this ledge.

"Time is running out Julie," Endora insisted. "Mark will take him and lock you away in the dark like Bunny did."

"Please, Mommy, please—I want my dad."

*"What if Andrew wants to stay with Mark? If he does, you must leave him—"*

"Stop it," I screamed. "For God's sake stop it." My aunt appeared in the stairwell and called up to me. *"Causing trouble again I see. If you don't stop I'll lock you in the attic."*

While my attention was centered on my aunt, Connie moved two steps closer. Now something had changed, and she no longer demanded but spoke softly, just above a whisper.

"You have to keep Andrew safe Julie. You have to protect him from evil. Are you going to let Endora harm him? She doesn't care if he's safe, she wants him dead by your hand. Nothing else will do."

"That's a lie," Endora cried out. "She doesn't know what she's talking about. I'm trying to protect him—to keep Mark from taking him. This is the only way. Jump and get it over with."

I turned on her. "What I do and when I do it, is my decision to make, not yours. It's always been my decision. The Council gave me the power to decide. If I say no—"

"How dare you try to deny me my revenge. Do you know how long I've waited? How long I've plotted and schemed for this moment, and now you have the nerve to tell me it's your decision?" Endora roared with laughter. "Everything you've done since the moment of your birth has been by my direction. Where you lived, who you lived with, even who you married was my decision. All to bring you to the moment when you'd jump from that ledge. You will not deny me this victory." Again, she laughed, and the sound was like a thousand screaming magpies.

"No! Your lying. You're trying to confuse me."

"Do you know why your father killed himself Julie? Because I do."

"Leave my father out of this. You know nothing about him."

"I know everything about him. I was the woman who wasn't there, the one that showed him your future, but he betrayed me by warning you. Luckily my powers were stronger, my desires more intense."

"That's a lie. Father died because he couldn't live with what he saw, couldn't stand the suffering his visions foretold. It had nothing to do with you or anyone else."

"Yes, the suffering his visions foretold. It was your suffering that drove him, not the others. You were the one thing he cared most about in the world. It was seeing what was ahead of you and knowing he was powerless to stop it—that's what drove him to suicide. That alone."

Her words broke my heart. My father died because of what she allowed him to see. And all in the name of revenge.

"The Council didn't save me to fulfill your desires but to thwart them. Evil is defeated by love Endora. That's what the Council told me." Endora's eyes widened and darted quickly about the landing as if expecting the Council to appear any moment. "There's fear in your eyes. What are you afraid of ? Tell me!"

"Afraid? I'm not afraid of anything. Why should I be when I have all the power?"

"Endora's lying Julie," Connie said, her voice calm and reassuring. "She always lies. But this time it won't save her. You hold the power now and the thought that you could destroy all her plans horrifies her. Do you really want to sacrifice eternity and the life of your son to secure her victory?"

The entrance hall and now the stairs were crawling with those horrid bugs. Several laughed and waved the paper they had stolen. The paper I needed to write my note. "Give it back" I screamed but they only laughed louder. Now they were on the walls and falling form the ceiling.

I needed to think, to clear my mind of doubt and confusion but no one would give me peace. If only the bugs would go away maybe I could think more clearly—or are they here to distract me, to keep me from discovering the truth? Truth? It was too late for that now. I had already seen the truth. "I don't want to be here," I screamed. "I want to be left alone. I want my life back."

"No one forced you to stay. Endora said with a look of smug satisfaction. "I gave you every chance to leave. I can name at least five people that warned you of the danger in staying but you ignored then all."

"That's true," the bugs called out in unison. "She's right. You stayed to find the answer to your questions."

"You can run if you like but you'll never escape Thornwood. The end is already written. This is where your destiny lies. This is where your life has led you. You've burnt your bridges so there's no place left for you to go. You've no friends, no family—you don't even have your son. Death is your only way out," the bugs said in unison.

Everything they said was true. But what had Andrew done? His only failing was to be born and given to me. Why should he suffer for my mistakes? Slowly things were becoming clearer. Looking at Andrew I saw that like Endora my arms were covered in scratches from his fighting to hold on. For the first time ever I saw fear in his eyes. Fear of what his mother would do to him. The same fear I saw in Nathan's eyes whenever his mother was near. This was all wrong. Love doesn't kill. Love brings life. I could still save my son. Yes, I could save him . . . "Come and take him away," I called out to Connie. Get him to safety, I must remain behind."

Running forward Connie grabbed Andrew and hurried out the door. The moment he was away the house, as if in mortal danger began to shake and moan.

"You say you want revenge," I called out, "will so do I. Only my revenge will come not by dying, but by living. I have chosen life over death. The Council has granted me the victory."

"Poor stupid girl," Endora's voice echoed off the walls. "It's all been an illusion, a fantasy. You've been living a dream. Even Bunny—all in your mind. Remember the day you watched as I became Matilda? Did you never suspect I was trying to give you a clue? A chance to understand. How could you have been so naïve?"

An unseen hand came to rest on my shoulder and whispered in my ear,

*"Doubts unfounded, doubts concealed,*
*Deception surrounds and blinds what is real,*
*Trust in your knowledge of things as they are,*
*Be not deceived by lies from afar,*
*Lies can destroy you, trust will reward,*
*Truth is the answer, truth will endure."*

There was only the two of us now, alone in a house crumbling around us. Plaster fell in chunks from the ceiling, windows shattered sending shards of glass flying through the air. Flames crept up the stairs and caught the curtains. Finding a door and believing it to be the way out I pulled it open only to find myself on the sandbar at Shingle Street as the tide rose around me. How was I to reach the shore? What had they said? *"Deception surrounds and blinds what is real."* But how to tell deception from reality? Grabbing hold of the banister I thought to pull myself to safety, but the floor gave way, and I fell.

"Only a fool would believe a mere mortal could destroy me. My survival assures your destruction. I'll be in you, around you, through you. Until I'm free, neither will you be." Endora cried out, her voice deep and filled with malice. "You shall never be free of me till one of us is dead."

"But you won't be free either, Endora. Every day you will think of me and what could have been if only I had done what you demanded. But I didn't Endora, and never will. I will trouble you every day till one of us is dead."

Her screams echoed like thunder through the universe and then all became silence. Our destines would forever be intertwined."

A great emptiness swept over me as my words came back to haunt me. Neither of us would be free till the other was dead. How was I to live with that or the shame I felt for attempting to kill my child. Crying out I pleaded for forgiveness, but the answer never came. I had been judged and found wanting.

# CHAPTER THIRTY-FOUR

The squeaking of rubber soled shoes on a freshly waxed floor woke me, and in the haze of waking I realized I was no longer at Thornwood but in the hospital. Mark sat over in the corner staring off into space. His skin was pale, his hair disheveled, and his eyes lacked sleep. Finally noticing that I was awake, he stood, placed the chair back against the wall and without speaking left the room.

Next day things were different. This time he had a list of questions. The first being why didn't I show up for the hearing? Since I didn't have a believable answer, at least one that would satisfy, I said nothing.

"Is silence all I'm going to get? No explanation or attempt to lie your way out of it as usual? Then I'll tell you what I've been doing. I've been trying to ignore the crazy wife jokes being told behind my back. My son, refusing to speak to me shut me out of his life. My job was on the line and I was inches away from being grounded. Then just when things start to get better you reappear and ruin everything." It was a long emotional speech filled with anger and hurt but he wanted something I couldn't give, a truthful answer.

Connie arrived shortly after lunch. I assumed she came to gloat. She placed a small gift on the tray table and took a seat without being invited. "I thought you might be bored. There's not a lot to do in the hospital."

"Have you seen Mark?" I asked ignoring the gift.

"Yesterday, but not today."

"And Andrew?"

"He's with me at the moment. But yeah, he's fine. Eager for you to come home."

Connie chattered on, but I was stuck on the words 'Come home?' Home to where? There was no home for me anymore, at least not that included my son. Any chance I had of getting him back I had carelessly tossed away. I was moments away from killing both of us and all the while believing it was the right thing to do. You'd have to be crazy to do something like that. Crazy like Endora. But at least when they locked her away she had me to care for her—who would care for me? They would lock me away in that house with no one to talk to but myself. Day after day, night after night—alone. With only my guilt for company.

Reaching out I grabbed Connie's arm. "Promise me you won't let Mark send me back there. Not to Thornwood. Not on my own. Promise me. I can't be there alone, not in the dark. I'm going to be sick."

Connie called for a nurse and afterward sat a box of chocolates on the table. "Settles the stomach," she said. Unwrapping the box Connie removed the lid and took a piece with nuts. Her favorite, then moved her chair closer to the bed.

"So why are you here?" I said once the nurse was gone.

"I guess because I'm your friend." I almost chocked. Friend? She couldn't wait to run and tell Mark what I said. She was here to spy. "I know what you're thinking but you're wrong. What do you remember after going back to Thornwood?"

"Why do you care?" I asked.

"I was there. I saw what happened."

"You were there?"

"Yep. Right in the middle of it and it wasn't pretty." She reaffirmed what Mark said about Andrew and his job, then moved on to Mrs. Gilbert calling to say Andrew was gone. "I'm sorry about what I said on the phone."

"You only said what you thought."

"I was so angry. To just go in and take him. Anyway, after you hung up the room got all misty and this shadowy figure appeared. I didn't know whether to defend myself or run. These things don't happen every day. I'm standing there trying to decide what to do, when this voice tells me I'm needed at Thornwood. That something terrible was about to happen that required my help. I started to say no, but I never got the chance. 'If you were ever her friend now is the time to prove it. You're the only one who can help them. Go now before it's too late.'

"Well you don't say no to something like that do you? When I got there, everything was dark and sort of spooky. I was at Thornwood, but nothing was familiar. Then I thought of course, this is how Julie sees it. I've gone back in time. It was so weird.

"Anyway, I checked several rooms, then coming out into the hall I saw you standing on the ledge. At first I didn't think it was you. You looked—if you'll forgive the expression, like warmed over death. Hoping to talk you off the ledge I called up to you, but you told me not to come any closer. Talk about being scared."

"Why because I was crazy?"

"Don't interrupt. It's getting to the good part. So, I'm yelling at you not to jump and Andrew's crying and calling for Mark and then Endora appears. At first I didn't know who she was, but then you said her name. No wonder your—"

"Crazy?" I interrupted.

"Stop saying that! Things were way out of control, and I start saying stuff that makes absolutely no sense except to you because your whole expression changes. Endora understood as well because she goes berserk and starts flying around screaming all kinds of stuff about revenge and destiny and right away you turn on her. You tell her she's lying, that you have the power not her. That's when the you-know-what hit the fan big time.

"'You have no rights,' she screamed."

"'My rights come from the Council. The decision is mine, not yours.' Anyway, things go on and suddenly you call for me to come and take Andrew away which I did. I tried to find a way back in, but the house locked me out. There was nothing I could do.

"Thornwood was coming apart. Pictures were flying off the walls, plaster was falling from above, furniture was spinning around. Then all the clocks began chiming at once and wouldn't stop. It was like something out of *Dante's Inferno*. I'm standing there trying to figure out what to do when Mark comes out with you in his arms. Only it wasn't Mark—Andrew starts shouting Edmund and breaking away runs to him."

"'Moms going to die and it's all my fault because I wanted her to come and get me.' So Edmund lays you down and tries to calm Andrew."

"'Andrew, stop—listen to me. Your mother will be fine. Trust me. It's not your fault. It's Endora's fault and no one else's. It's going to take time and you're going to have to be very brave, but I promise everything will be fine in the end, and you know I wouldn't lie to you.'"

"'Can I stay with you?' Andrew asked throwing his arms around Edmunds neck."

"'No, because your father needs you now. He needs you to love him. You have to be a man now, it's what your mom would want. Now stop crying and blow your nose.'"

"Once Andrew was seen to, Edmund came and spoke to me. Said he was grateful that I came and made it clear that he was very worried about you. 'She's been through some real horrors over the past year, but it's up to her to decide whether she wants to share that or not. All I'm asking is that you watch over her. She's still very fragile both in body and mind and needs someone she can trust and depend on.' He was absolutely torn."

"I promised to do whatever was necessary, then he turned his attention back to you. Lifting you into his arms he began to weep. 'I begged them to let me stay. To let me see this through to the end but they refused to listen. I understand why but it doesn't make it any easier. Trust Connie, she'll be there for you. I couldn't have done this without her. And you my darling girl. You were marvelous, but then I never doubted you'd be otherwise.'

"He stopped for a moment as if listening, then said, 'Mark is coming so I must go.'"

"Moments later Mark pulled in the drive. How I was to explain all this I had no idea, but then I notice the blood on your wrist. Of course, you tried to kill yourself. I was trying to get you into the car, but you were too weak and passed out. Mark seemed ready to question my explanation when Andrew distracted him by begged Mark to save you."

Visiting hour over Connie promised to come again next day. My aunt was right. It would have been better if I hadn't been born.

# CHAPTER THIRTY-FIVE

Mark arrived mid-morning and his inability to settle said this wasn't a social call. Drawing back the curtains he stood for a time staring out the window. Then without looking at me said, "I've filed for divorce, and sole custody of Andrew." He appeared calm but his voice betrayed him.

"When?"

"When you didn't show up for the meeting with Dr. Connelly."

"What am I to say to that?"

"I don't want you to say anything. You said it all when you didn't show up. What I can't understand is why you'd rather see Andrew dead than with me? Do you hate me that much?"

"No, I don't hate you. I could never—" but I had hated him. Hated him for not believing me. Then I remembered Endora. *Never say never.* "I guess desperate people do desperate things—"

The hard line of Mark's jaw betrayed his struggle to keep his emotions in check. "I tried to convince myself that if you came back—but now that you have, I can't. Not again. Andrew and I need someone who cares about us and you don't." I did care about him, more than he knew, but to say so now, what good would it do?

Dr. Connelly arrived as Mark was leaving. They stood huddled together for several minutes, each glancing furtively in my direction before Mark left and Dr. Connelly came over and took a seat. At first it all seemed rather ordinary, but then he took out his notebook and started writing things down. I didn't like notebooks. Bunny wrote things down in a notebook. How loud I screamed, the number of lashes, my reaction to electrical shocks, the weight of the sand . . .

"Stop writing everything down," I demanded. "Can't you see it upsets me? I won't talk to you if you keep writing things down."

When asked why, I just repeated that it scared me. That people put things in notebooks they later use against you. He nodded but refused to comply. Fine, I would refuse to answer. We had reached an impasse.

For a moment he read over what notes he had, flipped back and forth between the pages, pushed his glasses further up on his nose and told me I suffered from a severe delusional disorder which would require spending time at the mental health facility at Dunmore. How long I'd have to stay depended on my progress. When I asked to speak to Andrew, his short answer was no.

\* \* \*

The transfer took place two days later. A nurse escorted me out to the car, and off we went to my new home. That none of what he believed was true didn't matter, he'd written it in his notebook, and everyone knew notebooks were sacrosanct. I didn't think it fair that he should believe Mark when he had yet to hear my side of the story, but there was little I could do about it.

Every afternoon at 2 p.m., sharp I'd be escorted to Dr. Weaver's office. Dr. Weaver specialized in delusions, but since I had my own, I never needed his. He asked questions, and I'd answer. Most questions centered on feelings— but over time believing he had gained my trust he started asking more personal questions which I refused to answer. I didn't like this man and I didn't want him delving into what I considered private. Often my visits deteriorated into shouting matches which would end with me being sent back to my room to as he said, "Think things over."

Five months past and the routine never varied. Then one afternoon things got out of hand and I shouted that it was he and not me that needed therapy. Without waiting for permission I ran from his office and back down the corridor to my room. The longer I ran the longer the hall became until I found myself in the churchyard of the old Celtic church of my visions.

People were milling about in an agitated state and when the doors creaked open everyone pressed forward hoping to get a seat in which to watch the event. Carried along I found a place near the back to sit unnoticed and settled down to watch the proceedings.

"What's going on?" I asked the woman seated beside me, who shrugged her reply. Two men, one in black and one in white, entered from the vestry. A hush fell over the assembled as everyone waited to see what would happen. The man in white took his place at the lectern while the one in black with a wave of his hand, ordered the guards to bring Endora bound in chains to stand before the people.

"Now it begins," the man sitting behind me whispered.

"Will anyone speak for the accused?" Endora hopefully scanned the crowd, but no one responded. The man in white raised his hand for silence then opened what he called the *Book of Deeds* and read a list of Endora's offenses. Once finished, the man in black stepped forward, and asked if anyone wished to add to the accounting. A moment of silence passed before Nathan, his face pale and expressionless, walked past his mother and addressed the man in white.

"This woman was my mother. A singularly cruel woman she hated both me and my father. She tricked my father into marrying her, then killed me believing that he would grant her a divorce once I was gone. When Father refused, she attempted to kill him and then took her own life." His testimony completed he took a seat in the first-row pew.

"Are there others?" The man in white called out.

Now it was Andrew's turn. "I'm not here to condemn Endora, her crimes speak for themselves. I'm here seeking justice for my mother who was imprisoned, and sorely abused so that Endora could attain the revenge she sought against her husband. I'm only a nine-year-old boy, but what the Council did was wrong, and should never have been allowed." Fighting not to cry Andrew took the seat next to his friend.

"Let me to speak," a young woman in a blue dress cried out from the rear. My name is Jennifer Glenn and Endora is responsible for my death. Pregnant with her brother-in-law's child, Endora sought someone to blame. She chose Edmund, but I stood in her way. On the day we were to announce our engagement she pushed me down the stairs to my death."

"You're all lying," Endora screamed, as Jennifer came and led me to the front of the church.

Pointing to the *Book of Deeds*, that lay open on the lectern Jennifer said, "It's all there for everyone to see. Unbeknown to Julie, the Council had entrusted her with my soul. When Endora discovered what they had done, she attempted to destroy Julie in hopes that I would be destroyed as well. It was only because of Julie's great love for her son that she was able to stand firm and say no to Endora's entreaties and threats. Without that love we would all have been lost."

Murmuring voices filled the church as everyone wanted to hear what the man in white had to say. With a thunderous voice that caused clouds of dust to fall from the rafters, he pronounced judgment.

"Because you lied to the Council and made a mockery of the rules, because you sought revenge rather than redemption, the Council has no alternative but to declare you guilty as charged and to reinstate your earlier sentence."

"No! None of what they've said true. You must let me speak." The two judges conferred and finally agreed to allow her to speak. Using her most beguiling voice Endora began. "Since childhood Edmund and I have loved each other. But Jennifer wanted him for herself, and when she couldn't have him sought Julie's help to destroy us. I begged her to leave us alone, but she refused. So upset was I by her continued schemes and plots that when my son became critically ill she convinced me that it would be a blessing to end his suffering by smothering him with a pillow. I loved my son and would never have done such a thing if they had not driven me to do so."

Finishing her tale those in attendance murmured angrily amongst themselves and moved toward us in a threatening manner. At once the heavens parted and a light as brilliant as the stars lit up the church causing the crowd to cover their eyes and fall to their knees. "Sin is all around you," said a voice filled with authority. "Julie is innocent of the charges. Endora is the once and forever beguiler."

"Please," I pleaded, "tell me. Is Jennifer a part of me?"

"You are who you are, another and the same. All part of the mystery. There is yet another to be revealed."

"Did Edmund know Jennifer, and I were one?"

"He did."

Embracing me Jennifer whispered, "It is well with us. We shall be again as before, but the time has not yet come."

"Declare what you will," Endora screamed shaking her fist toward the heavens, "I belong to a stronger power. A power that will someday rise up and rule the universe."

The shadow of a man appeared on the wall behind her and a terrible fear spread amongst the congregation. "Call upon the powers of heaven, it will do you no good. Victory is mine." Exhaling, Endora created a whirlwind that tore through the church, blew open the Book, and shredded its pages.

Then spreading wide her arms she blocked the sun. Fire and brimstone rained down upon the gathering and screams for mercy filled the church. Bunny with his chains and ropes beckoned me to come and though I tried to find a way of escape, the doors sealed themselves against me.

Someone was shouting my name and demanding I lie still and stop fighting. Didn't they understand I had to get away, to find somewhere safe to hide? A needle was thrust into my arm and suddenly I was floating up and out of the building. Below was a field, and in the field a fresh mound of dirt, and on the dirt, a tombstone without a name.

When I came to Dr. Weaver was standing over me and both my arms where tied down. "It's for your own protection. You were thrashing about and we were afraid you'd hurt yourself. We've given you medication to help you sleep. I'll come back in the morning and we'll talk."

* * *

From then on I was continually medicated. Losing the will to fight I no longer argued or try to persuade; I was docile and agreeable and never questioned their methods. Whatever they wanted me to do, I did regardless how degrading. My visits with Connie were monitored and any mention of Andrew ended the visit. If Mark came, I never saw him. For all intents and purposes, I no longer existed. I became a name on a door kept locked. Then twelve months later and without fanfare I was told I was well enough to become an outpatient. I was to report twice a week to Dr. Connelly and if I missed an appointment I'd find myself back at Dunmore. The question no one answered was where was I supposed to go?

Connie arrived while I was packing. "I thought maybe Mark would come."

"Afraid you're stuck with me." Connie laughed but not much. Once in the car I told her to drop me at the Crown Hotel in Woodbridge.

"The Crown? You're kidding right?"

"I have a little money."

"Show me."

"I can't."

"That's what I figured. You'll be staying with us. At least till we can find you a place. You can bunk in the spare room. Charlie said he didn't want you roaming the countryside like a waif of the storm."

"Are you sure?" I asked, as we headed home.

"I don't say things I don't mean. Well—not always."

I spent the next several weeks looking for a place of my own and by chance found one that would suit my needs and was will within Mark's ability to pay. For the first time in more than a year I was free, and the feeling was intoxicating. Though I still had nights when I would wake up screaming—I was finding it easier to cope.

When the weather was fine I'd take long walks through the surrounding fields with sketch book in hand or sit quietly and enjoy my freedom. One thing however nagged me and that was Endora saying that everything had been an illusion. Was it possible? My head said no, but I had to be sure. As always I asked Connie.

"Let's think about this for a moment. You said Bunny had a title." Connie sat a bowl of vegetable soup and crackers in front of me and after telling me to eat, considered. "So the first thing to do is to see if he exist. If he does, we go from there. There must be a list for these people? Or what about old newspapers? If he was murdered, wouldn't that be front page news? I'll get a babysitter and well go down to London tomorrow and check out the libraries. They're bound to have stuff like that on file."

So, off we went to London to scour the libraries looking for anything that might help us discover the truth. After hours of searching Connie found it on a roll of microfilm. "Mysterious Death of English Lord." It read;

"*Charles Ambrose Lester, Baron of Kilgore, only son of the Duke and Duchess of Downcaster, was found dead in his Paris flat late on the evening of the twenty-fifth. The method used was, according to the police, bizarre. Shortly after five that morning a neighbor saw two men leaving the premises. No positive identification has yet been made, but the police are continuing their enquiries. The body will remain in French custody until further notice.*"

"At least now I know it wasn't my imagination."

Pleased with our success I was rewinding the microfilm when Connie yelled stop.

"Go back. I thought I saw—no, keep going. There!" Connie pointed at the screen. I couldn't believe it. It was the article about the break-in at Thornwood. Connie was almost giddy and insisted we photo-copy both items.

I hadn't told Connie about my time with Bunny, but that night as we sat talking over what we found, I told her what happened. Sparing no details, I told her everything, and when finished she broke down in tears.

"I don't know what to say. I mean after all that and still you called to talk to me—to talk to me, and what did I do? I don't even want to think about it. How could you stand it? We all thought, but you know what we thought. I swear I'll never let you down again. Ever!" She threw her arms around me and hugged me so tight it hurt.

As we headed up to bed I questioned why the story of the break-in differed from what I remembered. But Connie feeling quite proud of herself said, "How can you be in a story that took place before you were born? I guess we'll just have to consider it one of life's little mysteries." Then she laughed out loud and I along with her. "I think I'm catching on to how this stuff works."

# CHAPTER THIRTY-SIX

On the sixth month anniversary of my leaving the hospital I was granted a supervised visit with Andrew. Though excited, I worried he might refuse to see me. "Why wouldn't he want to see you?" Connie asked. "You're his mom for Pete's sake."

True, but my stomach didn't know that and by the time I arrived at Mark's place it felt as if my entire body was tied in knots. A daunting looking woman answered the door and said Mark would be late. I could come back another day or wait in the car for his return.

Fearful of jeopardizing my visits I returned to the car. Mark showed up an hour later and without offering an apology showed me into the house. No one invited me to sit down, so I stood off to the side while Mark and Miss Snooty discussed his schedule for the following week. She threw me one last icy glance before leaving.

A long uncomfortable silence followed her departure and we were both relieved when Andrew arrived and ran headlong into my arms. I was filled with such a sense of joy I could barely contain myself.

Eager to show me his new bike he led me out into the yard where his happy demeanor turned into tears. He disliked Miss Snooty and hated school. "The kids make fun of you and say mean things. It's not fair. Sometimes I get so mad I hit them."

Crushed by the pain I saw in his eyes I pulled him into my arms. *"No, Andrew will as well."*

"I've loved you since the first moment I held you in my arms and it breaks my heart knowing how badly you've been hurt by all this. I'm so sorry my darling. So very sorry."

As we sat talking Andrew shared Edmund's promise to send a sign. "But how do we know Mother, and what will happen to Dad?" They were questions I couldn't answer. I didn't know what would happen. Hoping to cheer him I surprised him with the Christmas gift from the servants. "Wait till you're alone to open it. I wouldn't want Miss Snooty to take it." Andrew laughed out loud and told me he loved me. Getting late we headed back to the house. I told Mark about the trouble at school and he promised to talk to his teacher.

Having proved myself harmless, I was now granted a three-hour weekly visit. I couldn't take him away from the house, but it didn't matter. We were together and had a grand time. Then Mark went to Italy for a month and our visits were put on hold. I was making breakfast when he called to say he was back and that my visits could continue. He suggested we go out to dinner the following evening. I agreed hoping we'd go somewhere quiet and out-of-the-way. A place where we could talk about increasing my visits and perhaps allowing Andrew to have sleepovers at my place. Instead, Mark took me to the Officer's Club. The moment we entered the whispering began. Some intended to be overheard. Others just stared as if I were Lizzie Borden. If Mark noticed he never said.

"What would you like?" he asked studying the menu.

"I'd like to go home."

"But we just got here."

"I know, but everyone's looking at me."

"Oh, for God's sake. They couldn't care less if you're here or not. What would you like to eat?"

"Nothing, I'm leaving." I pushed my chair back upsetting it as I did and headed for the door. Mark followed me out into the parking lot.

"Julie you're being ridiculous. Come on, wait up," he called out as I hurried down the drive. "Julie, stop." At that point I stumbled on the uneven pavement and fell. "Are you all right? Let me help."

"Get away from me. I can take care of myself." Getting to my feet I staggered down the drive and out onto the road. It didn't take long to realize I'd made a monumental mistake. My ankle was swollen, my coat still hung in the club's cloakroom and the night had turned bitter.

Attempting to get out of the wind, I struggled up the bank and used the hedgerow as a shelter. All this and I didn't even get a chance to eat. Several cars passed, one even slowed down, none stopped. Later another car came and this time it slowed, pulled over and stopped. "What are you doing up there?" Mark called out, "I've been looking everywhere for you. Come on, I'll take you home."

He helped me into the house and down the hall to the kitchen. "Sit still while I get some ice for that ankle." He opened the freezer and then the frig. Where's all your food?"

"I don't have any."

"So why didn't you buy more?"

"With what?"

"The money I put in your account every month. Didn't Dr. Connelly tell you?"

"No one said anything."

"Where do you eat?"

"I've been eating at Connie's because there's no money left for gas. Otherwise I'd go down and get something at the charity food kitchen in town."

"Dear God Julie, why didn't you say? I had no idea. I'll be talking to Dr. Connelly about this. All this time . . . Look, the base store is still open," he said looking at his watch. "I'll go get something and we'll eat here."

Mark returned with a week's worth of groceries and Chinese takeout. Not until we finished eating and Mark had cleared away the dishes did I discover the real reason for his invitation. Whisking me off my feet he carried me into the bedroom and before I could say no, began to undress me.

"Mark, stop it," I said struggling to get up. "This is wrong."

"Convince me you don't want it and I'll stop."

But I couldn't because I did want him. I wanted the closeness, the touch of his hands on my flesh—but when it ended I felt weak for having given in. To make matters worse, he chose that moment to describe how badly I had hurt him. Astonished by the crass assumption that he was the only one to come out of this with scares, I hobbled to the door and demanded that he leave.

"After all this, you can't be serious?"

"Get out and take your self-pity with you."

"What was I supposed to say? Did you want me to lie and flatter you by saying how glad I was that you came back? For a whole year I had no idea where you were, what you were doing or who you were with. Then you waltz back into our lives like nothing happened. To make it even worse you kidnapped Andrew.'"

"I shouldn't need permission to take what's mine."

"He's not yours, you gave up that right when you ran off for a year."

"And what about what you did Mark? You said I was a danger to my son and had me committed. How many times did you come to see how I was? I had to beg to see my son. Beg Mark. Do you understand how degrading that was? You didn't even check to see if I had money to live on. You left it to someone else. If it hadn't been for Connie I don't know what I would have done. And since you didn't ask, I'll tell you now. Once I get Andrew back, and I will, then it's over, done. I'll wave goodbye and you'll never have to see me again."

Mark looked at me as if I'd stabbed him in the back. "You could walk away as if we never meant anything to each other?"

"Do we mean something to each other? It doesn't appear that way to me. I thought you'd be happy to have me out of your life."

"You don't understand, I—damn, there's so much I need to say, so much I need to tell you but damnit, I always get it wrong. I never wanted any of this tonight, all I wanted was to talk. To try and work things out between us, but then there you were, all small and helpless, and I just had to be with you. All I ask is for you to hear me out."

At that point I just wanted him gone, but there he was looking like a lost little boy, and suddenly that inner voice of mine was telling me to give him a chance. "All right, fine, I'll hear you out, but I'll make no promises."

Relief flashed in his eyes, and his features softened. Helping me back over to the bed he sat down beside me. "I realize now that a lot of what happened was my fault. I was so busy at work I didn't take the time to really listen like I should have—to realize how scared you were. I thought being together was enough, but I see now I was wrong. You won't believe me but the day I met you I knew we had to be together. You gave me something to live for. I've failed in so many ways where you're concerned and for that I'm sorry—"

The softness of his touch and the gentle tone of his voice tore down the wall I had built around my heart, and forced me to realize that regardless the past, I still needed him. Still loved him and that he still loved me.

"How about this. What say we put all this stuff behind us and start over fresh. We'll go out to dinner; take Andrew to the shore. We'll just enjoy each other's company. No overnights, no commitments just be together. Maybe that way we can work ourselves back to what we had in the beginning. Please say yes. Without you in my life I'm lost."

He made it sound so simple. Wipe the slate clean and start again, but how do you do that? How do you overcome what went before and promised to come again? Still, not to try would be unfair to both of us and to Andrew.

I'm not saying it didn't take time, or that there weren't moments when one or the other of us thought it wouldn't work, but then Andrew would come bounding in and we'd go on. Returning to the states we renewed our vows and made a life together. For Mark the past was just that, but for me, having gone through so much I found it hard to relate to the normal everyday affairs of life.

As for Andrew, I thought being young his memories would fade, but I was wrong, and as he grew he would talk to me about what took place and if Edmund would ever come back. After high school he followed his father into the Air Force, and three years later was killed when the plane he was flying crashed. They said it was an accident . . .

# CHAPTER THIRTY-SEVEN

I'd been writing almost nonstop for the past month and throwing down my pen I stretched and sat back in my chair. Writing though painful had kept me sane over these last nerve-racking weeks but now I was finished and wondered what to do next. Connie offered to come, but with her daughter having a difficult pregnancy I couldn't bring myself to ask. Besides, there was nothing left to do but wait for the end. All hope of recovery had gone, and though miracles happened, everyone said so, miracles seemed in short supply at the moment.

I spent a good deal of time just watching him. At first hoping he'd recover, but then I began having nightmares. I was locked inside one of Bunny's tiny boxes, so small that movement of any kind was impossible. Even expanding my lungs to breathe was difficult. And I wondered—was that how it was for Mark, trapped within himself unable to move or scream? Lying there praying that someone would open the box?

It was clear to everyone but me that my vigil was taking its toll both on my mind and body, so when the doctor insisted I take some time off, I didn't have the strength to say no. Gathering my things, I returned to the hotel where a note was waiting from Captain Donaldson. He'd received a call from Bedford Manor asking if I could go round and pick up Mark's belongings? To be honest, I hadn't given much thought to Mark's things or even where he'd been staying. To discover he was staying in her house changed everything. This was the incentive I needed to get myself moving again. It also put to bed the idea that Mark's accident was in fact, an accident.

Next morning, I called to check on Mark, then drove the ten miles to Bedford Manor. If I wanted to somehow convince them to allow me to see where she was buried, it was imperative I stay calm and chose my words with care. At least that's what I thought till I met the current Lord Spencer the spitting image of his grandfather and my friend Richard. After that all my well thought out plans went out the window.

"To be honest, I didn't realize Mark was staying here."

"That was the weather's fault," he said escorting me into his office. "The day he arrived we were in the middle of that horrid storm and all the other hotels were full. Because we're a little off the beaten path, we had one room left. Please, take a seat." He indicated where I should set then offered me tea and biscuits both of which I excepted. By the way, we don't stand on formalities here so please, its Richard. "Your husband said this wasn't the first time you lived in England."

"No, Mark was in the Air Force and we were stationed just outside Ipswich. We lived in a house called Thornwood." Richard's reaction was immediate.

"Did you say Thornwood?" he asked quickly sitting his cup aside.

"That's right."

"I think we should find someplace to talk were we won't be disturbed." I came to Bedford Manor with hopes, but no expectations. No real plan other than to speak to Endura. Now this man wanted to talk in private.

"Now," Richard said, having escorted me into the library. "Tell me everything you can about the place. Then I'll tell you."

His tone sounded rather ominous, so I gave him a summary rather than the whole story. To verify my acquaintance with the family I mentioned the birth mark on Stewart's back, and that Lady Barbara played the flute but only for family gathering. Unsure how much of the truth he could handle I left it there, fearing to go further would get me thrown out before I got a chance to talk to the lady.

"Well, Richard said, you realize you've laid waste to everything I assumed true."

"I understand it's hard, but—"

"You'll stay for lunch won't you?" he interrupted.

Without waiting for a response Richard called down to the kitchen and ordered for both of us. Once that was seen to Richard relaxed and spoke in a more open manner about his family. He confided that his grandfather spoke often of Edmund, but seldom if ever of Endora. "If she hadn't been buried here at the Manor, I'd never have known she existed."

"Putting her here was your great grandfather's decision."

Again, Richard interrupted. "Then I can only say she must have done something rather horrid. Only the black sheep come here."

"That pretty much sums her up," I said.

"Now here's where we come to a parting of the ways. You say you lived at Thornwood for just over six years, and that a Mr. and Mrs. Black rented the place to you with the stipulation that you'd stay for at least two. Have you any proof of that transaction?"

I did and showed him the lease. He read it through than sat silent for a time. "This is impossible," he said handing it back. Completely impossible. Let me tell you why. According to several family members who heard it from grandfather, the Blacks had purchased Thornwood at auction when she and her husband first married. She sent them a letter stating that with the death of her husband, the place was simply too big and wondered since we had a past connection to the house if we'd like to purchase the place.

"Grandmother was an emphatic no. She wanted nothing to do with the place having heard rumors of its past. Never one to say no to what he thought a marvelous idea he bought the place sight unseen. 'It can't be that bad if people are living in it,' he told Grandmama, but he couldn't have been more wrong. When he finally saw the place, he was appalled. Even tried to back out of the deal, but the papers had been signed and Mrs. Black was nowhere to be found."

"When was that?"

"Let's see—Uncle James must have been about sixteen at the time, so I'd say sometime around the end of 1935 or 36. Uncle said it was the only time Grandmother ever threatened to leave my grandfather.

"Anyway, Father barely got started on the repairs when weird things began to happen. Tools went missing, repairs were undone, painted walls mildewed overnight. The workers were beginning to refuse to come to work. The contractor said he'd never seen anything like it and swore the house was haunted.

"In time we finally made the place livable and several times managed to rent it out, but the tenants never stayed long. Maybe six months but no longer. They all said the place was haunted, and they refused to live there. In the end we were out a great deal of money and had nothing to show for it but a house with a bad reputation. In the end the family boarded the place up and that's how it remained. So when you said you lived there it knocked the wind out of me."

Rooting through my purse I showed him several pictures of the house both inside and out, and all he kept saying was how impossible it was.

We continued our conversation, but time was pressing. I took a chance and explained the real reason why I came. Perhaps it was the direct way I went about it, but Richard acted as if Endora was somewhere in the room. When I explained I needed to go to the mausoleum, he was visibly relieved. He would wait for me in his office.

* * *

The path was as he said overgrown, so it took some effort to fight my way through the jungle of weeds, and brambles. The gate was another obstacle. The hinges having rusted shut it was almost more than I could do to move them. Finally however, I shimmied my way through and went in. In the semi-darkness I could see a figure standing next to a marble sarcophagus. On top was a life-sized copy of the person inside. There were two others, one on each side.

"It's about time you got here," she said over her shoulder. "The Stonemason didn't catch the real me. What do you think?"

"I'm here to get Mark back, not to discuss how you've aged."

"No need to get nasty. If you hadn't wanted me to have him you shouldn't have allowed him to come. I mean having him stay here was rather daring on your part." She blew the dust off her marble likeness and studied it more closely.

"I had no idea he'd be staying here. It's the storms fault not mine."

"Tell you what. Since I know what a curious creature you are, how about I show you what happened. You know, walk you through it." I agreed and we were there.

Mark was sitting in the far corner of the dining room studying the menu when a bolt of lightning momentarily short-circuited the lighting. When it returned Endora was standing behind the chair opposite Marks.

"Would you mind sharing your table. They'll be closing soon, and this is the only table with an empty seat." Mark agreed and introduced himself.

"Mark Hammond? That name? It sounds so familiar. I know I've heard it before." For a moment she sat as if trying to recollect. "Yes, of course. You leased my home. The one called Thornwood, outside Ipswich." She held out her hand. "I'm Lady Endora Stanley."

Mark at first appeared bemused. "Julie put you up to this didn't she? A Halloween joke? Well, you can tell her for me this isn't funny."

"Now don't get upset, Julie knows nothing about it. She's still at that ridiculous party you forced her to attend. I mean all those people dressed up like ghost and goblins. You don't even believe in ghost."

Mark's expression hardened. "I don't know who you are, or what your trying to prove, but this has gone on long enough. I suggest you go find someone else to play games with."

"Games? This isn't a game. This is about what took place at Thornwood." Refusing to listen Mark left the dining room and headed back upstairs where Endora was waiting.

"Get out or I'll throw you out!"

"You can't throw me out, I haven't finished confessing."

"Then go find a priest."

Endora laughed, "I'm afraid that wouldn't work for me. Come on, be honest, aren't you the least bit curious."

"No, I'm not. As far as I'm concerned that all over and done with."

"Julie doesn't think so."

"This whole thing is preposterous. I want you to leave."

"I'll leave but you're coming with me." Before he could argue further he found himself standing in the entrance hall at Thornwood and watching what took place. "Why was I never allowed to see any of this?"

"Because it wouldn't have served my purpose. Sadly in the end it didn't really matter as nothing turned out as planned. Of course there's still more to come, so it might turn out all right after all."

"What do you mean there's still more to come?" Mark asked, taking hold of her arm.

"I mean exactly what it sounded like. It's not over. All I can say is that if you had moved her like she begged you to, if you had believed her even one time, none of this would've happened."

"I did care. I tried to get her to see someone."

"No, no, no, no, no! Getting her to see someone only proved you thought she was lying and worst maybe going crazy. Come," she said waving him toward the window. "Look down there." Below him the street was overflowing with wagons, omnibuses, street vendors and people of all sorts going about their daily business. "That's the world she tried to explain to you. The world she saw every day. Andrew as well. We met him months before Julie. He was our connector."

Mark stood for a moment looking out onto the world of the eighteen-seventies. "Wait a minute," Mark said turning to face her. You said she tried to tell me, right? Then when she said it wasn't her I was talking to but you, she was telling the truth."

Endora began to laugh. "Now you get it."

"And it wasn't Julie talking in her sleep. It was you flooding my mind with lies and innuendos."

"Problem was you kept insisting, 'It's not the house it's you Julie. You and your ridiculous fantasies.'"

Defeated, Mark stood motionless in the middle of the room. "If there's more, show me."

And so, she took him to Hellborn and Bunny's torture rooms. In the first a woman, naked, lay moaning on a stone slab. Unrecognizable Mark asked who she was. Endora answered with one word. "Julie."

"Mark swallowed hard and struggled to speak. "How did she—"

"Someone called Bunny brought her here. You remember her saying that name don't you? She was on her way to your meeting when Bunny tricked her into going with him."

"Dear God. I've seen enough. I can't do this anymore. Please, let's go back."

"Not yet," she took his hand and led him down a dark corridor running with damp. "There's one more thing you need to see."

When he hesitated Endora pushed him through the door and across the room till he was standing only inches away from me.

"Why would he do this to her?"

"He hoped by killing her he'd destroy me. Absolute foolishness, but that's what he thought. Come now, time is of the essence, reach out and touch her," Endora demanded. "Can you feel the chill on her flesh? That's death approaching. Oh, you have her blood on your hand." Frantic, Mark tried to wipe his hand clean, but the blood remained.

"All right, you've shown me what a fool I was. That if it wasn't for me none of this would've happened." His voice faded away and was replaced by bone racking sobs. "I need to get back to her, tell her I'm sorry. That I didn't understand—" Within moments he was back in his room and I was back in the mausoleum.

"I need to go back to Thornwood. I've been away too long," she said looking somewhat shriveled.

"No, not till you tell me about the accident."

"Wasn't it enough I forced him to realize the part he played in all this?"

"No—I want to know." I demanded.

"Fine—but then I have to go back. That evening I returned to his room and found him packing to go home. When I mentioned why he came he said the only thing that mattered was getting back to you. The problem was, that silly storm was still raging, and though I warned him the roads were treacherous he was beyond reason.

"I knew how he had to go, so found a spot where the road ran close to the loch and waiting till he was almost on top of me stepped out in front of him. He swerved to miss me, his car jumped the guardrail, hit a tree and slid down the bank and into the loch. Semi-conscious he tried to free himself, but the water rushed in and it was over."

I thought she'd fade away back to Thornwood, but instead she began to laugh. "How stupid you are Jennifer. I told you I'd have him in the end, and now I do, and you have nothing. Do you know how I despise you? That I loathe the very sight of you. I warned you what I'd do if you got in my way."

"That wasn't me, that was Jennifer. I never did anything to you."

"You kept her alive when she should've been rotting in her grave. You gave Edmund hope when he should have remained desolate. You want Mark back so you can live happy ever after. Will it's not going to happen. Soon I'll have you as well and then I'll be victorious, and you'll be in hell. Seeing you beg has been a balm to my soul."

"You don't have a soul. You sold it for the thrill of getting even."

Squeezing through the gate I ran back to the house where Richard was waiting. He listened to what I had to say then poured us both a large scotch. "I think before this is over we will need a lot more of these."

# CHAPTER THIRTY-EIGHT

On the drive back to town, I thought of stopping at the spot where Mark went into the water but couldn't bring myself to do it. As my father would say, *"better to remember a happy moment than a tragic one."* Instead I thought over my conversation with Richard concerning Thornwood's history. As I suspected Tom and Maggie had told the truth. The house had sat empty for more than forty years. Our arrival in England was the catalyst that set it all in motion. That's why Mark never saw the sign. They weren't ready. Only when the time was right was he led by a so-called stranger to see what they wanted him to see. If only Maggie were still alive I could tell her how right she had been.

* * *

It was going on seven by the time I reached Inverness so drove directly to the hospital to check on Mark. A message from the doctor said that Mark's condition had worsened, and internal bleeding was suspected. Surgery would be required. Sitting beside him I began to wonder if perhaps I should refuse permission. Why keep him alive if living meant being suspended between life and death indefinitely? He told me several times while in the service that if anything happened not to keep him alive if he was in a vegetative state. Of course I would be the one that had turn off the machines. *"Death comes to all at the prescribed time?"* my father would say and so I agreed to the surgery.

Worried and unable to sleep I went down to the hotel lounge and made a cup of coffee which I carried back to my room. The time was 4:15 a.m.

much too early to go to the hospital so while I waited for my coffee to cool I brought my diary up to date. At 5:00 a.m. I took a shower, then made a note to call Connie when I returned. By 5:45 a.m. I was headed back to the hospital.

At this early hour, the place was still yawning itself awake, but by six, its eyes would be wide open and the bustling urgency of caring for the sick and dying would resume. By seven

Mark would be in surgery. Following the arrows to the surgical ward, I signed in and sat down to wait. As the wait dragged on Endora came to mind. It was good that Mark was finally shown the truth, that he saw what I said was true, but what good would it do us now?

As for Richard, he couldn't have been kinder, and I left there feeling I had made a new friend. The fact that it went so smoothly surprised me, and that he believed what I told him a miracle. I guess miracles do happen on occasion.

* * *

Lost in thought, I paid no attention to the man who came and sat beside me. It was hearing his voice that changed everything. "I don't have much time my love, but I want you to know you can trust Richard to help you, and shortly another will appear as well. They will be there for you until the time comes to face Endora one last time. I must go, but you know where I am, come." He laid his hand on mine then was gone.

"Mrs. Hammond—Julie," the doctor's hand on my shoulder nudged me back to the present. "We need to talk before Mark goes into surgery." He explained the risk then asked the question I was dreading. If it's bad would you like us to let him go? I quickly said no. Do what you can for him. If he dies during the procedure, it will be God's will not mine.

The doctor joined me two hours later with a bemused look on his face. "Everything went more smoothly then I thought possible. There was this however." He handed me what looked like the tip of a knife. "When you consider all the scans we did after the accident it's baffling that no one saw it."

I drove back to the hotel, then walked down Castle Road to Ness Bank and the river. Finding an unoccupied bench near the river's edge I allowed myself to think of nothing but the sound of the water rushing past on its way to the sea. The quiet seemed almost blissful after the turmoil of the past few days yet my fingers kept toying with the metal point the doctor gave me.

Looking at it more closely I saw that it wasn't a knife point but the point from a pair of scissors. Endora's scissors. There was only one way it could've gotten there. Did I dare even consider what it might mean? Was that the reason for Edmund's unexpected visit? Why he wanted me to come to Latham? Where they in fact one?

Till now the evening had been clear and the temperature comfortable, but a chill had swept down from the north causing a mist to form above the river. Something about the way it snaked along the bank and up onto the grassy area around the fort reminded me of death coming to call and I shivered. Walking hurriedly away, I returned to the warmth of my hotel room. Tomorrow I would answer Edmund's call to come to Latham.

Laying a map on the counter I asked the desk clerk for directions. "Latham you say? Wouldn't advise it. The weathers expected to turn this afternoon and the roads up there can be treacherous at the best of times. Tomorrow would be better."

"No, it has to be today."

In that case, I'd best show you how to go. After leaving the main road here," he pointed to the turning, "it gets a bit twisty-turny, and the road narrows. Carry on another four miles and you'll see their sign. The main house is closed for the season, but the rest is open though you won't see much once the rain starts." I thanked him, gathered up the map and set out for Latham.

Despite the state of the secondary road, I made good time. As for the weather, the clouds were looking more menacing by the minute. Rain was coming, I could smell it in the air, but would it hold off long enough for me to accomplish my mission?

I found the sign without a problem and stopped to read what it said. Latham Hall, open April 1—November 30. Hours, 9 a.m. till 5 p.m. daily. Grounds open year-round. Well, that's that. There it was, the grounds were open and since Edmund was buried under the oak in the garden, there shouldn't be a problem.

Passing through the gate I could sense Jennifer was with me. This was where she grew up, met Edmund, and where she received her first kiss. It was also where she died. Now she was back and couldn't contain her joy.

The road leading up to the house was long and winding and just before cresting the hill that ran down to the house I was forced to stop to avoid hitting the herd of fallow deer that dashed across my path on their way down to the meadow. Edmund often spoke of its beauty, but nothing prepared me for what I was seeing. The main building was Elizabethan, but the Stanley's made extensive alterations during the reign of Queen Ann and again in 1876 by Sir Owen.

Parking the car at the top of the rise I hurried down the path toward the house. I could see the oak, a huge giant of a tree peeking out from behind the main building. It wasn't till I reached the rear of the house that I found my way blocked by a locked gate and a large sign which read, "Garden Closed Until Spring." There was nothing for it but to inquire at the house. It took three pulls of the bell cord before a not unpleasant looking man appeared.

"Yes?"

"My name is Julie Hammond, and I realize the sign says the garden is closed till spring, but I was wondering—"

"We don't make exceptions I'm afraid."

"Would it be possible to talk to the Curator?"

"He won't be back till Tuesday. If you want to see him, call back then."

"Who is it James?" a woman asked coming to stand beside him. "What's she wanting?"

"Says she wants to talk to MacKenzie."

"He's not here," the woman said, giving me a look reserved for strangers.

"I already told her that," the man said.

"You need to come back Tuesday like my husband said. Now please, you're keeping us from our tea."

"Oh, I didn't realize." Then one of those miracles I was short of, happened. The skies opened, and the rain fell in torrents.

"Is that your car at the top of the rise?" the woman asked.

"Afraid so, but if I run—"

"Then you might as well come in till it passes. No sense you drowning yourself."

They led me back to the kitchen and pointed to where I should sit. They were having scones and marmalade and invited me to join them. I introduced myself, and they returned the favor. "Blair's the name. I'm Katherine, and that's James," she nodded in his direction.

We talked about the weather, and the number of people that came to visit, but then Katherine mentioned that her family had served the Stanley's since 1860.

Without thinking I blurted out, "Then they were here when Edmund and Jennifer were— The look on Katherine's face said I had gone too far and was hoping to change the subject when footsteps were heard coming down the hall.

"Sorry to interrupt," he said extending his hand. "I forgot my briefcase. The name's Mackenzie, Donald MacKenzie, I'm the curator here." Paul

Bunyan sprang to mind as he smiled down at me, but once James explained my reason for being there, MacKenzie's smile changed to a skeptical frown.

"Did ye no see the sign?" he asked.

"She saw it," Katherine said, "but now she's here, you might as well see what she's after."

We traveled down three hallways and a flight of marble steps before reaching his office. He offered me a chair then disappeared into an adjoining room to hang up our coats. In a moment of madness, I took advantage of his absence and with Jennifer's help made a dash for the garden. If the rain was cold, I didn't notice and was about to wipe the dampened leaves off Edmund's gravestone when a powerful hand came to rest on my shoulder. MacKenzie . . .

"What are you doing?" he asked, as he stood over me like a great woolly mammoth.

"I only wanted—"

"Do you realize you're now in a good deal of trouble?"

"I didn't mean to—"

"Let's get in out of the weather." I didn't mind the weather and would gladly have told him so but never got the chance. "Here, dry yourself off," he said handing me a towel. "I'm not sure whether to show you the door or call the police." Sitting down behind his massive desk he swung his chair around to face me. "Now what were you about out there?"

What I should have done was to state in a calm, quiet manner why I was there, but fearing he'd turn me out, I babbled on and made no sense at all. If it hadn't been for the stupid gate, I'd be out there now and none of this would be necessary and unlike Richard this bearded Scotsman had no family ties to fall back on.

"Well, that's quite a story. Would you mind starting again?" he said tapping his fingers on the desk."

I took a deep breath and began. "Several years ago, I lived in a house called Thornwood. The Stanley's owned the place and we became close friends. Anyway, yesterday at the hospital, Edmund appeared and told me to come here."

"Edmund Stanley was in the hospital?"

"No, Mark was, but Edmund appeared and told me to come, that I'd meet a new friend, so I came." MacKenzie looked incredulous.

"I thought that's what you said but wasn't sure. So, let me get this straight. You're saying that a man who's been dead more than a hundred years appeared out of nowhere and told you to come here." I nodded. "And that's why you're here?"

"That's right." Why I didn't think of it before I'm not sure. "You can call Sir Richard Spencer. He'll vouch for me."

"I'm not about to bother Sir Richard with a yarn like that. Besides, if it's the dead you're wanting to talk to, since they won't be answering, you can come back when we're open." I could feel Jennifer's frustration growing and mingling with my own. How was I to deal with the man? Unable to constrain myself, I made a break for the door.

"I told you to sit down," he said, blocking my way.

"And I told you I needed to go to him."

"If any of this sounded plausible, I might consider it, but you haven't said one coherent word since you came in."

"Then call Sir Richard. He knows me and will vouch for what I'm saying." Anger was turning into frustration. "Mr. MacKenzie please. I realize all this must sound impossible to you, even crazy, but two years ago I lost my only child and now I'm about to lose my husband. My life is in shambles and all I ask is a few minutes alone with Edmund. Is that so terrible? What could it hurt?"

He sat for a moment mulling over what I said. "I've been curator here for over ten years, and every year someone comes claiming the money or title. But none of them wanted to talk to him."

"I said nothing about money or title. All I asked was a few moments alone at his graveside which you refuse to allow. You sit there playing God without having the slightest idea how important this is."

Outside the rain had let up. "No," he said, getting up, "I've given you all the time I can spare. It's too preposterous to even consider." He retrieved our coats then escorted me back the way we came. Halfway up the stairs, I slipped on a wet marble step and grabbing for the railing, lost hold of my purse which tumbled down, spilling its contents as it went.

"I'm so sorry," I stammered. "I didn't mean—"

"Don't fret yourself." He interrupted. "I'm the one that dripped water all over the place. Are you all right?"

"Yes, just clumsy." MacKenzie picked up my license, glanced at it, then about to hand it back, stopped and took another look.

"Mr. MacKenzie, Is something wrong?"

"Aye—would you mind coming back to the office for a minute? Something you said earlier, I need to think about this."

"Are you going to call the police?"

"The names Donald and I'm not calling anybody." The rain had started again. Hurrying toward the bookcase on the far side of the room he mumbled something about a book. "Blast it MacKenzie, get your wits about you, it's in the history section." Finding what he was looking for, he opened it to page ten and told me to read the first entry. I began,

*"Am writing from Thornwood. We arrived early last evening for the sad and painful duty of attending Nathan's funeral. Edmund is bearing up, but*

*Endora as usual is making things difficult for everyone. The woman has locked herself away and refuses to show herself. The Duchess arrived after lunch and makes up for her daughter's absences by taking every opportunity to denigrate Edmund in front of the guests. If I weren't a gentleman and the occasion so solemn, I would confront the lady for I find holding my tongue difficult. I have yet to discover where Julie is hiding. Regardless I shall find her for its imperative that both I and Lady Beatrice thank her for the love and concern she has shown for our grandson. Ah, they're calling for us, I must go down."*

MacKenzie then directed me down to the last paragraph.

*"Have located Julie's hiding place. Believing her presence a distraction, she has been watching from an alcove off the middle landing. I was surprised to learn that she intends to leave directly after the funeral. For a moment I thought she was mad with grief, but she assured me that it would be best for everyone if she returned home. Edmund must dissuade her of that notion. Julie is his rock and without her I'm afraid he might go to pieces. Well, must close, it's time to take Nathan north to Latham. A sad task.*

*"Before closing I must report a disturbing occurrence. Edmund, just in from outside, is in a terrible state and refuses to explain. Undeterred, I hope in time to discover the cause of his sudden inexplicable behavior. He slammed several doors because of it and is now in a very black mood. From what I could glean from Silas, it concerns Bunny Lester of all people. He'll say no more so we're off."*

For a time, I couldn't find my voice, and with the greatest effort managed to keep my tears at bay. That Lord Owen had written about our encounter never occurred to me, but I thanked God that he had. My surprise turned to amazement when Donald handed me the photo album.

"That's Jennifer Glenn without a doubt. Her father was Sir Owen's land agent. She was a servant here and intended to marry Edmund but died on the day of their engagement. So tell me this than, how did your picture wind up next to hers? And how if you know the answer, did his signature which I am quite familiar with, get on the back of both pictures?"

"I think I already explained that. I traveled back in time, and Edmund came forward."

Donald roared with laughter. "By God the whole thing's daft, but I'm inclined for the moment to believe you. Seeing how I can't disprove what you're telling me, or for that matter what Sir Owen wrote, there's nothing I can do but follow along and see where it leads. And you say Sir Richard knows?" I nodded.

He returned the books to the shelf and insisted we go back up to the kitchen for tea. "I'll tell you straight," he said as we walked along, "seeing Edmund's picture in the pocket with your license gave me quite a start."

"That's not Edmund. That's my husband Mark."

"Thank God I have a strong heart."

We found James and Katherine busy in the living room. He asked if there was any possibility of tea. Katherine said there was. The two of us took a seat at the kitchen table and waited for them to join us. The tea served; he could barely keep from laughing. "You probably both thought I'd be throwing this little lass out on her ear—and under normal circumstances would have done, but damn, these aren't normal circumstances. James, remember when I was searching through the archives trying to find the woman Lord Owen's kept mentioning in his diaries, and how frustrated I was when I couldn't find anything other than her picture."

"Yeah, so what about it?" James asked.

"Well, I'll tell you what. This is the girl Sir Owen wrote about." He passed them the two pictures, and unable to hold it back any longer, roared with laughter. Naturally they wanted proof so I described in great detail things that only someone who knew the family intimately would know. What convinced them was my description of the dress Lady Beatrice wore to Nathan's funeral. It turned out that Katherine's great-grandmother had sewn the lace for the cuffs and collar. She brought out a picture to show us.

"I wondered why her eyes lit up the minute I mentioned Edmund's name. It was like she was talking about someone she knew, not just someone she read about in a guidebook. But I still find it impossible to believe," Katherine said, with a nervous glance toward her husband.

The rain continuing Donald suggested that instead of going out in the weather, I visit Edmund's room instead. At least you'll be dry, and all his things are there. To suggest such a thing meant Donald believed a dead person was upstairs waiting for me. No wonder he seemed hesitant to say it. It wasn't something a sane person would contemplate, regardless what just happened.

# CHAPTER THIRTY-NINE

Standing outside Edmund's door I was overcome by a whirlwind of doubt. What if all this was just another of Endora's tricks. Was that really Edmund at the hospital? Did he tell me to come or was it a dream? Refusing to give in to my fears I opened the door and went in.

At first I thought I'd gone back in time. I was standing in an exact replica of his office. There was the desk where he did his work, his squeaky leather chair, the leather sofa he sometimes slept on, and over on the book-shelf all stacked alphabetically, his favorite books and novels. In his wardrobe his clothes hung neatly on their hangers clean and ready to wear. But there was one item that was new. Above the fireplace was a portrait of him I'd never seen before.

A portrait is supposed to reflect the inner person, but if that were true then whoever put brush to canvas for this portrait failed miserably. Where were the straight shoulders, the soul piercing gaze, the hint of a smile? What this artist painted was a portrait of a broken man. A man weighed down with sorrow. A sudden sense of guilt overcame me. It wasn't the artist fault, he painted what he saw, and that's when the tears came. What could possibly have happened to cause him to look so grieved? It had to be more than our parting as he knew in time we'd see each other again. I located the bell cord and gave it a tug. Mr. MacKenzie appeared almost at once.

"Mr. MacKenzie, I need to ask you about that picture. That's not the Edmund I knew, that's a picture of a broken man. Did something happen after I left?"

"Please, call me Donald, and the answer to your question is yes, a great deal happened I'm afraid. It was painted shortly after the troubles began."

"Troubles? I don't understand."

Owen's father, the Duke of Cambrea finally did everyone a favor and died. Probably you heard about the Duke and how cruel and demanding he could be. When he was in his forties he went off to India and from there to Africa where he picked up a near fatal illness that left him weak and partially bedridden for the rest of his life. Everyone thought he wouldn't make it to sixty but too stubborn to give in managed to hold on till he was ninety."

"But what does that have to do with Edmund?"

"Hold on, I'm getting to it. With the Dukes passing Owen decided it was time to tell Edmund the truth."

"What truth?"

Donald rearranged the pillows on his chair and settled back. "That Edmund was not and never had been illegitimate. Owen and Sarah had been secretly married before he left for the continent."

"Oh dear God."

"Fearful of Owen being disinherited, they decided to keep their marriage a secret."

"Edmund must have been devastated when he heard the truth."

"He was—and wasted no time condemning his father for withholding the truth. 'We were living hand to mouth while you were living it up on the continent. Mother was seventeen—seventeen, with a child to care for. A child you created. Every day, she'd tell me that once you came back we'd be right as rain. Only we weren't were we? Mother was dying, and I was sent away.

"And yes, I grant that you came and found me, but was it out of love or guilt? Where were you when family members mistreated me and laughed at who my mother was? When the boys at school shunned me and called me names and cruelly beat me. What sort of man allows that? What sort of man puts title and money above his families well being? Were you so afraid of Grandfather and what he might do that you'd rather my entire life be a lie than to cross him? What you've done today—no, I can't go on. From this moment on you're dead to me. Dead! I don't want your money and I don't want your title. I'm my own man and will remain that way.'"

"I think I can add a bit to that if you like," I said sick at heart. "Owen came to talk to Edmund about getting his leg seen to, but Edmund stubbornly refused, and a heated argument ensued. When Owen came down he seemed very depressed and I asked if there was anything I could do. Out of the blue he told me he was thinking about a promise he made. One he didn't want to keep but felt he didn't have a choice. That it was just taking so damn long, but regardless he would keep it. And then he said good-night and left to catch his train. Could that have been what he was talking about?"

"It certainly could have been. What I can't figure out is why Owen thought that Edmund would be thrilled by the news. Was he so naïve as to think that Edmund would simply forgive and forget? Because if he did, he badly misjudged his son's reaction. As far as I can see his reaction was completely justified. What's sad is that Edmund died believing his father had betrayed him. That's a terrible burden to take to your grave."

"When did Edmund die?"

"August 10, 1903. In the spring of 1900, he grew despondent and could settle at nothing. Sir Richard ventured that a trip abroad might raise his spirits, but it only served to add to his depression. Ignoring the advice of both Richard and Dr. Wood, Edmund insisted on returning to Thornwood saying, 'If she can get back, that's where she'll go, and if I'm not there, she'll assume I abandoned her.'"

"If she can get back—"

Donald embarrassed, quickly apologized. "Oh Julie—I'm so sorry. I didn't think—forgive me."

"There's nothing to be sorry for, honest."

"Edmund returned to Thornwood a month after arriving home from the continent. He sold the mill to the American's and for all intents and purposes became a recluse. If he ventured out at all, it was to go to Shingle Street, a place he said you loved."

The rain having stopped Donald urged me to go out to the grave site. "You need to get out and get some fresh air. There's too much gloom and sadness here. Come on, I show you the way." He escorted me back to the kitchen and told me to take all the time I needed.

* * *

The sun, too shy to show itself, remained hidden as I made my way out to his grave. Wiping away the rain-soaked leaves covering his name I had to fight the urge to fall upon it and beg him to appear. "A peace that passes all understanding," I whispered, as the cold wind caused the old oak to shiver and send tiny droplets of moisture tumbling down onto the stone. Teardrops of the soul I thought as the sun growing braver seized the sky and turned the damp meadow into a giant prism of light and color. Once again I was at Thornwood.

We were sitting together on the top step of the stairs. Taking my hand, he pressed it to his lips. "I've missed you Julie." he said as the light shining through the stained-glass window turned the stairwell into a kaleidoscope of color. I turned to respond but instead of Edmund, I saw my father.

*"Don't let the darkness consume you my daughter."*

The sky darkened, the rain returned, and I hurried back to the house. "Are you all right?" Katherine asked when I came in. "You look pale."

"No, I'm fine. Just a little tired."

"Tell you what—why don't I fix up a room for you and you can come and stay whenever you like. You're one of us now," she said. Donald coming in overheard our conversation.

"That sounds like a wonderful idea. The roads around here can be treacherous at night and we don't want you ending up in a ditch. Come whenever you can," he added walking me to my car. "You're always welcome."

It was late when I arrived back in Inverness. Too late to visit Mark, so I returned to the hotel, had a quiet dinner and a long hot bath. I was exhausted and wanted only a good night's sleep, but my insomnia was unrelenting.

Over the coming months Donald and I became friends and spent many hours discussing the past. One warm mid-summer evening Donald and I were out on the veranda sharing the last of the days warmth, when I asked if he knew that Richard's family had purchased Thornwood?

"Yes, my grandfather was Lord Owen's accountant. He arranged it so the estate would go to Edmund along with an annual annuity for its upkeep. Later my father was appointed estate manager. I was born in the cottage by the gate, a gift from Lord Owen.

"Anyway, Mrs. Black if I remember correctly offered the place to us but grandfather refused saying it was too expensive a proposition. I believe the Spencer's lost money on it in the end. Couldn't get anyone to live there. Funny thing was they had no room to keep half the stuff that was sent up, so we offered to store it for them in one of the spare rooms at the back. What we didn't realize was that when they said boxes they really meant large crates. Eleven of them.

"You mean they're sitting up there unopened?" he nodded. "And you waited till now to tell me?"

"Never thought you'd be interested." Donald took a quick glance at his watch then continued. "It's too late to get started now, but if you want tomorrow you can look through them to your hearts content.

Next morning with crowbar in hand I made my way upstairs and got started. Most of the things were of little interest. It was crate number eleven that loosened the demons and sent me running down the stairs to get Donald.

"Come," I said tugging on his arm.

"I'm in the middle of something."

"That can wait. This is important. Look," I urged, going into the room. "There on the side of the box."

"It's the number eleven, so what?"

"No, the one inside. That's my name and the date. It proves I didn't lie. That I was there." I laughed out loud. "Now just let them try and take him. I have the proof right here. I'll show them—I'll show them all. When Mark sees this, he'll be sorry. They can call me crazy all they want, they can even lock me away, but now the laugh's on them. I have to show Mark."

"What are you doing? Julie! come back!" But I didn't come back. I grabbed the box and made for the stairs. Donald caught me at the front door, but I fought my way past him and started down the drive toward my car. Halfway there I stumbled on the loose gravel and dropped the box. Donald caught up with me, but I fought against him until finally he was forced to pick me up and carry me back into the house. Going up the stairs he yelled for Katherine to bring a pot of tea laced with brandy.

"Julie! You need to stop! Julie—listen," he said as I struggled to get away.

"I don't want to listen I've listened long enough. I've got to get Andrew before Mark takes him again."

The harder I fought the tighter Donald held me until he was forced to slap me to bring me to my senses. "Calm yourself. None of that matters anymore. It's done, over. You don't have to prove anything to anybody."

Katherine, with a tea tray in hand stood just behind Donald with a look of concern on her face.

"Is she gonna be all right Donald? Should I call the doctor?" she asked.

"She'll be fine, she's just had a bit of a start." Then he addressed me. "Here, drink this and try to relax." He said it was tea, but if there was any tea in it, I couldn't find it. "You're to stay here and not leave this room till we bring up your supper. Do you understand? I want you to rest. And I mean it. I don't want you out of that bed till I come back."

Donald brought my dinner up just after six and I found it almost impossible to face him having made such a fool of myself. I thought I'd grown stronger, more able to cope, but Father was right. Once evil takes hold it doesn't let go. So many mistakes, so much pain. "I'm so sorry Donald. I've upset everyone."

"There's nothing to apologize for. But this afternoon . . . the things you were saying. I confess I'm afraid for you. When I watch you out by the grave, I get such a sense of dread. Whatever you're doing—do you think it's for the best?"

"It doesn't matter what I think. It's all about destiny."

\* \* \*

I'd been in the north going on six months but having found a hospice for Mark near our home I was able to return to Wiklesbee. I was anxious to get home but sad to be leaving my friends. I spent several days with Richard and was now on my way to Latham to say my goodbyes and thank them for their kindnesses. We said little during dinner and once everything was cleared away, I made what I thought would be my last trip up to Edmund's room.

Next morning I visited his grave. It was a calm, peaceful, morning, with not so much as a breeze to stir the trees. I hoped that this being my last visit maybe he'd take pity and come, but once again I was disappointed. Lingering as long as I dared, I finally gave up and was about to return to the house when a magnificent young stag came out of nowhere and stood only a few yards away from me. That he would come that close amazed me, but there he stood, proud, fearless and unmoving. Sensing my eyes upon him he turned and looked into mine. It filled me with such a sense of joy I almost laughed out loud.

Below in the meadow, a doe and her fawn moved out from the protection of the trees. The stag, noting the deer's movement stood head erect and muscles quivering, as she led the fawn further away from the safety of the trees. Barely audible the snapping of a twig sent the stag bounding down into the meadow where he ushered the young mother and child back to safety.

I must have been blind not to see, but now I did—clearly. I hadn't been abandoned. Edmund, like the stag moved unseen, but was always nearby to give me courage and protection. Kneeling down I laid my hand over his name and found it warm to my touch. Did I hear him sigh? No, just the wind.

# CHAPTER FORTY

Over the following months a sort of dullness crept over me. I was drifting, mentally and emotionally until one day I found myself standing in the weed ravaged driveway of Thornwood. Hidden behind a jungle of unrecognizable plants and uncut grass, its windows shattered by vandals, its roof tiles scattered in the weeds, I couldn't help but feel sorry for this once proud home. Across the front door, someone had nailed a board with the words "no trespassing" written in red letters.

As I stood looking up at this wreck of a house I wondered. Was this how it looked before we arrived? Did it appear as hopeless and forlorn as it did now? But what about the inside? Had it remained timeless?

Hanging off the porch railing I was able to see enough of the inside to have my hopes confirmed. Everything was just as I had left it. It was as if I'd never been gone. The smell of bread baking sent me round to the back where I hoped to find a way in. What I found was Matilda hanging out the wash.

Delighted to see her again, I rushed forward calling her name.

"Matilda, it's me—it's Julie, I'm back." I thought she'd be as happy to see me as I was her, but her smile faded, and her eyes grew wide with fear.

"Get away from me. You don't belong here." She said backing away.

"Matilda, don't you know me? It's me Julie Hammond, your friend. Don't you remember?"

"I don't know anybody by that name. Now go away and leave us in peace. Go back to the grave where you belong." Dropping her basket, she ran for the house and slammed the kitchen door behind her. I ran to try and catch her, but she was too fast, and she locked the door against me.

"Matilda please, I'm not dead. Open the door and let me in. I want to talk to you."

A sudden gust of wind swept through the courtyard and with it a warning. "*Leave this place. Your time has not yet come, leave the dead to their troubles.*"

Unnerved, I stepped back and losing my balance fell onto the stony area around the porch. The sudden pain in my knee brought me to my senses.

Hurrying toward the front gate, a sudden memory made me stop and look up at the house. There she was. A young woman more gossamer than flesh and blood staring down at me. "Yes," I shouted up at her. "I remember. I understand." Smiling, she turned away from the window and left the curtain fall back in place. The moment she was gone the house shuddered and shook the ground where I was standing. It remembered as well, and the memory was frightening.

\* \* \*

In early April Connie arrived for a surprise visit and as usual had a list of things to do. Over the course of the next two weeks we saw every historical building, museum and play she could think of. We ate fish and chips in the park and dined at an expensive restaurant. By the time she was ready to leave we were both exhausted and ready for a quiet evening at home.

"I'm leaving tomorrow and I'm still waiting to hear what you intend to do about Mark. You can't go on like this forever."

"You make it sound like he's a car that needs trading in."

"No I don't."

"I am doing what I think best. I'm letting nature take its course. He'll go when he's ready and not before."

"But I can see what it's doing to you," she said.

"Really, I'll be fine—honest."

"I'm not saying you won't—"

"It's what happens afterward that keeps me up at night." I said clearing off the table.

"So, leave the dishes and talk to me."

"I went up to Thornwood last month. I'm not sure why, but there I was standing in the drive looking up at this sad old house. The place was in a terrible state with the windows broken out and weeds waist high. It was terrible. Anyway, several strange things happened."

"When don't they?" she interrupted.

"Very funny." Connie sat back folded her hands on her lap and waited. I started with first impressions and ended with the woman in the window.

"And you left nothing out?" I nodded. "Well—how about this? It will sound crazy, but what if, and I'm thinking outside the box here—what if Matilda wasn't Matilda, but Endora? You said she could be anybody."

"But then why try to frighten me away? I think Matilda thought I was Endora back from the grave. Anyway, I was halfway to the gate when a memory just seemed to pop into my mind. I turned and looking up at the house saw the women looking out the window just as she had the first night I was there. Our eyes met and for the first time ever she smiled, as if to say 'finally, you've got it, you remember,' then she was gone."

"So, what was it you remembered?"

"I'd rather not say right now. I need to think it through. When I've got it sorted I'll tell you. I promise."

\* \* \*

The plane was still at the gate, but I already missed her. Before board-ing she asked again about Mark and what I intended but my answer was the same. Wait on God. Four days later he gave me the answer. Mark was fading and had only a few days left to live.

From then on, I never left his side. Pastor Boswell, the hospice Chaplain was a devout man who understood what grieving was about. He saw it on a daily basis. His job was that of comforter, of finding words of hope and redemption for those departing and strength and reassurance for those left behind.

For three years I had longed for and dreaded this day. Now it was here and the pain I felt was unbearable. There were so many questions that never got answered. So many things that should have been said but never were. Now it was too late. Hoping to keep him with me I climbed in beside him and held him to me.

"Julie," Edmund said as he appeared next to Mark's bed, "don't be sad over his leaving. Mark's part in this is over now. He was part of the mystery. One that became two will soon be one again. When you're ready, come to where it started. I'll leave the timing in your capable hands." He said nothing for a moment, then, "it's time Julie. We must say goodbye for now." Edmund laid his hand over Mark's heart. "Come to us when you're ready. We'll be waiting."

I checked Mark's pulse than called for the nurse who called the doctor. I explained what was to be done with his body and signed the required doc-uments. The hospice staff wished me well, and I thanked everyone in turn. As I walked toward my car, the clouds gave way to the sun. Mark loved the sun. Another sign I told myself, another sign.

I flew Mark home and buried him beside his parents and our son. Connie and Charles attended and afterward invited me to stay with them for a time, or at least until I came to my senses about returning to England. I understood their concern, and I loved them for it, but England was where it began and where it would end. A month later I said a tearful goodbye to my truest friends and boarded the plane back to England.

Over the ensuing months I lived quietly. I read books long put off, finished several paintings I'd started but never finished and spent time at the shore relaxing to the sound of the waves rolling up onto the beach. In March I traveled up to Scotland to see my friends. Both as usual were more than accommodating and for the first time in a very long time I actually laughed out loud.

* * *

Almost unnoticed, summer arrived with all its lush green splendor. I reached for the phone and called Richard.

"Are you still interested in selling Thornwood?"

"Tomorrow if I could find someone dumb enough—"

"I'm dumb enough."

"Wait a minute . . . what's this all about?"

"I want to buy Thornwood?"

"Why?"

"It's complicated."

"Nothing new there, but since you refuse to explain the answer's no."

"Richard—"

He laughed. "You don't have to buy it I'll give it to you as a gift."

"No," I interrupted. "I have to pay for it."

Richard disapproved of the idea and threatened to burn the place down. "There's nothing for you at Thornwood but trouble, and I refuse to be responsible."

"No one said you had to be responsible. That's all on me. I just want to buy the house." We argued, but three weeks later, realizing I wouldn't be put off, he called to say he'd talk to the estate agent and tell her I was coming. He had other news as well. While rebuilding the reception desk they found a letter stuck behind the mail drop addressed to me. He sent it on and figured I'd get it in the morning post.

I spent most of the night wondering what it would say and knowing Endora was capable of anything wondered if I should even open it. Besides I had plans for tomorrow. I was going up to Ipswich to talk to Mrs. Anderson about Thornwood. Believing the house was more important the letter would just have to wait.

I arrived in Ipswich full of enthusiasm. I hailed a taxi and instructed the driver to take me to the Brown and Wilson Estate Agency on Princes Street. I admit I was nervous. I'd never done anything like this before. We were to meet in her office at eleven o'clock, but when I arrived found she wasn't there, and they had no idea when she'd return.

I decided to have lunch and perhaps see her later that afternoon but again she wasn't there and was told she'd call.

I thought she'd be glad to be shed of such a dilapidated property, but obviously not. Disappointed I boarded the train back to London. The letter and a box from Donald were waiting when I arrived home.

I assumed it would start as all his letters started with a description of his trip, where he was staying, and if he'd had a meal what he ate. It was always the same. This time however there wasn't anything at all about the hotel. Not even its name. He did mention the weather and how it might force him to stay longer, but then everything changed. His writing became hurried, harder to read. He said he was desperate to talk to me, but felt it needed to be discussed face to face and that's where it ended. Not even his usual, 'I love you' and signature.

There was just enough to let me know he must have seen and perhaps talked to her, but nothing more. Overcome with frustration I banged my hand down so hard on the table I spilled my coffee.

Frustrated, I turned my attention to Donald's box. Lying on top was a short note.

*"Julie, got thinking about those boxes after you left and decided to go and have a proper look see. Inside the last one was a package addressed to you. It's in the box with a few other items I thought you might want. Anyway, let me know what you find.*

Inside the package was a diary that required a key. A key given me years ago. So why wouldn't it fit? I tried several times without success and finally giving up used a hairpin. I admit I was nervous. After all, he'd made a point of saying I should read it, though by page three I had no idea why. This wasn't a diary; it was a confession.

It was definitely Edmund's neat script, but other than that there was nothing of him in it. Rather it was a blow by blow account of every deceptive action they took to destroy me. What they hoped to achieve, and how they planned to go about it. There was a whole section on how to trick Mark into believing Endora's lies.

Unable to deal with any more I grabbed my coat and though it was cold and growing dark took a walk around the town. A woman on a bike hurried passed me on her way home from the store and waved. Across the street a man looked on impatiently as his dog debated on which spot of grass to use. Everyone seemed to have a reason for being out. Everyone that was but me. I was a ship adrift at sea with no way to find my way back to the shore.

The longer I walked the more confused I became. I was drowning in an ocean of questions that had no answers. Numb to the bone I decided to call it quits and go home. I could walk all the way to London and still not find the answers I was searching for

* * *

Endora was sitting on the foot of my bed when I woke next morning. "Do you always sleep this late?"

"Why what time is it?" I reached for the clock and was surprised to find it was closing in on noon. "Why do you care how long I sleep."

"Because I'm your friend."

"Yes—well—you always say that don't you. It's getting sort of stale." When I didn't get up she began wondering around like a lost sheep looking for its shepherd.

"My word, isn't that's Edmund's journal?" She picked it up and began leafing through it. "It's all true you know, though I'm not sure why he felt the need to tell you."

"Why don't you get on your broom and fly off somewhere." She left in a huff but returned that evening. "What are you playing at?" I asked.

"I'm moving in mysterious ways, like it says in the Bible." She picked up a figurine left to me by my mother and studied it.

"Put that down before you break it. And what would you know about the Bible or its author for that matter?"

"I won't break it, and I know plenty about him. In fact, you might say I've got firsthand knowledge. And I'll tell you something else," she said pointing the figurine at me, "all that talk about love and forgiveness—forget it. There's a lot of Thou shalt not's, in his vocabulary, and though I hate to admit it, I'm not very good with those."

"Now there's a surprise."

"So, where's Edmund?" she asked looking behind a chair.

"How should I know?"

Knelling down she looked under the bed. "He's here, I can feel him."

"I thought you felt nothing for him."

"Your becoming quiet the comedian. Ought to go on the stage, but Edmund's a man of his word and if he said he'd come back, then he will." Endora opened the closet door and rifled through my things. "And don't go assuming that book was my doing. Far from it," she called from inside the closet, I put nothing in writing. No sense doing something that will later condemn you. Besides, after Mark's tragic accident, the Council demanded an end to the trickery. Play by the rules or forfeit. Well—you don't have to be brilliant to realize when the Council's had enough. Cross them again and I'll reap my just rewards." Disappointed not to find him, Endora took a seat on the sofa. "*Just*, was their word, not mine."

"I don't know their rules."

"Yes, but I do, and when they get serious, you listen. Push them on if you dare, but cross the line, and you'll wish you'd never known them." It was there in her eyes that same fear I saw at Thornwood when they intended to lock her away.

# CHAPTER FORTY-ONE

It took Mrs. Anderson two days to return my call, and when I asked why, was told someone else had already made an offer. Something about her tone set me on edge, so I insisted on being allowed to do the same. Without giving her a chance to say no I told her I'd be in her office at ten next morning and that I expected her to be there.

A blue haired woman wearing too much make-up, and far too many bracelets escorted me into her office and though not rude, wasn't friendly. She repeated what she said on the phone and added that the bid he made was quiet substantial.

"But has he put any money on the table?"

"No, but he signed a promissory note stating his intentions."

"Then I guess Sir Richard was wrong. He said it was still available."

"You a friend of the Duke?" I nodded and smiled. "I see, I didn't realize. That puts a different light on things. You're aware of the house's condition?"

"It's condition is unimportance. I'm more concerned about the other party. What can you tell me about him?"

She went to her file and pulled out a rather thick file. Let's see—" she said dumping its contents on the table. "I'm really not supposed to do this but since you're a friend of Sir Richard. Naturally I can't give you his name it wouldn't be ethical, but he's a single gentleman of some means. A little too flamboyant for my taste." Anyway, I only met him once and that was at the house. Seeing how I'm the agent I shouldn't comment, but the place gives me the creeps. He wants to turn it into a haunted bed-and-breakfast type establishment, you know, like those games where someone dies, and you have to discover who did it and with what. More power to him I say but I won't be staying there. Can't imagine why anyone would. But here's the problem. If there's nothing untoward in his offer and he doesn't withdraw it, I must allow him to have it. I might be able to offer other properties, I have several of similar quality, but in the end it's his decision."

"In that case, I guess we'll have to wait and see. Sir Richard will be disappointed I'm afraid." I thanked her for her time and made as if to leave.

"Look, I'm not sure why you'd want to, but go ahead and make your offer. That way we're that much further along." I filled out all the papers, signed my name on the dotted line, and went to get something to eat. So why after all these years did they want to buy the place. Had they heard I was interested? Maybe they thought Richard would sell it to a land developer or something. I laughed. That would upset her for sure. Trapped in the frozen food section. Oh well, I needed to catch my train.

I found an empty compartment and took the seat by the window. Mark and Andrew joined me. "Daddy, what does that say?" Andrew asked, holding up his book. Mark read while Andrew snuggled closer and rested against Mark's arm. When Mark asked if Andrew could see the pictures, it set me to wondering if that applied to me as well.

"Be wary, be wary," the hum of the wheels intreated. "Wait and see, wait and see, wait and see," they warned. "Don't be fooled, don't be fooled, don't be fooled," they screeched coming into Paddington Station. "Easy for you," I said stepping out onto the platform.

"So," Richard asked when he called that evening. "How did things go? I know Mrs. Anderson can be difficult."

"She was fine once I mentioned your name. Did you know there was another offer on the place? Wants to turn it into a haunted bed and breakfast of all things. I can't see—but then it might work. People enjoy being scared half out of their wits if it's not real."

"Why didn't I think of that?" Ricard said. "I could make a fortune and seeing that the witch is already in residence. Maybe I need to rethink this thing. A little extra money would come in handy."

"It's too late to back out now. A promise is a promise. According to Mrs. Bangles and Bows, our mystery buyer was charming though a little too flamboyant."

Richard couldn't help but laugh. "Has she looked in the mirror lately?" Turning serious, "I should never have agreed to this. The whole thing sounds dangerous to me and you're right in the middle of it. Why I didn't burn it to the ground when I had the chance God only knows."

* * *

The following Monday Connie called from Heathrow Airport. She missed her connecting flight to Warsaw and needed a place to stay. I found her standing curbside. "Can you believe it?" she said the moment she got in the car. "I ran the entire length of the airport, which isn't easy at my age. I'm trying to catch my breath and at the same tell the ticket agent I'm the one they were calling, and she just stares at me. So I show her my ticket and I start to head toward the plane, but she calls me back and says it's too late. They've already closed the gate. Then smiling, she says I'll have to wait for the next flight. So get this. The next flight that has a seat available is four days from now. Four days! My luggage was on that plane. What am I supposed to wear?"

I was about to comment when the phone rang. "Mrs. Anderson . . . How are you? Yes, I'm still interested . . . That's great . . . Tuesday the twenty-fourth . . . I'll be there." I put the phone down and punched the air. Life is good. I downed my drink, poured another and called Richard.

"Hi, it's me . . . Yes, I heard . . . I can't tell you what this means . . . Next month if I can. I've gotta run, a friend's visiting, and Richard—don't worried, everything will be fine. Honest."

"All right," Connie said. "What have you done?"

"After dinner I'll explain everything." She wasn't happy but her hunger overrode her desire for news. I waited till everything was cleared away than broke the news.

"You can't be serious, but you are, aren't you?" I nodded. "So, tell me why."

Ever since Mark died, I've felt unsettled. Adrift I guess you could say. I feel old beyond my year and worn out. Everywhere I look I'm haunted by the past, so I've decided it times to go home."

"Thank God for that, but then why purchase Thornwood?"

"Because I want a say in what happens to it."

"You could always sell it to a land developer or some such. It is a great location and you could maybe get two or three houses on a lot that size. You might be able to make a good deal of money. I mean it's not like you're rolling in dough."

"Thanks for reminding me. Take a look at this. "Richard found it while rebuilding the front desk. Tell me what you think." I handed her Mark's letter.

"Well, this verifies that he saw her, and that something took place that greatly upset him. So there's that. In fact it so upset him he was willing to forget about his work and come home. That isn't the Mark I know. Work always came first."

"That's what I thought," I called from the kitchen while making coffee.

"I don't know Julie," she said when I returned. "In the greater scheme of things does it really matter. Mark's dead, and she killed him. The important thing now is to make sure that so-called Council of yours sends her back to where she belongs."

"I guess you're right. What he wrote could mean a million different things if he wrote it at all. Worry about what's going to happen not what has." Connie looked at me in astonishment.

"If only you had said that years ago."

"Don't be smart or I'll send you into the street with nothing clean to wear." I handed her Edmund's diary and waited.

"Good grief Julie, you don't believe this do you?"

"I'm not sure. Maybe he wanted—"

"Stop right there, and don't say another word. I swear that woman must have seen you coming."

"Actually, she did."

"But that's neither here nor there. Think about it. The letter and this on the same day—never. If you weren't so damn gullible, Endora couldn't do this."

"I'm not gullible."

"Oh, yes you are. Where she's concerned, you're deaf, dumb and blind. Did you call Donald to ask if he sent you anything?" When I said no, she handed me the phone.

\* \* \*

Next morning, Connie insisted we go shopping for clothes and perhaps take in a movie. I tried to tell her she didn't need a whole wardrobe just something to change into since washing what she was wearing appeared out of the question.

"You can't expect me to buy a top and not the bottoms and besides Charlie likes to see me looking good." The fact that Charlie was still in the states and the only one who would see her was her mother, never crossed her mind.

We were fighting our way across Piccadilly Circus to the bus stop when Connie said, "You're asking for trouble buying that house. In fact, I'd bet the farm on it, and I don't even have a farm. Though I've always wanted one with chickens, and pigs, maybe horses to ride. And a garden—"

"Connie—"

Time, as it always does when most precious, slipped away, and before we realized, Connie and I were once again waiting at the airport to say our goodbyes. We lingered as long as possible, then after another long hug I watched her disappear down the ramp, and onto the plane. I would never see her again.

# CHAPTER FORTY-TWO

Donald, having been away from home called me three days later. I wanted to ask about the package, but he kept interrupting.

"That's all fine and good but let me tell you what's happened. Last week, I got a call from the freight office. They said they had an old steamer trunk with the name Julie Hammond stamped on it and our address. Not recognizing the name, they wondered if perhaps it was mislabeled. I assured them it wasn't, and they sent it on. It's here now waiting for your arrival. I would've called sooner but I'd been sent on a fool's errand."

"A fool's errand. Donald I owe you a kiss. Can you meet me?"

"Don't I always? As for the kiss, I'm not sure my wife would approve."

As usual we met in the baggage claim area. Filled with nervous energy I urged him to drive a bit faster. "I could walk faster than this."

"Now look here lass," he said, glancing over at me. "That trunks going nowhere, and we'll get there soon enough."

Katherine was waiting at the door when I arrived, but I had no time for tea and a chat. I shouted my hello and raced up to my room where the old trunk sat waiting. I couldn't help but smile. We were old friends that trunk and me.

As usual, the faint smell of lavender filled the room when I opened the lid. Most of the contents where memories Edmund had shared the day

Nathan died. But on the bottom, wrapped in cloth and almost overlooked, a diary identical to the one that required a key. A key that fit perfectly.

Unlike last time there were no plans, no talk of deception or making things work in Endora's favor. Instead it was all about his childhood, his inventions, and some very painful pages concerning his father's betrayal. He wrote about me as well, but more importantly he explained the exact reason for everything that happened, and why I was chosen.

*"Endora said she picked you out, and in a way she did but not in the way she thought. It was the Council who had followed you through year of mistreatment that allowed her to find you. They need someone brave and strong of character and heart to stand up against her. They watched how you endured years of hurt and abuse under your aunts care and the heartbreak of losing you unborn child. Seeing the way you lovingly accepted Andrew as your own, they knew you had enough love to survive this."*

Then he spoke about Mark, and why he wasn't allowed to understand and how important it was to the outcome. What I didn't know however was that Mark, though unaware, was the lynch pin that held it all together. His steadfast refusal to move, though it cause a great rift between us, made what was coming possible.

*"The Council and I understand the suffering you've faced, the pain and the hurt you've experienced, and though at times you thought Mark was being unkind and unfeeling it wasn't true. Even in the hardest of times his love for you was true. You were hurt physically, but his hurt, though you'll laugh when I say it, was more internal and sometimes internal hurt is harder to endure than the physical. And just to ease your mind Andrew as he grew to maturity was well aware of his father's love for you and also his difficulty in trying to show it. Andrew loved you both deeply.*

*"Just as Mark and I were separated for a reason, so to were you and Jennifer. If all goes well when the final battle takes place we will be rejoined and hopefully Endora be returned to hell where she belongs.*

His last entry was on June 10, 1903, the day I left Thornwood.

*"Since the moment this farce began I dreaded the day I knew was coming. I hoped it would turn out differently, that somehow the Council would look on my plea's more favorably, but since they haven't, we must once again be parted. If there was some way to save you from the trials ahead I would without question, but the Council has spoken. What you decide now will determine the destiny of all involved. Think before you act and act only when you're sure. Use love as a weapon and you will succeed. All this you know but I would be remiss with all the years that have passed not to remind you. Till we're reunited I leave you with all my love."*

As I pressed his words to my lips, a small piece of paper fell into my lap. I read it aloud.

*"My dear Julie, I found this among the master's things after he passed away and I thought you should have it. With love, Silas."*

The note said; *My dearest girl, Five-years have passed since we were together, and though I've tried to carry on, I find it impossible. The past haunts my nights and refuses me rest. I see you everywhere. On the swing, sitting on the porch, going up the stairs, caring for Nathan, yet when I cry out for you, you run away. The pain of our separation has grown so strong I can no longer stand against it. Since I can't stop my mind from thinking, or my eyes from seeing, dying is preferable to living. Our time is coming of that I'm certain, but it moves at such a slow pace. I only hope that all goes well, and you come out of the darkness victorious. Until we are one again,*

*Always yours,*

*Edmund*

A soft tap at the door announced Donald's arrival. He poked his head in and ask to join me. Carrying a plate of sandwiches and tea he sat it down on the small table next to me. "Katherine thought you might be hungry."

I managed a few bites, but it all got stuck in my throat. How could I eat after what had been revealed. I had made so many mistakes, said so many hateful things that couldn't be fixed. I felt a failure for not seeing the pain Mark was having to bear. I knew what having your heart torn apart felt like, yet I didn't see it in Mark. Perhaps they didn't want me to, perhaps I was deliberately blinded to his situation. *"If you'd think about me once and awhile . . ."*

"Are you all right Julie, you look so broken."

"Yes, I guess I am. I feel old, worn out, and used up. I've lost everything I ever loved, and now all I want is for it to end."

After the incident with the box I called Richard. I was upset, we all were by what took place and I had to know, to see if there was anything I could do to make it better."

"I'm so sorry about that."

"I have to say that what Richard told me was hard to believe and if it hadn't been Richard telling me I wouldn't have believed it. I'm so dreadfully concerned for you. You have no family to call on and though I'm a friend I realize it's not the same."

"You and Richard are family. You've both been so kind and understanding. Most would have thrown me out on my ear or worst; assumed I was crazy."

"Please, Julie, tell me what all this means. I'm sick with worry for you."

I took his hand and held it. He was a dear man, but this wasn't the time. "I know you're upset and I'm very sorry for that, but until it's over I can't share it. Once it is everything will be explained, but for now it must remain with me."

Two days later Donald drove me to the train station. As the train roared to a halt Donald unexpectedly hugged me. A big Scottish highlander hug that lifted me off the ground. "Is there nothing I can do—"

I smiled and looked up into his tear-filled eyes, "No my friend, I'm afraid this is something I must do on my own."

# CHAPTER FORTY-THREE

Two messages were waiting when I returned. The first from Connie, glad I went to visit Donald, and the second from Mrs. Anderson suggesting I stop by at my earliest convenience to finalize the sale. I traveled up on Thursday, and what a wonderful day it turned out to be. Thornwood was mine. From the wine cellar to rooftop, from the front gate to the back garden. All mine. Now it was just a matter of breaking the news to Endora.

She showed up as I was sitting down to dinner. "Oh, how quaint. You actually cook."

"There's plenty if you'd like to join me." Surprised by my offer she took a seat and for the next hour we actually enjoyed each other's company. I even made her laugh. After clearing away the dirty dishes, I gave her the news.

"Guess what I did today?" I said putting the last dish in the dishwasher.

"Why would I care what you do?"

"Because it involves you."

"Then stop playing games and tell me."

"I'm the new owner of Thornwood."

She looked bemused. "That's not funny."

"No, really. I signed the papers today. Thornwood is mine. Aren't you surprised? Some guy named Black put a bid in as well, but later backed out. Isn't that wonderful. Even better I was told I could make a good deal of money selling the place to land developers. You know, to build a shopping mall or some such thing."

"You're lying."

"Afraid not."

What I expected wasn't what happened. I was prepared for her to throw one of her fits, but instead, she pushed herself away from the table, stood, straightened her dress and left. Poof, just like that. I found it quite a disappointment.

So now it began. I contacted Mr. Blunt a local builder who agreed to meet me at Thornwood on Saturday morning to discuss what needed to be done and how. In the meantime, I wrote down what things I wanted to go to whom, made sure my diaries where up to date then called Connie. She asked when I'd be home, and I said soon. There were a few loose ends I needed to tie up. We spoke about the old days how anxious she was to see me and then we said goodbye. I did many hard things in my life, but this was one of the hardest.

\* \* \*

Storm clouds were building in the west, and soon the rain would come. I took one last lingering look around, then locked the door and drove away. All my papers were neatly organized along with instructions concerning what I wanted my lawyer to do. Also included were three copies of my diary. I arrived at Thornwood just after sunset. I unlocked the gate and drove the car up the drive to the house. There were no more weeds, no roof shingles laying scattered in the grass and no broken windows. Thornwood had been reborn.

The woman stood at the window watching, she'd been watching for a long time. This time however she looked down to where I was standing, smiled. She knew what my arrival meant and was happy the day had finally arrived. I guess I was as well.

As usual Silas greeted me. *"Miss Julie, how good to have you back. We've missed you."* I smiled and made my way up the stairs, reciting my father's favorite poem. *"Yesterday upon the stairs, I met a woman that wasn't there."* I crossed the landing and continued, *"She wasn't there again today, I wish, I wish, she'd go away."* I reached the second floor and looked around. *"When I came home last night at three, she was waiting there for me."* Everything was just as it was the day I left. *"But when I looked around the hall, I couldn't see her there at all."*

I didn't see her, but I saw Mark. He was standing in the doorway of the living room and seeing me hurried over and took me in his arms. It felt so good to be with him again. To feel his arms around me and his lips warm against mine. Leading me over to the sofa he said he had something he needed to tell me.

"Do you know how dangerous it is for you to be here?"

"There's just as much for her."

"If you don't leave and soon, it will be too late, and we'll be lost."

"I'm not leaving. This is where the Council said I should be."

"The Council or Edmund?"

"All right. Edmund told me, but does it matter? It's time to end this once and for all."

"I thought by now you'd be over him, but I guess that was a foolish hope. If he really cared he wouldn't have brought you back. He knew what you were facing yet he couldn't leave well enough alone. By calling you back from the grave he made it possible for her to have a second chance."

"But Mark, can't you see that it gives me a second chance as well. A chance to finally send her back to hell where she belongs. I'm tired and worn out. I can't do this any longer. Constantly looking over my shoulder waiting for her to come and try to destroy me has taken its toll. It's time we had it out. One way or the other it has to end. It started here, and it will end here."

"What makes you think you have that sort of power? You didn't decide all this on your own. Be honest. Someone kept hinting this is what you should do and once again it was Edmund. Always Edmund. What other things did he tell you? Did he say that you and Jennifer were one, that he and I were two halves of a whole? How can that be? How can one person be split in half?" I tried to interrupt but he didn't give me a chance. "They said you were caring for Jennifer's soul. How can that be? The soul belongs to one person and one person only. Only God can deal with the soul. But Edmund's convinced you otherwise."

"No, that's not true. I know Jennifer is with me. She speaks through me. I've seen her, talked to her. She's real."

"Are you sure it wasn't Endora pretending to be Jennifer. You can't see a soul Julie, and you can't touch it, what you hugged at the church was flesh and blood, but whose?"

I was confused by this unexpected onslaught of questions and being unprepared had no defense against it. I needed to think, to regroup, but he kept on until his words blended together and became just a series of unrelated sounds.

Mark, shoulders slumped, hands stuffed in his pockets, looked the picture of dejection as he stood staring out at the approaching storm. "It was always Edmund, wasn't it?" he said over his shoulder. "From the moment you saw him, it was over for us. I tried to pretend it wasn't true, that you still loved me, but you didn't. All those years, it was always him you were hoping to see again, not me. Even when I was dying. I was trapped inside my body with no way to speak or move, I was totally alone yet you chose to go to Latham in hopes of seeing him again."

"I was trying to force Endora to give you back. I didn't want you to die and I thought if I could see her—"

"And you did see her, and she explained how she took me back and showed me what happened. But she lied. What she showed me was you with

Edmund. In bed, making love while I was away at the beach with Andrew. She showed me how you were more concerned about getting back in his good graces than mine."

"No, you're wrong, she said she showed you the truth."

"Yes, she did. The truth that you slept with him behind my back, that it was him you wanted to see while I was dying, that even at the moment of my death he was there. That was the truth she told me. Can you deny it happened as she said?"

"No, but you—"

"I don't want to argue, I want to save you. Can't you just for once do what I want? I love you so dearly. Please, leave before it's too late." Mark said, his eyes pleading. "I don't want you to face her. I want to know that in the end we'll be together and she'll be burning in hell."

"You don't understand. One of us must destroy the other or we'll all lose. It's too late to turn back now. Not when the end is in sight. We all have a destiny, and this is mine."

Mark came to where I stood and took me in his arms. "Is there no way I can persuade you to leave? No way at all?"

"I'm afraid not."

He sighed heavily as if giving in. "All right. If staying is what you want, then I'll stay as well. I love you too much to let you face this alone." He put his arm around me and led me out into the hall. Taking his hand I reached to kiss it and there it was on his fourth finger. The ring.

The same ring that sparkled in the candlelight while I hung from the ceiling begging him to stop. Breaking away I ran for the door, but he caught me and dragged me back.

"I told you she'd notice," Endora said coming out of the shadows.

"Well, what difference does it make? Three times she was given leave to walk out the door and each time she refused," Bunny said. Then laughing, "for a time she really thought—"

"Yes, a born actor," Endora interrupted before turning her attention toward me. "You've done me a tremendous favor."

"How?"

"By purchasing Thornwood—One of my many punishments was to be locked inside the walls of Thornwood and there to remain till someone came and released me. That's what you did. You bought the house which means you own it. Like most seller or homes I'm free to take and leave behind whatever I choose. And—" she said for emphasis, I intend to leave behind my sins trapped within the walls. You will now be responsible for them."

Bunny, stepping between us said, "There is a way out if you're willing to take it. All you need do is call Edmund and Jennifer to come, and when they arrive we'll tear up the deed and you'll be free to go."

"The Council warned that deception surrounds and blinds what is real. Truth they said was the answer. That I should trust in the knowledge of things as they are. That knowledge tells me that the moment they arrived you're promises would be forgotten. Just as your promise to help me was nothing but lies."

Shoving him aside, she screamed in my face, "Damn you! Quote whomever you like. The Council's words are just that, words nothing more— now call out to Edmund and Jennifer and tell them to come."

Endora was scared, I could see the slight shaking of her hands. These weren't just word's they were weapons. Weapons that wounded deep inside where eyes couldn't see, and Bunny knew it.

"Enough," Bunny shouted as he took hold of me. You won the first battle, when you refused to jump, but you won't win this one. Now it's all or nothing. Either you survive or they do. It's your choice. Give them up or be lost. Tying my wrist together with a stout cord he ran it over the chandelier hook then hoisting me up tied the end to the newel post. From the first I wondered if I'd be strong enough, worthy enough to do what was needed. Now I saw that as Edmund said, all my previous sufferings had been for one purpose—to make me strong enough to face the end.

"If I stay strong, if I say no, it's over." There was a sort of peace in that. They could take my body, Bunny had already done that, but never my soul. Only God could take that.

"Call out their names Julie. That's all you need do," Endora encourage.

Below me, a small fire burned, but like the flames of Revelations, though they blazed white hot, they did not consume. If you don't relent, you alone will pay the price. A simple nod of the head will suffice. Do it, Julie and live."

"No . . ."

Walking into the flames Bunny took my face in his hands, and demanded I yield. Yield or join me in Hell."

"I can't offer what I don't own."

"What is wrong with you?" Endora said losing control, "the Council has turned its back on you. My sins are yours and damnation awaits. Do you see it, Julie? Can you see Paradise? Look at it Julie and realize it will never be yours. Day and night your shattered dreams will haunt you. Peace will be impossible. There will be no night, no day, just eternal torment. In time the love you have for them will turn to hate and your one driving need will be to visit upon them the pain they've allowed you to suffer. Are they worth it Julie? Are they worth an eternity of unrelenting damnation?"

My silence only served to infuriate Endora further. Hovering above me she spread her arms wide and engulfed me in darkness. The wind blew in great heated gust and pushed me toward the gates that like a yawning cavern, opened wide before me. From within came the smell of brimstone and the tortured screams of the damned. I shuddered knowing soon I would join them.

Off in the distance my loved ones stood watching. Desperate, I called for them to help me, but they refused to come near. How could they abandon me when I was facing an eternity in hell to save them? Inside a small flicker of hate began to grow. I was being torn apart as I struggled to remember that love not hate was the only thing that mattered.

A breeze as if someone opened a door turned me so I could see the girl standing on the middle landing watching me. As our eyes met, a look of surprise changed to horror as she realized she was looking at herself. I saw the revulsion; felt the bile rise in her throat. Holding her gaze, I remembered that day and smiled, a soft little victorious smile and whispered,

"My life for theirs."

At once Endora's laughter turned to horrified screams as the demons of Hell appeared, and wrapping her in chains, dragged her back into the abyss. Bunny with a wry smile and a sweeping bow in my direction slammed shut the gates, locked them with seven keys, and returned to rule over the damned until his time of judgement arrived.

The weight of Endora's sins were lifted from my shoulders, and as it was in my vision by the sea, I saw it. A light, only a glimmer, but a light none the less. As it drew nearer its brightness increased, as the singing of hymns and the chanting of prayers could be heard drawing closer. I had done what they asked and now I stood on solid ground. Jennifer stepped out from behind the Council and running toward me with outstretched arms, made us whole. Mark and Edmund followed, and as they hurried forward, became one. Shouting for me Nathan and Andrew came running. My heart overflowed with joy and for the first time since arriving at Thornwood, I was truly at peace, absolute joyous peace. My long painful journey was over, and once again I was reunited with those I loved most in the world. As the Council led us away I smiled, knowing in the fullness of time love overcomes all, and evil is nothing to fear.

# EPILOGUE

It was just after 8 p.m., when Richard called to tell me that Julie had passed away. According to the police, Mr. Blunt, a local building contractor, found Mrs. Hammond lying dead in the entrance hall of the home she had recently purchased and intended to renovate. From all appearances it looked as though the second-floor banister had given way and she fell to her death.

Richard and I flew down for the funeral and afterward her lawyer handed each of us a large brown envelope with instructions we weren't to open it for a year. Today was that day.

I made myself comfortable, and after some considerable time of reflection opened the envelope and read what she wrote. At times I laughed, then cried at the pain and losses she suffered. To be honest, I felt ashamed that I hadn't done more to ease the burden she was carrying. As I went along there were times I thought I couldn't continue and would stop to regain my composure.

"You didn't give me an easy story to read my friend, but I'm grateful you cared enough to share."

Looking over to where she sat that first day I smiled remembering the complete hash she made of trying to explain the unexplainable. Did Richard find this as painful a read as I had? I'd call him tomorrow, but for now I needed time to break the spell of the past and bring myself back to the present. Was she here I wondered? She often talked about coming back. Did she find her peace? So many questions...

"Tomorrow Julie," I said aloud. "Tomorrow the demolition will be complete. Thornwood will no longer exist. Everything has been carried out as you directed. Every single brick, window and piece of wood has been ground into powder and hauled off in different directions. There's no way Thornwood will ever be rebuilt."

As evening approached, I took one last look around the office, found my coat and headed for the door. "Are you here Julie? Are you happy?" Enough, I told myself, it was time to go home to my family.

"Donald—I thought you'd already gone," Katherine said coming out of the kitchen.

"I'm on my way now." Katherine followed me down the hall to lock up behind me.

"Good night then."

"And to you Katherine."

Sitting out on the terrace Julie watched as her two boys played in the yard. As the sun slowly disappeared below the trees that lined the meadow Mark came and placed his hand on her shoulder. "It's growing dark my love, time for you and the boys to come in."

"Yes, Julie said smiling up at him. It's time."